House
of Shadows

Also by Misha M. Herwin

Dragonfire

Juggler of Shapes

Master of Trades

Misha M. Herwin has written short stories, novels, plays and books for children. She has two grown up children and lives in Staffordshire with her ever patient husband and a very demanding cat. When not writing she likes to bake. Muffins are a specialty.

House
of Shadows

Misha M. Herwin

PENKHULL

House of Shadows
copyright © Misha M. Herwin 2014

Cover design by Peter Coleborn

Published by Penkhull Press 2014

All rights reserved

First edition

ISBN 978-0-9930008-0-5

Published by Penkhull Press
Staffordshire UK

www.penkhullpress.co.uk

ACKNOWLEDGEMENTS

House of Shadows has taken a long time to write. Over the years many people have helped in the making of the book. My thanks go to:

Jan Edwards my excellent editor; my beta-reader
Rachel Swindells-Hallett

Renegade Writers and Room-in-the Roof for their comments
on the various drafts of the book

Lucy Harrisis, Natasha Molloy, Carole Thornley, Heather
Steele and the members of the Tuesday Reading group for
feedback on cover design

Anuk Naumann for help on artistic matters

Posy Miller for the original blurb

Peter Coleborn for his technical assistance, over and above
the call of duty

And my mum Danuta Chmielinksa, who took me to
tea in Kingsweston House

DEDICATION

For Posy Miller

CHAPTER ONE

Kneeling at the attic window, the child pressed her face against the glass. Her thin body shivered in the bitter cold. The bare floorboards bit into her knees, but she kept her eyes fixed on the distant river where the last rays of the setting sun touched the water with a silver light. The dark was rising. It had covered the salt marshes, shrouded the trees on the slopes of the hill, swept over the broad lawns that surrounded the house. Once that thin, luminous band had gone, then the darkness would creep from the corners of the room, where it was waiting for her. The child dug her teeth into her lip. She would not cry or scream for a servant to let her out, for she knew they would never dare go against her cousin's orders.

Whenever Sophia locked her in the attic she had to stay there, until her punishment was complete. The last time it had been all night. When the candle stub had died, the rats had come out of their holes. She heard the patter of their claws, felt the whiplash of a tail against her leg. She screamed and screamed until her throat was raw and still no one had come. In the morning, Sophia had found her huddled up against the door, wet and shaking and laughed at her for being a dirty, stinking brat who should be sent out into the streets where she belonged.

A hot wave of shame swept over her. Clenching her fists so hard that her nails tore at her palms, she vowed that she would never be laughed at again. Sophia could keep her here for days, starve her, beat her, but she would not show her fear. The child lifted her chin proudly. One day she would have her revenge then Sophia would be sorry. All she had to do was wait until she was grown up and mistress of this house. When that day came, the first thing she would do would be to rid herself of her cousin. It would be easy enough. Sophia was the poor relation, she had no money, nor with her swarthy skin and tangled hair could she have any hope of ever marrying.

If only she didn't have to wait so long. She was only ten years old. Her head drooped, her lips quivered. Like the faint touch of a finger, a wisp of chill air slid down her back. The child gasped and shuddered. She must not look round. Sophia said the house was haunted by the ghost of her godfather, who spent his nights searching for naughty little girls, for girls who wet themselves and scratched and swore when they were scolded. For girls whose mothers had died when they were born, whose fathers had been lost at sea. For children who showed no gratitude for being taken in and given a good home when they could have been sent away to school and left there without any loving relations to take care of them. One day if she went on being a bad girl, he would come for her.

A scream rose in her throat. To choke it down she beat her forehead against the window. The pain was comforting. Rocking backwards and forwards on her heels calmed her. The thumping of blood in her head dulled, then became louder and louder like the sound of hoof beats on flagstones.

Could it be? Was it? She stopped, leaned forward, listened. There were voices, the sound of doors being thrown open and then the bright flares of torches. He was here. She rubbed the dirt from her face and straightened her skirts. Then standing as tall and as still as she could she waited.

The door opened. Candlelight threw great shadows around the walls. The rats scuttled away.

"I have decided you have served your time." Sophia stood in the doorway, her gown as red as blood. Over her arm she carried a blue silk dress. Face twisted with contempt, she thrust it at the child. "What a disgrace you are. Come, make yourself presentable. Cousin Nicholas is home."

"I'll tell him. I'll tell him what you have done to me. How you treat me when he is away," the child muttered as Sophia tore the dirty dress from her back and forced the clean one over her head.

"You think he'll believe you? A scruffy little urchin like you. The orphan his father was forced to take in because she had nowhere else to go?"

- 8 -

"He loves me. He cares about me."

"More than me his foster sister?" As Sophia bent to grab her by the shoulders, the child sidestepped avoiding her grasp.

"Yes," she cried triumphantly as a man's voice called,

"Where's my Annabel, my dear sweet little Ann?"

"See," she hissed and raced down the attic stairs, along endless corridors and into the domed entrance hall where he was waiting for her.

He held open his arms and she flung herself into them. He lifted her up and swung her round and she breathed in the scent of his journey, of winter wind and horse and the spicy perfume he used and she wanted to bury her head in his shoulder and have him hold her tight for ever and ever. The entrance hall with its glittering candelabra and marble statues whirled in a maze of colour and light and she cried out with dizziness and joy.

"Have you missed me?" he murmured his breath sweet against her ear.

"Oh yes, more than I can say," the words trembled on her lips, but before she could speak he was setting her back on her feet. Sick with dizziness, she stumbled towards him, half falling against the warm cloth of his riding coat, but instead of holding her close and letting her regain her balance, he was moving away.

"Sophia," he breathed, his eyes on the woman in the scarlet dress standing at the top of the staircase. Her dark hair tumbled about her bare shoulders and when she spoke her voice was sweet and warm as honey.

"Nicholas, welcome. It's been too long, far, far too long."

He started up the stairs towards her. He caught her hand in his and raised it to his lips. She smiled down at him, her eyes narrowing like a cat's. Straightening up he slid an arm around her waist. Two dark heads bent close together, talking and laughing, they swept past the child, who sank down on the bottom step and put her head in her hands.

CHAPTER TWO

Jo Docherty stood and looked at the wedding ring on the black granite worktop. It would be so easy to leave it there and go. On a practical level there was nothing to stop her. She had kept her own name, had her own career and since buying The Granary she had her own house. As she hesitated a shaft of late afternoon sun caught the circle of diamonds. Refracted light threw an arc of colour onto the stark white wall in front of her. A rainbow, a symbol of hope, a promise never to be broken, or so she remembered from the nuns' Religious Instruction lessons at school. It was a sign. It must be, or even if it wasn't she'd take it as such. Now was not the time to make a decision. She was still too raw; too full of grief.

Sliding the ring back on to the finger where she had worn it for the past eleven years she walked over to the blackboard that hung on the wall. Beside it a piece of chalk dangled on a length of string. "Gone to," she wrote then stopped. The message took up so little space; she wanted to write more, to begin to try and explain how there was only one place she wanted to be. How she had to spend time there to give herself, to give them both, a chance. But she didn't have the words. Instead she drew a quick sketch of an old house, high on a hill, surrounded by trees, overlooking a wide river.

White on black the drawing took on the look of a woodcut in reverse. Richard would appreciate that. Her husband liked things to be simple and clear-cut. The buildings he designed were structures of light and air, even the conversions he planned for Kingsfield would strip out any unnecessary detail. Life however was more complicated, full of misunder-standings and long cold silences.

She needed to work and she couldn't do it here in this cold, white riverside apartment. Going into the bedroom she threw a few essentials into an overnight bag then took her brushes and makeup from the slab of marble that was her dressing table.

The face reflected in the mirror was thin and pale, her silver blonde hair hanging like wire, accentuating the whiteness of her skin, the shadowed, haunted eyes.

"Get a grip you look terrible," she told herself. "Your clothes are falling off you. Thin is thin, but this is too much." She tightened the leather belt that held up her skinny black jeans and looked around to see if she had forgotten anything; her iPad was in her shoulder bag, her car keys on the console table by the door. There was nothing else she wanted, or needed. One last glance around the empty echoing space of the penthouse, then she re-set the security system and took the lift to the ground floor of the converted tobacco factory.

The day was on the cusp of evening when she turned the open top Mercedes onto the Portway. The Suspension Bridge hung high over the steep sides of the gorge, the river flowed grey green, the traffic fast on the wide road. The air was warm and thick with the smell of mud, water and petrol fumes. Jo's hands were tight on the wheel, her eyes fixed ahead. When she came to the hill leading up to Kingsfield, her stomach tightened as it always did. Looking to see that there was no one in front of her she put her foot down and shot under the iron bridge that arched over the road before taking the left turn to dip down between the high walls that ran around the estate. Only then did her grip loosen, her shoulders relax, her foot ease off the accelerator.

The lodge cottage was boarded up, its door covered with graffiti. On either side of it, marking the entrance to the drive were two stone gateposts, their surface worn and leprous, mottled with lichen and moss. Jo eased the car between them and drove into a shadowy twilight. Trees linked their branches overhead, forming a latticed tunnel, which seemed to have no end. Somewhere soon was the turning to the outbuilding conversion they had called The Granary, but in the dappled light Jo could see no gap in the thick wall of rhododendrons that pressed in on both sides. Frowning she changed down into first gear. The drive wound and twisted through the foliage. Trees and bushes closed in on her, cutting off the remaining light, sucking in the air. Any further and they would reach out their branches, entangling the car in a deadly embrace.

She could already feel them in her hair, around her shoulders. She had to get out of here and soon. How could she have missed the turning? She knew the way so well. Jo swore loudly to shut down the first stirring of panic. She had to go on. There was no way back. A wall loomed up in front of her. Blank windows stared emptily out of crumbling stone. She gulped, edged forward and then, as if she had no control over it, the car shot forward. Her foot came down on the brake. She steered wildly round the final corner and came to a halt at the very edge of the terrace. Far below her were the streets and houses of Weston Ridge. The council estate where she had lived as a child, stretched out over the salt marshes reaching almost as far as the line of factories that edged the bank of the Severn.

Elbows resting on the steering wheel, she let her head fall into her hands, the tension drain from her shoulders. After a while, she sat up, took a deep breath and leaned back in her seat to let the warmth of the evening steal over her. Sun sparkled on the surface of the river. Thin plumes of yellow smoke rose from the factory chimneys. In the distance the Welsh hills rose blue and misty into a darkening sky. Jo stretched a little awkwardly then got out of the car. Standing by the low wall that surrounded the terrace, she took in the view. Already she could see ways in which she would use it in her work. The dark shapes of industry etched against the silver water, bisected by streaks of sulphurous yellow. Should the house, with its classic portico and mellow golden stone provide a contrast? Acrylic, watercolour, or collage, which was the right medium for what she wanted to convey?

Pondering the options, Jo turned to look at the house. Painting Kingsfield seemed such a natural thing to want to do. For as long as she could remember she had loved this place. The house overlooking the wooded slopes of the hill, the half ruined outbuildings, the follies, the ancient stones that stood at the end of the west avenue. Instinctively she turned her head in their direction.

In spite of the heat, a shiver slid between her shoulder blades. The blood pounded in her head like the start of a migraine. Jo pressed her hands over her eyes, holding them there while she made herself relax. When she looked up again, the headache had gone and her vision was clear. Almost too clear. The details of the house stood out as if freshly carved. The windows were clean, the stone steps leading up to the front door showed none of the dips or misalignment of age. She blinked. The sun beating down on the back of her neck, made her skin prickle with heat. The air was heavy with the scent of lavender and honeysuckle, the drone of traffic muted, non-existent. It was as if everything had stopped and she was suspended between two states of being.

Needing to ground herself, but unable to take her eyes off the house she stepped back. Her hands feeling for the car met empty space. Her head jerked upwards and she saw high above her in the row of attic windows, a small, white face pressed against the glass.

Then her palms met warm metal, her legs nudged against the bumper. Light drained from the landscape, everything blurred and when she looked again she saw the decaying façade of a neglected country house.

She leaned against the Mercedes trying to make sense of what she had seen. Was it a trick of the light? Of some half remembered story from childhood of a princess locked in a tower? Jo pulled a face. That was the least likely explanation. Nan, as far as she knew, never read her bedtime stories and even if she had, her memories of childhood were vague. Unlike Richard, or their friends she found it hard to remember anything that had happened to her before the crash. So if not a story, then what?

Unable to decide, she slid into the driver's seat, her hands shaking a little as she turned the key. As the engine ignited she gave a snort of laughter. The explanation was so simple. She'd been thinking about work and had had a vivid idea for a painting. It was not her usual style, but maybe there was something in what she had seen that she needed to explore.

As soon as she got to The Granary, she'd go straight to her studio and begin. Swinging the car around the corner, the turning to her house was so obvious that she could not think how she had missed it. From this angle it was easy to see that the trees had been trimmed back, the track levelled and in the gathering dark, the security lights stretched out to greet her.

The key slid easily into the lock, turned smoothly in her hand. Stepping inside, she hurried through the empty hallway. At the door of the studio she stopped, taking in the darkness of the night as it pressed against the glass structure. For a brief moment she hesitated, then flicked the switches. The dark retreated, the space was filled with light and she was standing at her worktable. She opened her sketchbook, grabbed tubes of acrylic, squeezed and spread, using her fingers to mould the shapes of the buildings, her thumbnail to etch in details. She worked fast letting her hands translate what she had in her mind, then stepped back to see what she had managed to capture. The house was there, golden stone roughly delineated, an indigo sky rising behind it. But there was something else. Jo frowned and squinted at the paper to make sure she was not mistaken. She remembered the sweeping movement of her hands as she spread the deep blue over the page. She did not remember drawing the figure of the girl with wide spreading skirts running towards her, arms outstretched as if pleading for help, or rescue.

Jo shook her head. The girl in the blue dress was not what she had envisaged. It was the house that interested her, the graceful Georgian mansion, which contrasted so starkly with the brutal shapes of the industrial buildings along the river. There was no room here for figures.

She pulled out the page, set it to one side. Thinking that perhaps the medium she had chosen didn't suit her subject she picked up a pencil and began again. This time the house faded into the background and the focus of the drawing became a girl's face. The girl in the blue dress.

Jo drew in her breath. In the garden, something moved against the darkness of the glass. Glancing up, she caught a flurry of skirts, the briefest glimpse of blue. An after image of her drawing? Jo pressed her palms over her eyes to clear her vision and when she looked again there was nothing there. The house was silent and still. Then it came. A faint tap against the window. A small, white hand pressed against the pane, reaching out towards her.

CHAPTER THREE

Standing under the harsh lights of the studio Jo watched the small white face looking in at her. Against the dark glass it appeared disembodied, ghostlike; then it was gone. She flung open the door and stared out into the night.

"Who are you? What do you think you're doing?" she yelled. Somewhere in the woodland, a twig crackled. Jo let out a pent up breath. Kids from the estate, it must be. How dare they? Coming up here so late and scaring her half to death.

"Get out of here, go on. This is private property." There was more she wanted to scream, but she choked down her fury. Now was not the time to antagonise the locals. Expecting, almost hoping to hear a barrage of taunts and giggles, she waited.

Nothing. Either the kids had made their escape, or they had never been there. To banish the second impossible thought she stepped out into the garden and flinched as the security lights swept an arc of bright white light over the rough lawn. Clenching her fists, Jo strode over the grass towards the trees. She called out again, but as far as she could see the garden was empty, nor was there any sign of an intruder, whether human or animal. The trees were too close and tangled for an easy exit, the undergrowth undisturbed.

Wrapping her arms around her waist, Jo stepped back into the light. Inside the house she felt calmer, safer.

I must have imagined it, she thought. *I was caught up in what I was doing, that's all. And it's late and I'm tired. That's why I thought I saw her.* She made herself walk over to the table and look at the drawing. The girl with her fair, almost white hair scraped back from her pinched face stared back at her. There was a look in her eyes that was both demanding and pitiful. *As if she needs something so badly that she can't bring herself to ask for it. In case he says "no".* Jo caught her bottom lip in her teeth. *I know how you feel.* Her eyes wandered to the dark glass that formed the wall of the studio and she looked quickly away. This was getting crazy. Here she was projecting her feelings on some mirage when what she wanted to do was to find her way into a new painting. It was the contrast between eighteenth century elegance and the brutalist structure of the factories and the fluidity of the river that she had been striving for, not a portrait of a kid who looked as if she'd been sucking lemons. Ripping her sketch from the pad, she threw it into the waste bin and stared at a clean new page.

The air in the room closed around her, heavy and still, clogging her thoughts. What she needed was a cool night breeze, but she could not bring herself to open the doors and windows. Here behind a triple thickness of glass she was safe, out there anything could be lurking.

Giving up any attempt to work, she wondered if there was some Sauvignon left in the fridge. She couldn't remember buying it but her head was so full, her thoughts so bizarre, that it was possible she might have forgotten. If not, there was always the twenty-four hour supermarket. Jo glanced at her watch and decided that this was not an option. It was past midnight; too late to go out, too late to do anything but sleep. Keeping her eyes from the expanse of darkness that surrounded her, she switched off the studio lights and went into the kitchen.

There was no wine, only half a carton of milk. First thing in the morning she would go shopping. If she were going to stay here she would need food. As she had not planned to move in so soon The Granary lacked basic supplies. It had never been intended to be more than a studio with sleeping accommodation she could use if she were working late, or had a project she could not bear to leave. Or so she had told herself.

Her phone signalled a new message. Looking at the screen she saw it was Richard and wondered whether to let it go to voice mail, then relented and took the call.

"Darling are you OK? I know this is late but I only just got in and found your message. Is everything all right, or do you want me to come over?"

Alright? Jo's skin prickled with irritation. Didn't he know what she was feeling? Couldn't he at least try to imagine?

"I'm fine," she said coolly. "Don't worry about me."

"You're sure you don't want me?"

"Not tonight."

"Tomorrow then. I'll see you tomorrow."

Jo's stomach clenched.

"Tomorrow," she murmured.

"Love you." The words hovered between them. Were they his? Or hers? Trotted out without thinking as their usual way of ending a conversation.

Her footsteps echoed on bare wood as she went upstairs. A row of small windows along the corridor reflected a darkness unbroken by the orange glow of streetlights and there was no moon. The bedroom window was a dark arch in a white wall. The room was empty except for the bed. There were no curtains to shut out the night, but Jo felt cocooned in the warmth and light of The Granary. All the evil and menace that was out there was held at bay by thick, stone walls and reassuring layers of glass and solid wood. Slipping off her clothes, she showered and got into bed. Curled under a single sheet, she wrapped her arms around her pillow and slept.

She woke to a flood of early morning sun pouring through wide windows and a riotous chorus of birds welcoming the dawn. Stretched out in the wide bed, thin and flat-chested as a boy, her hands rested on the dip of her stomach, the empty space between projecting hipbones. For a moment she let them rest there. If she had not miscarried that last time, if the child had stayed snug and safe in her womb, her baby would have been born by now. He or she would be four months old, asleep next door in the bedroom she had thought might be a nursery.

Jo screwed up her eyes against the pain of her loss. She had to stop thinking about it. Brooding would do no good. The consultant had said that early miscarriages were very common. Some women suffered a number, before a successful pregnancy. There was nothing to worry about. If she lost another baby, then he would run a series of tests. In the meantime there was no reason not to try again. Jo bit back a sob. If only it were that simple.

She threw off her sheet and walked naked to the en-suite. What had happened, had happened and after the miscarriage she had spent too much time lying in bed too weak to move. She needed to work and by starting now she could take advantage of the early morning light. Dressing quickly in her customary black jeans and white T-shirt she went downstairs.

The house, her house, bought with the money left by her mother and stepfather, smelled of new wood and sawdust. Her footsteps padded on dusty floorboards as she went into the kitchen area. There was no furniture yet. The Granary was always intended as a studio not a home. The apartment at Wharfside was where she had lived. This was where she worked. Now of course it was different. She was going to stay here, at least until she knew what she wanted to do next. Or had she always known that this was the place she wanted to be? Was that why she had been so inexorably drawn to it and why she had been so keen to buy it?

As soon as it had come on the market she knew she had to have it. She had sold her old studio and Richard had reluctantly agreed to convert the outbuilding. As a hugely successful architect with a world-wide practice, he'd been sceptical of the whole idea. Once he had viewed the site, however, he had changed his mind and when quite suddenly and unexpectedly the rest of the Kingsfield estate had come up for sale he had bought it as an investment. The main house would be turned into luxury flats, the other outbuildings into single dwellings.

She'd been angry with him at first, furious that her special place would be invaded by strangers, but he pointed out that this was inevitable, Kingsfield was a prime site. It was within easy reach of the city, yet at the same time curiously isolated and so was bound to attract developers. At least if he was doing the work she could have some input. Much as she doubted he would listen to any suggestion of hers, Jo knew that he was right. If it were not Richard's firm then someone else would buy the estate. They might even turn the main house into a hotel or wedding venue. In the meantime Richard was busy with other more prestigious international projects and Jo was alone at Kingsfield.

Although she had always lived in a city the isolation did not worry her. She was used to working alone and the joy of her house was something she savoured. She had wanted a space that was airy and filled with light and this is what Richard had given her.

The Granary's ground floor was open plan. As Jo stood in the kitchen waiting for the kettle to boil she looked out into the living area. At the furthest end of the empty room a single arched window looked out on woodland. On the adjoining wall there was a wood burning stove. In the winter it would warm the whole fabric of the building. A similar stove stood in the studio, which Richard had designed as a glass extension along the whole length of the house.

As soon as her coffee was ready, she went to work. The pages she had discarded the night before lay crumpled in the wastepaper basket. She ignored them. The shapes that had seemed so tantalisingly out of reach in the dead of night came to her in total clarity. Deciding against paint she picked up her pencil and began to draw. She worked so fast it was almost as if there was no need to think. Sometimes when the ideas flowed, her hands worked of their own accord and when this happened Jo had learned to abandon herself completely to the process. She drew rapidly, with purpose and a sense of rightness, a feeling of being carried on an unstoppable wave of creativity. It would not be until she had finished that she would be able to see what she had achieved.

When finally she was done, she stood back to view her sketch. She had intended blocks of industrial buildings, set against the elegant details of the old house, the suggestion of sun on water, a rugged surface of distant mountains; what she had drawn was an exquisite little picture of a domed summer house. Built like a Grecian temple it was an eighteenth century folly set in parkland. Pretty enough, innocuous even, but it was the figure of the girl sitting on the steps that sent her heart pounding. It was the girl in the blue dress; the girl she had drawn in spite of herself the night before.

The pencil slid from her fingers. Her hands flew to her mouth. Backing away she stumbled out of the studio into the sunlit spaces of the house.

What was happening to her? Whatever it was it would have to stop. With shaking hands she filled the kettle. A cup of tea that's what you needed for shock, Nan always said, with lots of sugar for the blood. Jo looked helplessly around her empty kitchen. There was no sugar; she was lucky she had teabags and milk. Whatever would Nan have said? Noreen Docherty's whole life ran on hot strong builder's tea. The sort you could stand a spoon up in and laced with enough sugar to keep the industry going for a year. Jo laughed shakily at the thought. There wasn't much she remembered about her childhood, in fact she had amazingly few memories compared with everyone else she knew, but Nan and her tea were imprinted on her brain. Jo's shoulders relaxed and she smiled. Perhaps she should have a go at drawing her? Perhaps that would help her remember. It was odd that she'd never thought of that before. Maybe the girl in the blue dress was some residual memory too.

Whatever she was, she was not going to address it this morning. There were other more pressing matters like buying food. Jo cast a quick glance around the empty living space, if she were going to stay here she needed some furniture; sofas and chairs to sit on, a table to eat at, rugs to soften the floors, curtains to keep out the night.

*

The antiques market was full of stalls selling everything from comics to commodes. Jo lingered at one selling lace, until she caught sight of a christening gown displayed over the back of a nursing chair. Cutting off her conversation with the stall-holder she moved quickly towards the jewellery. Sunlight trapped in amber calmed her. An amethyst set in silver tempted her. She remembered reading somewhere about the stone's healing properties, then reminded herself that what she really needed was something to sit on. She wandered towards the exit, weaving through the narrow passageways between the stalls until, turning an unexpected corner, she was brought to a halt by a display of oriental rugs strewn across the floor.

"You can walk on them if you like, my lover. They've lasted for hundreds of years, so they'll hold out a little bit longer," the stall holder, a small, round, gypsy like woman called in her languid Bristolian drawl. Jo knelt to examine a rug its original scarlet mellowed to a deep claret. She bought it and a pair of cushions, made from camel bags, their colours faded into a rich patina of crimson and cobalt.

"Now all I need is some furniture," she said as the stallholder's teenage assistant helped her load her purchases into the car.

"You want 'elen's for that. She's got good stuff. You'll find her in Alice Court, just off Princess Victoria Street. It's not five minutes walk from here," he advised, jerking his thumb in the approximate direction.

Jo slung her bag over her shoulder and set off down the road. Beyond the main shopping area, the buildings had been painted in bright colours. None were taller than two storeys; some were shops, some offices. The one or two still lived in were like tiny dolls houses with bright shutters and highly polished door furniture. Their windows looked straight onto the street and glancing inside Jo was so absorbed in deciding how she would change the décor of each room that she almost walked straight past the notice.

"Helene Bonheur and Daughter" was written in plain script on the sign that hung to the side of the wrought iron arch spanning the entrance to Alice Court. Three sides of what had once been a small mews had been transformed into a shop. The buildings were painted a pale terracotta, their shutters a deeper shade of burnt sienna. Vines and creepers were trained over the walls and a selection of furniture had been set out in the sunlight.

"Can I help you?" The woman who approached her was of medium height, with a strong face and short dark hair shot with silver. She wore elegant slacks, a loose denim shirt, a red scarf tied like a bandana around her neck and gold studs in her ears. There was a thick gold band on the index finger of her left hand.

"I have an empty house that needs to be filled," Jo said.

"Immediately?" The second woman was a softer presence. Younger and fairer, she wore a lilac shirt over blue loose cut jeans. A Navaho necklace studded with turquoise hung between her plump breasts. "You need to blot out the echoes. Empty spaces are full of the most unpredictable things."

"Cecile," sighed the older woman affectionately.

"No. It's OK. She's right," Jo let herself be guided into the shop. At the entrance they were greeted by a large orange cat, which led them through a cornucopia of waxed pine, polished mahogany, burnished brass and pewter. There were tables and chairs and cupboards with glass fronts, and cupboards with plain doors, linen chests and rocking chairs and Welsh dressers and beds and over-mantles and fire surrounds. They followed dutifully until suddenly the cat jumped onto a table and settled down for a wash.

"Thank you Monty." Cecile waved her hand at the animal, which lifted a leg and applied himself to more intimate regions. "Wretched creature. He is so rude. In spite of his terrible manners, I think you'll find he's right. This is the one for you."

Jo ran her hand along the wood. It felt good beneath her touch. The table was sturdy and with the matching chairs would fit well into the space she had in mind.

"I'll take it." The cat lowered his leg, yawned, stretched and jumped onto the floor.

"Does he do this with everyone?" Jo asked. Cecile smiled.

"I know it's crazy, but he seems to have some sort of

instinct. If he doesn't take to somebody, they don't buy anything. Mum says it's because he's Leo come back and it could be. Leo used to own this place. He had a shaggy orange beard and he was huge and he never sold you anything unless he liked you. So," she shrugged. "Who knows?"

I don't believe in reincarnation, Jo thought, picking up a small wooden figure. *Or ghosts.* Remembering the pinched, white face, pressed against the attic window of the empty house, the hand knocking at the studio window, she shivered. Her fingers tightened round the squat figure of the goddess.

"If it's too much, you can pay in instalments," Cecile was saying.

"Oh no, it's fine. Any chance of delivery before the end of the week?"

"I'll see." Helene went over to the desk and opened a large leather bound book. "I'm sorry, we normally do next day delivery, but we're fully booked for tomorrow. The first slot I have is the day after tomorrow and it will have to be after four when we close the shop. Will that do?"

"That's fine. I've got a rug, some cushions and a bed. So I'll cope." Jo nodded. "Do you do the delivery yourselves?"

"How else did we get these muscles?" Cecile rolled up her sleeves and, bunching up her fists, held her arms above her head in a parody of a prize-fighter.

What a shape, all curves and dips, Jo thought appreciatively. *I'd like to draw her and her mother, but with Helene it's the face that is interesting. With that narrow chin and aquiline nose she's like a hawk.*

"What's the address? I have to stick labels on everything to make sure you get the right set, or Monty will never forgive us."

"Jo Docherty, The Granary, Kingsfield."

The two women exchanged glances. Helene lifted an eyebrow and for a moment Jo thought she frowned.

"Kingsfield House, I know that name. Hang on a minute." Cecile disappeared into a room at the back of the shop and came back carrying a tattered pamphlet. "If you're living there, I think you'll be interested in this."

"The Antiquities and Curiosities of Kingsfield and Surrounding Parishes, by the Reverend Edwin Marriot written in the year of Our Lord 1721," Jo read.

"It's a copy. It says so somewhere on the inside of the cover. It has the original illustrations, though. Look." Cecile flicked through the pages. The print was cramped and stained with damp, the drawings crude and out of proportion. The Neolithic stones that stood at the end of the west drive loomed above the treetops dwarfing the two countrywomen with their basket of flowers who stood before them.

"The Satan Stones," Cecile said. "At least that's what the good Reverend calls them. But then he's a man and a clergyman and the Church has to knock anything it doesn't control, so what's new?"

"Cecile" Helene's voice carried a warning tone.

"Sorry. I hope that didn't offend you. All I wanted to say was," she stopped as if searching for the right words.

"You didn't," Jo burst in quickly. "I'm not religious. I never have been, or at least I went to church when I was a kid, Nan made me, but once I could make up my own mind, I decided that all that stuff wasn't for me."

"You don't believe in anything?" Cecile prompted.

"No. I mean. Yes." Jo was uncertain where the conversation was going. Were they talking, ethics, or morals, or philosophy? There was a pause as she gathered her thoughts, during which she thought she saw another of those brief glances between mother and daughter.

"The supernatural, ghosts, that sort of thing?" Cecile said at last. Jo shook her head vigorously. Helene smiled and said briskly,

"I'll put the pamphlet with your delivery shall I?"

"No. I'll take it with me. It looks interesting." Jo was strangely reluctant to hand back the booklet.

"It's all just superstition," Helene said as they waited for Jo's card to be processed.

"Of course," Jo said. Yet some distant memory nagged at

the back of her mind. As she dismissed it, she remembered glancing down the west avenue in the direction of the Stones the previous night and something cold slithered down her body and a feeling of dread lodged itself in the pit of her stomach.

CHAPTER FOUR

The Satan Stones were evil. That's what Nan had always said. Or had she? Driving back to Kingsfield Jo tried to remember. She knew that when she was a little girl Nan had forbidden her to play in the woods at the back of the house. This wild tangle of trees and shrubs stretched right up to the terrace where she had parked her car last night. No one had cared for it for years. So although it belonged to the mansion, it became the perfect playground for kids from the council estate. During the day, the younger ones made dens, waged war with rival gangs, smoked and dared each other to sneak up to the big house. In the evenings the woods were used by courting couples and the occasional tramp.

Jo shook her head and smiled wryly. Was that why Nan didn't want her to go up there? Noreen Docherty had always striven to better herself and her family. As soon as Jo could understand, Nan had made it plain that a council estate wasn't good enough for her granddaughter. If she'd had her way they'd have lived anywhere rather than Weston Ridge. It was Granddad with his job at the docks who had insisted they stayed close to the port at Avonmouth.

None of that however explained the name that had been given to the Stones, or why they were associated with the devil. When she was little, did she even know they were there? Jo's hands tightened on the wheel. Frowning with concentration, she dredged her memory, but as usual whenever she tried to bring back the past she simply could not remember. Absorbed in her thoughts, she turned into the drive at the wrong angle, missed the entrance into the courtyard of The Granary and had to drive on to the front of the house, just as she had the night before. Once again, Jo found herself facing the avenue of ancient oaks leading up to the Satan Stones. She was wondering whether to get out of the car and take a look at them, to see if the reality came anywhere close to the exaggerated picture in the pamphlet when she caught a movement somewhere just beyond her field of vision.

In the warm light of a different afternoon, two figures were walking on the terrace. The girl in a long dress was in her teens, the man in satin coat and breeches was older perhaps in his thirties. Her face upturned to his was alight with joy. His stance toward hers protective, caring. They stopped and he murmured something gently, tenderly and she rose on tiptoe for his kiss. Her dress was blue as the summer sky, her hair touched with gold by the sun. He was dressed in black, dark as the sudden shadow that raced across from the west. The wind gusted. Jo looked up expecting a flurry of rain and they were gone.

They look like lovers, was her first thought. They were so close, so easy with each other. She should draw them. A quick sketch. Charcoal, or pencil. A few brief lines to suggest his dominance, her openness, the way she reached up to him, offering herself and her life. Just as she had with Richard at the beginning of their relationship.

When they had first met she had felt so alone. She had been sitting beside the hospital bed, where Kit the man she loved and worked with was dying. Surrounded by friends and hangers-on, his life was draining from him yet he was determined to party to the end. Jo had found his refusal to face what was happening to him unbearable. Everyone else had thought he was being so brave. Only Richard, Kit's cousin, had understood how it was tearing her apart.

Jo ran both hands through her hair, and clenched her fingers as if tearing the images from her brain. What had this to do with what she had seen? If indeed she had seen anything. There was no one there now. There never had been. She stared through the windscreen at the crumbling terrace, the weeds thrusting their way through the flagstones, the line of factories along the estuary. Putting the car into gear, she drove away as fast as she dared.

Turning into the courtyard she came out into dazzling sunlight. Bees buzzed in lavender beds, there was a whir of insects in the fringes of the woodland, the air smelled of new mown grass and the thick stone walls of the building soaked in the sun.

The cobbles were warm under her feet, the heat seeping through the fine slippers she wore. Muslin skirts clung to her legs and her body felt different, fuller rounder as if all the hollows had been filled in. There was a basket over her arm, a large brimmed straw hat on her head. She walked slowly, her hips swaying, towards the half open door of the barn. The air was dusty with grain, heavy with the scent of hay. She put her basket on the floor, undid the ribbons and threw her hat down beside it. Raising her arms, she unpinned her hair and shook it over her shoulders, where it lay, thick and dark, curling over her coffee coloured skin. She leaned back against the wall and waited. Above the tightness of her bodice, her breasts rose and fell.

"I could not keep away." His shadow in the doorway blocked out the light.

"You grow tired of her," she murmured triumphantly, winding her arms around his neck.

His lips came hard on hers, her mouth opened, her body rubbed against his. His kisses grew deeper. His hands traced the line of her hips, pulling her into him. She opened her legs, her nails digging into his shoulder, her breasts hot against his chest. Flushed, drunk with desire, he raised his head.

"I must have you," he breathed.

"It is forbidden. You are bound to another," she mocked and twisting away, moved deeper into the shadows.

"I must."

"I know," her voice was low, inviting.

"I will run mad, if I do not."

A shaft of sun pregnant with dust shone in under the eaves. She slid her dress from her shoulders, reached down and unfastened her laces. With a whisper, the muslin fell to her feet and she stood naked before him, her body creamy brown in the dusky light, her waist narrow, her breasts high and firm, nipples upright. He sank to his knees before her and she wound her hands in his hair as he buried his face in her dark curls. Her face as he pleasured her was savage in its ecstasy. Nostrils flared, eyes half closed, her teeth bit deep into her lips as she shuddered to her climax. He tore at his britches, flung away his shirt and took her where she stood.

She loosened her grip. A trail of blood slid from the scratches on his back. A bruise rose at the base of her throat, another on the curve of her neck. She took his hand and led him to a fall of hay. They lay there, her arm around his shoulders, his head on her breast, his tongue playing lazily around her nipple, licking, teasing, sucking. Her hands flickered through his hair. Her breathing changed, her hips arched towards him and laughing she pushed him away. He rolled over onto his back and she was on him, head flung back, hair snaking down her back as she rode him. His hands gripped her hips and they climaxed.

Spent, she lay along him, fitting her body into his, covering his face and shoulders with her hair. The light changed, the mellow afternoon deepened into a golden evening.

Heart racing, flushed and shaken, Jo found herself back in The Granary, her car keys in her hand. The house was as she had left it; empty of furniture, still smelling of new wood. Dropping her bag on the kitchen unit she gripped the edge of the surface. This was real. Solid. Whatever she thought she had seen was her imagination, or her need. It was so long since she had felt desire. Since the last miscarriage, she couldn't bear to be touched. Even a brief kiss on the cheek made her flinch. So why all of a sudden was she conjuring up these fantasies? If that was indeed what they were.

This is stupid, she told herself, *you've got to stop it. Nothing happened, you saw nothing. It was a trick of the light, that's all. A trick of the light.*

A car drew up outside. The door opened then clunked shut. Relief swept over her, so powerfully that for a moment she had to lean against the unit to prevent herself from falling. A key turned in the lock.

"Richard." She ran to him, holding out her arms and he

caught her and held her close.

"You're early," she whispered.

"I came as soon as I could. I wanted to see you." His breath tickled her ear, his kisses were soft on her mouth. Her body stirred. The blood pounded through her veins. She wound her arms around his neck. Half shutting her eyes, she let her lips open beneath his. His hands cupped her buttocks, pulling her into him. She wriggled closer, pressing herself against him, her hands at his buckle loosening his belt, her fingers exploring.

"Jo?"

All her doubts forgotten, she flung back her head and smiled, slowly, provocatively, grinding her hips into his.

"Come upstairs," she whispered.

In the bedroom she pulled away from him. Still smiling, holding him with her glance, she let her hand fall to her crotch, let her fingers tease at the zip. She could hear his breathing quicken, but she would not hurry, slowly, slowly, she unzipped her jeans, then raising her arms slid her jumper over her head. Her nipples stood firm and erect beneath the silk T-shirt, straining against the delicate lace of her bra. Sliding her hands down her body, she pushed her jeans from her hips, stepped out of them and sat on the bottom of the bed, legs apart, her eyes challenging him, as she pulled off her boots and lay back against the pillows wearing nothing but her briefs.

He flung off his clothes and lowered himself onto her. Her legs curled up around his back, her nails dug deep into his flesh and they climaxed.

Bodies slippery with sweat, bed hot with the smell of sex, they lay side by side.

"Jo," he said shakily. "That was…"

"I know." Something flickered at the back of her mind. An image of two bodies entangled on a dusty floor. She bit her lip and leaned over him. A thin trickle of blood trailed down his back. "Did I do that?"

"Who else?" He tried to grin, but she could hear the note of unease in his voice.

"I'm sorry. I didn't mean to hurt you." *I never hurt you. I've never done anything like this before. It's not my style.* Again the almost photographic flash. A woman's face, savage in its ecstasy; long dark hair snaking down her back. Jo pushed back the duvet; swung her legs out of bed.

"I need a shower."

He did not follow her. He lay with his hands behind his head, silent and preoccupied.

"Do you want to…" she stopped. There was nothing to say. Their lovemaking had left them with nothing but silence.

Standing under the scalding water, she felt the pleasure drain from her. It was as if she had made love with a stranger. No, that was not it. It was as if she had made love as a stranger. In spite of the heat, she shuddered. Washing herself quickly, she wrapped a towel around her body and went back into the bedroom. Richard was already out of bed. Usually after they made love, he would drift off to sleep until she woke him with a cup of coffee. Today he was already up, waiting impatiently for his turn to use the shower. Did he too sense something strange about what had happened? She wanted to ask him, but some deep instinct held her back.

She went downstairs and made coffee. Richard joined her, his hair still damp. Standing opposite him at the kitchen counter, she noted how drawn his face looked. The lines on his forehead deeper, the silver grey hair that she had thought so distinguished now made him look much older than a man in his late forties. Bending her head, not wanting to meet his eyes, she let her hair fall over her face. Richard stared out of the window at a blue tit pecking at the feeder. Their silence hung around them like a shroud. The sunlight leeched from the lawn and the shadows creeping in from the wood wrapped themselves around the house.

CHAPTER FIVE

Richard did not leave that night. Neither he nor Jo were hungry. He had brought wine and they drank until the bottle was empty and they staggered up to bed. They woke as strangers. Two people who'd had a night of rough sex. Lying side by side, Jo's skin was tight over her bones, her limbs ached, she moved awkwardly, not wanting to aggravate the soreness between her legs. Beside her, Richard stared up at the ceiling, where the morning sun made patterns on the new plaster. He did not watch her as she dressed and waited until she had left the room before he got up.

When he joined her, she was sitting on the step between the kitchen and living area, her hands wrapped around a coffee cup.

"I thought you'd be in the studio," he said, half bending as if to drop a kiss on the top of her head as he sometimes did, then moving away without touching her.

"No," Jo said flatly, her eyes fixed on the squirrel racing up the trunk of a tree.

"If you're not working, come home."

"I can't." She heard the faintest in-drawing of breath and added. "Sorry. I need to work. I've an exhibition coming up. I want, no I need, to be here."

"OK," he said stiffly. "If you're staying at Kingsfield, then why don't we go and have a look round the house. You can give me your opinion on the plans."

"Today? Now?" Jo thought of the months Richard's firm had owned the estate. "You must have been round it countless times."

"Not that many, and not with you." Jo nodded, recognizing the truth in what he said. At first she'd been too weak, then nothing seemed to matter anymore. The silences had stretched between them. They spent little time together, both losing themselves in their work. For Richard to ask her to go around the main house, for him to want to know what she thought was a break through the barrier they had erected.

"All right," Jo got to her feet. "Let's do it."

Outside the air was cool and fresh. A blackbird sang, zealously guarding its territory and sunlight dappled the front of The Granary. They crossed the cobbled courtyard, where their cars stood and turned into the drive. They walked side by side, not speaking, until hidden by trees the back of the house loomed up in front of them. It stood in deep shadow, the windows cracked, the walls stained with damp.

"It needs some work, but the front elevation is magnificent," Richard said.

"I know. We used to live down the hill. Remember."

"Of course I do. I may be older than you, but I'm not senile yet. My little Bristolian."

"There's nothing wrong with Bristol," Jo said fiercely.

"Did I say there was?"

"No," she admitted.

"Come on then," his voice was warm, more natural, as if they were slipping back into their old easy relationship.

"What if I don't like what you're going to do?"

"Then you'll tell me."

"And?"

"I'll ignore you."

"As always," Jo tried to keep her voice light, made herself smile and he was smiling too as they turned the corner and stopped in front of the building.

"Look at the sweep of those steps. That double bank of doors and rows and rows of windows. Perfect proportions, crowned by the balustrade along the top of the house and those classic urns standing at each corner. They've been up there for over two hundred years. God, they knew how to build. And it gets better inside." With a flourish Richard was up the steps and holding open the door. "Let me show you."

She hesitated, reluctant to leave the sunlight and step into the shadows.

"What is it?" Richard said sharply.

- 34 -

"Nothing," Jo shook her head unwilling to break the fragile connection between them. "I'm…" as she spoke something pushed against the small of her back.

Come to see the treasures of Kingsfield, a voice whispered in her ear. The air snagged in her lungs and shaken by a bout of dizziness she stumbled up the last two steps. Regaining her balance she said, "Sorry, I didn't catch what you said."

"I didn't say anything."

"But I thought I heard…"

"What?"

"Nothing. It doesn't matter."

He slipped his arm around her waist and guided her gently through the doors.

"Look at it. Isn't this something," he said.

A shaft of sun from the upper windows funnelled light down the staircase, catching the crystal chandelier and refracting colours onto the statues, giving Dionysius a red nose, Aphrodite blue hands. Jo blinked in surprise. She thought the house was empty. Then, as she was about to say something, the picture vanished. Dust hung in the air of the empty hall.

"No one's lived here for years. At one point the university thought about buying it. Ironically, they were going to use it for their school of architecture. Instead they decided to leave it to decay."

"And now it's yours." Was it the damp or the cold creeping up from the floor that made her shudder? Jo forced a smile. "Living down there as a kid, I never ever thought I would marry the man who owned this place." She took his hand, grateful for his warmth.

"Too grand for you?"

"Never. It's what Nan would have said was our just deserts."

"Your Nan was a prize snob," Richard teased.

"No she wasn't," Jo was quick to defend the small, fiery woman that had brought her up for most of her childhood. He looked at her quizzically. "Well maybe a bit," she conceded.

"She didn't like me mixing with the local kids. She thought we were better than that."

I wasn't going to end up with no exams and pregnant at sixteen. Not if she had anything to do with it.

Jo bit back a sudden twist of memory.

"You proved her right," Richard smiled and she wondered if he had read her thoughts, then he said, "You've come a long way."

"I know. I wish she'd lived long enough to see it."

"You did her proud," he said softly. "Look at what you've achieved, look at where you are. Top collectors buy your work."

Not any more, not for the past year, Jo thought.

"That's why this exhibition is so important," she said.

"Only if you're sure you feel up to it."

"I am." Jo felt her irritation rising. "If I'm not working, I feel as if there's a part of me missing. You're the same." "I know," he gave a mock sigh. The sun catching his silver hair, he looked so handsome, so much the man she had married that her anger evaporated.

"I've always wanted to see inside," she said.

"You never sneaked up here?"

"Me? You know what a good girl I am," she laughed lightly.

"If you had, your Nan would have heaped the whole Catholic guilt trip on you."

Instinctively Jo touched the heavy silver cross she wore around her neck.

"She'd have clipped me round the ear, or rather Granddad would. They were very strict."

"And very Catholic. No doubt she didn't approve of the pagan remains up here. That's one of the things that makes the whole development unique. A New Stone Age monument in the grounds. Apparently it was part of a chambered long barrow. Archaeologists think it's the ancient tomb of some long forgotten chieftain."

"I don't know about that. I do know she didn't like me

straying far from home." Without thinking, Jo looked over her shoulder towards the open door as if checking that nothing barred her escape. "Let's see the rest of it, if we're going to," she said.

They crossed the hall, their feet echoing in the emptiness. Richard pushed open a door and looking back Jo saw the dust drift over their footprints. The room was dim, shrouded in cobwebs.

"We've had the windows boarded up in case of vandals," Richard said. "You'll get a better feel for the house upstairs."

"Oh. That's odd. Last night, when I first got here I thought I saw…" Jo stopped uncertain whether she wanted to go on.

"You saw what?"

"I thought I saw a face in one of the upstairs windows," she said slowly.

"A trick of the light. No one has been here since we did the last survey."

"Of course not." Jo blinked away the vision of the two people in the barn. "I was tired and thinking of work. You know I even thought I saw someone in the garden."

"Who?" Richard said sharply.

"Oh no one. Or at least when I went to look, there was no one there."

"You shouldn't have gone out, not on your own. You should have rung me. Stayed put and rung me."

"But I told you. There wasn't anyone there."

"There hadn't better be. This is private property."

"You're beginning to sound like the lord of the manor," she said, an edge of disapproval in her voice. To her surprise his face lit up with enthusiasm.

"It's a wonderful house. If money was no object I'd keep it for us."

"No," she said sharply. "It's not for us. It's too…"

"Too much for a little girl from the estate," he supplied. Jo ignored him.

"I prefer The Granary. It's right for me," she said and was moving away when she heard the crying. Loud, demanding, insistent. "What was that?"

"What?"

"There it is again." Softer now, further away. As if someone had carried the child to a distant part of the house and left it there. "Can't you hear it? There's a baby crying." The words were out of her mouth before she could stop herself.

"Jo," he said gently.

"No, I heard it. I really did."

He listened. She saw the concentration on his face, knew he was thinking of trespassers then he shook his head.

"There's no one here but us. Look are you all right? Or is this too much for you?"

"I'm fine," Jo said a little desperately. She knew what he was thinking, that the crying was the product of her grief but if she gave in to his demands to look after her, she would be lost. Wrapping her up in a suffocating blanket of counselling and therapy, Richard would try to convince her that what he wanted for her was what she needed.

"I can take you home, back to Wharfside."

"No."

"Are you sure?"

"I told you. I'm staying in The Granary to get some work done and I'm OK. Don't worry so much about me. I'm stronger than you think." She touched his arm briefly.

"In that case let's go upstairs. The views from the first floor are spectacular. You can see as far as the Welsh mountains." He gave her his hand and her fingers twined round his, grateful for his presence as they climbed the long staircase. She had told Helene and Cecile that she did not believe in the supernatural, but now she was not so sure. Whatever Richard said, there was something, or someone in this house.

The first floor rooms were tall and gracious. The light poured in through long windows, but the air was restless with scurries and whispers and half heard voices. Even Richard heard them. Jo saw him frown and look around for the broken pane, the gap in the stonework that would explain the swirls and eddies of sound. Her grip on his hand tightened then loosened as the world spun around her and vertigo overcame her senses.

"Got to get some air," she gasped.

"OK." Unusually, he seemed not to notice her distress and was already walking towards the half open door of the adjoining room, as if that would explain the disturbances in the atmosphere.

Jo ran down the stairs and across the hall to the front door. The doorknob was smooth and slippery and it took a couple of attempts before she could turn it and stumble out into the fresh air. Keeping her back to the house, she walked across the terrace and looked over the river to the Welsh hills. Their deep indigo merged into the sharp blue of the sky. So different from the pale blue of a girl's faded silk dress. Jo took a deep breath. The image vanished and Richard was standing beside her, his face creased with concern.

"Are you all right? I turned round and you'd gone."

"I'm fine. It was a little airless in there. I know it's silly but for a moment I felt as if I couldn't breathe." *The air was too full. There was no room for us there. You felt it too. I saw it in your face.*

"It must have been the lack of ventilation. No wonder you felt strange. The sooner the builders get in there the better, or we'll have damp to worry about."

"Mm," Jo muttered, hoping that he would take it as agreement. She didn't want to argue with him. She didn't want to talk. She still felt strangely disembodied, as if she were only partly here in this landscape. *I'm like a fading picture, or one of those images that haven't quite arrived on the screen. If I don't hold onto something firm and solid, I'm going to disappear.* The thought frightened her and she clutched at Richard's arm.

"Jo?"

She made herself laugh. A short false little bark of laughter that she was sure he would see for what it was. Instead his face relaxed. He smiled down at her and would have kissed her if she hadn't turned her head and said.

"There's something I'd like you to do for me before you go."

"Anything." She could hear the hurt in his voice, but she went on.

"I bought a rug and some cushions yesterday. They're still in the boot of the car. I could do with a hand bringing them into the house."

"Sure. Then I'll take you out to lunch."

"No. I've got work I want to do." His face fell and she added quickly, "I'll ring you. Later."

She could hardly wait for him to leave. When they'd unpacked the Mercedes, she walked him to the door and stood blocking the doorway, watching until the Porsche rounded the corner into the main drive and she could shut herself in. Alone in the house the burden of his caring slipped from her shoulders. No longer having to watch what she said or did in case he worried or fussed, Jo yawned and stretched luxuriously. As she lowered her arms, she felt a small, sharp pain in her side. Fleeting, momentary, but enough for her to know. Cradling her belly in her hands she smiled.

CHAPTER SIX

The late afternoon sun pouring into her studio bathed Jo in its warmth. She walked carefully over to her worktable. She was aware that at this stage in her pregnancy what she did would make little difference, but she was determined that this baby was going to stay. She would do whatever she must to protect it. If she was told that she had to lie flat on her back for the whole nine months she would. If she could never lift another paintbrush or palette knife she would willingly give up painting forever, if only she could carry this child to term.

For the time being all she could do was wait. She couldn't take a test, it was too early, but she knew that she had conceived. She always did and she had always been right. Jo blinked away the memory of those other pregnancies. This time it was going to be different. She was sure of it.

She flicked open her sketchbook, looked at the blank page and let it fall shut again. She should be concentrating on her work. She had an exhibition to prepare. Jo smiled and shook her head. None of that seemed important now. What mattered was the child. She gave herself a hug and wandered towards the door.

Standing on the threshold she looked out at the interplay of light and shadow, noting the variations in colour and tone of the leaves as the breeze rustled through the branches. There were deep rich emeralds and vibrant almost florescent greens. There were hints of maroon and purple too. Jo was about to go back to fetch her iPad when the cry came. Faint at first, then louder more demanding.

Shutting her eyes she shook her head, but the crying did not stop. Heart beating furiously, blood pounding in her head, she forced herself to breath in, then out, long slow breaths. She must stay calm, panic of any sort was bad for the baby.

Gradually her heartbeats grew more regular and all she could hear was the wind in the trees.

Leaning back against the doorframe, Jo swallowed hard. Was she going mad? Even as the thought crossed her mind, she thrust it away. There was a rational explanation for this. There had to be, even if it was only the projection of her longing for a child, or maybe it was a premonition.

A good sign, Jo told herself, as she came back into the house. She locked the studio door and went into the kitchen. What she needed was a cup of tea. Nan's cure all would restore her sanity. As she waited for the kettle to boil, it occurred to her that the sounds she had heard could be an animal. The logical thing to do would be to drink her tea then go and have a look, so that the next time she heard something she could not immediately identify she wouldn't panic and send her blood pressure soaring.

She started her search in the back garden. Skirting around the edge of the lawn she peered through the undergrowth, but there was no sign of even a fox run. If some creature were lurking in there it would be impossible to see, let alone find, it. One possibility discounted, she was walking round to the front of the house, when she heard a miserable, little whimper. She was right. This was no unborn child, no ghost of what might have been. Hurrying into the courtyard she saw, sitting on her doorstep, a small black kitten.

It looked at her with large, unblinking eyes and with a sudden release of tension Jo sank down beside it. The kitten scrambled up the leg of her jeans, perched on her knee and began to miaow.

"Was it you making all that fuss? You silly thing, you scared me half to death." Now she knew where the crying had come from, Jo could admit how frightened she had been. "It was you wasn't it?" The kitten gave a miaow of assent, then butted its head against her stomach and began to pummel her thighs. "Ow that hurt," Jo yelped as needle sharp claws dug into her skin. She slipped her hand under the kitten's soft belly and gently disentangled it from her clothes. The kitten opened its mouth and miaowed loudly.

"You're hungry aren't you? Let's go and see if I've got

- 42 -

anything for you to eat." She got up slowly; the kitten's cries growing louder and louder and her own stomach cramping with hunger, as she realised that she'd eaten nothing since the day before.

How irresponsible can you be? she thought as she opened the fridge. She was eating for two, and had to keep her body strong and healthy to nourish her baby. She found bread, butter, cheese and salad and put them to one side for a sandwich, while she looked for something she could give the kitten. Except for a carton of milk however there was nothing, not even a tin of tuna. Nor did she have a bowl she could use to feed the little cat, all she could find were two mugs but no saucers. The kitten's cries were becoming desperate. Jo took one of the mugs and balancing it carefully on its side, dribbled in a little milk. Diving straight in, the kitten's pink tongue lapped up the milk, until it had all gone leaving only a large smudge on its face. Then it nudged against her legs, as if to say it could do with something solid.

"Me too," Jo told it. Having devoured her sandwich she was still hungry, too hungry to drive to the nearest supermarket then come home and cook. What she needed was instant food. "I know what we'll do," she said.

Sometimes, on a Friday when she was small, Nan would buy fish and chips as a special treat. There was only one shop that would do and that was the one on The Parade, because the quality of the fish was better and you got more chips for your money. Nan had hers with salt and vinegar, so did Granddad, but the vinegar made chips soggy, so Jo's were always carried home in a separate parcel. Just remembering made her mouth water.

"You wait here. I won't be long." Jo slung her bag over her shoulder and car keys in hand shut the kitten in the house.

Going into the estate was to descend into a different world. After six in the evening most shop doors were barred and their windows protected by steel shutters. In The Parade, litter lay scattered over the wide pavement and a group of lads loitered at the corner, ignoring a skinny kid who rode his bike past them at speed, yelling abuse as he went. A little nervously, Jo parked the Mercedes where she could see it and joined the queue in the chip shop, behind a girl in a leather jacket. In front of her two kids argued about whether they wanted curry sauce or gravy on their chips.

Fish lay beached in glass tanks, skin puffed with batter. In the next compartment were the sausages, browned hunks of chicken and pale meat pies. Behind them the serving staff moved with excruciating slowness, turning the chips in the metal fryers with long slotted spoons. How much longer was it going to take? Was she going to starve first? To distract herself Jo read the list of quantities and prices. The kids decided on curry, the leather clad girl began a long complicated list, she had not yet reached the end when someone said, "Next."

"Small fish and chips, please." It was like being ten again, counting out the money, checking the change, then holding the hot package in her hand as she carried it home. Jo balanced the food in one hand, fumbled for her car keys with the other. Her mouth watering, she put the fish and chips on the passenger seat and drove back up the hill as fast as she dared. Her stomach was rumbling, the hot smell was too tempting, she had to eat. Drawing up in front of The Granary, she reached for a chip. Just one, then another, then a mouthful of fish, the flesh white and succulent under the crisp batter.

Making sure there was plenty left for the cat, she licked her fingers clean, locked the car and went into the house. The kitten greeted her by curling round her legs and miaowing frantically. She unwrapped the crumpled paper and spread it out on the floor. The little cat approached with caution. It walked carefully around the fish, sniffed, retreated then sniffed again.

"It's perfectly safe," Jo assured it. She took a flake of fish on her finger and held it out. The kitten licked out its tongue and took it from her. "See," Jo stroked its back and it lowered its head and began to eat. In the depths of her bag her phone rang.

"Jo," Richard's voice held a hint of reproach and she remembered that she had promised to ring him.

"Hi, I was going to ring," she lied quickly. "I've been out," she added hoping that would be enough explanation to satisfy him. "Oh and something's happened. I've found a kitten. Or rather it's, no I mean he's, found me. But that's what they say cats do, isn't it?"

Grief, she thought. *I'm burbling. Now I really do sound crazy.* "I think he's adopted–" there was a second of hesitation, then she said a little more firmly than she had intended, "–us. He's little and black with big, big eyes. You'll love him. You will, I promise, no one could resist him." She reached out her hand to stroke the little creature. "Anyway I think he's going to bring us good luck."

CHAPTER SEVEN

The kitten woke her at dawn, paws paddling relentlessly, head butting her face, until she reached out from under the duvet and pulled him in beside her, where he lay his whole body trembling with the intensity of his purring.

Sheets of rain cascaded down the window, water dripped from the eaves and the leaves hung limp from the branches. Overnight, the whole world had turned to water. "A Vale of Tears", Nan had called it. She believed that life being the way it was, nothing came without suffering. It had rained at her funeral, as it had the day they buried Granddad. The kitten curled its claws around Jo's fingers. She carefully withdrew her hand and got out of bed.

She drove to the supermarket and bought milk, skimmed for herself and full cream for the kitten, and several tins of cat food. She added fresh bread, butter, vine tomatoes, crisp lettuce, creamy brie and firm sharp cheddar. Red skinned apples with sweet pink flesh, dark purple grapes, plump brown onions, garlic, fresh pasta and a tall, slim flask of cold pressed olive oil. Moving down the aisles, she chose kitchen equipment; a chopping board, cutlery, plates, six brightly coloured mugs and a china bowl with CAT written across the front in bold, black letters. It was a beginning. It was enough.

The road back ran past the Catholic church. The rain streaked the windscreen and spattered the sides of the car. Without quite knowing why, Jo pulled up in front of Our Lady of Sorrows. It was years since she'd been there, many more since she'd been to Mass. The last time was Nan's funeral. The church had been filled with her friends, the women who had served on the cleaning rota, the ladies in charge of the flowers, neighbours and girls from the shop Nan had opened with the money that had come to her after Melinda's death. Her customers came too; women, who had been going to Noreen's for years, because they trusted her flair and eye for colour and they knew that Nan never let anyone walk out of her shop in something that did not suit her.

Jo pushed open the door and stepped into the porch. The parish newsletter on the notice board flapped in the draught. Inside, there was the familiar smell of polish and damp. The church echoed with her footsteps as she dipped her hand in the holy water stoup and made a quick sign of the cross.

This is for you Nan, she thought. *I don't know whether any of it's true or not, but if you can see me you'll be pleased I'm here. About time too, you'd say. When I was little I had to wait while you cleaned. Friday was your rota day so I sat in one of the pews at the back while you swept and polished and dusted. But on Sundays, at early Mass I had to be right there at the front, with you and Granddad on either side of me making sure I behaved. "Kneel up straight, don't turn around," you'd say. "Remember Jesus and His Holy Mother are watching you."*

Smiling at the memory of that little girl in her Sunday best coat, her hair brushed and shining, her hands joined in prayer, Jo slipped into the last pew. The church was empty except for two elderly women at the front. They sat hunched against the chill, one reading her missal, the other telling her rosary.

Almost without meaning to Jo knelt down. Leaning her chin on her hands, she stared blankly at the altar. What was she doing here? Reliving her childhood? Trying to make sense of some of the few memories she had? What was the point? She had long ago decided that if God did exist he did not seem to care what happened to her. Or if he did, he had determined that her life was to be one long punishment. She'd lost her parents, her step-dad, her grandparents, her lover. She was thirty-five and all her life had been surrounded by death. Was that why she could not carry a child? Jo cupped her hands around her stomach and fought back the fear that she brought destruction to all those who cared about her.

You have Richard, she told herself. *You still have him. And now it matters more than ever to make things right. Never mind what happened before. That was in the past.* Having made up her mind where her future lay, it was time to leave. Jo gave herself a little hug and pushed back her kneeler, but as she did so a bell rang and the sacristy door opened. The two women rose awkwardly to their feet and Jo realised that the morning Mass was about to start and it was too late to go without disturbing the worshippers.

Nan would never approve, she thought cursing her luck. *Let's hope it doesn't take too long.*

"In the name of the Father and of the Son and of the Holy Ghost." The priest's voice rang out firm and warm. Jo, huddled in her jacket, hands in pockets against the damp air of the almost empty church, looked up in surprise. A young man with dark hair scraped back into a ponytail faced the meagre congregation.

"Whatever is the world coming to? Don't they teach them anything in Rome these days?" she heard Nan's voice in her ear as clearly as if she were standing next to her. *"I expect he goes around in jeans and one of those T-shirts. In my day you never saw a priest without his collar."* Jo smiled. *Things have changed Nan. I'm sorry I didn't see much of you over the last few years, but ever since I met Kit I knew you didn't approve of the way I lived. You liked my success, but not everything that went with it. You wanted me to be settled to have a nice house and kids, but marrying Richard wasn't right either. You wouldn't come to the wedding, because he was divorced and it couldn't be in church. It didn't matter how good he was for me, or how much he loved me. You disapproved and he knew it. That was why, after that first time, I didn't bring him to see you. I had so little time to come on my own and you were always busy. I only wish I could believe it was all worth it and that you've got your reward in Heaven.*

"Go in peace to love and serve the Lord," the priest intoned and the two old women gathered up their shopping bags and began to chat. Jo reached into her pocket for her car keys.

"Jo Docherty." The priest loped down the aisle towards her. "It is you isn't it?"

"Yes," Jo said puzzled. "But how did you know?"

"The hair, the clothes, everything about you." He shook his head and grinned. "You haven't changed in all these years. You don't recognise me, do you? I'm Damien O' Conner. I lived in Myrtle Road and I went to school with Sean O'Callaghan, Bernadette's brother. She was in your class," he added when she looked at him blankly.

"Oh yes." Jo remembered a hot-headed freckle faced girl. "You're the one she fancied," she said without thinking. "Oh I'm sorry, I didn't mean…" she trailed away embarrassed.

"Did she now?" Damien ignored her confusion. "Enough to bring herself and that brood of hers to church do you think?"

Jo flinched. Everyone had a family except her. *Dear God,* she thought, *did it always have to hurt this much, even now when she had cause to hope again.*

"I'm afraid I have to go," she said stiffly.

"Are you visiting?"

"Yes, no. Sorry I'm," once again she was lost for words. What was she doing here in Our Lady of Sorrows? What had impelled her to stop at the church? She took a deep breath and tried to order her thoughts. "I'm staying up at Kingsfield. I've got a studio in one of the converted barns."

"You're part of my parish then."

"I suppose I must be." Already she was moving away.

"Then I will include you in my visits."

"Thanks." *What else was there to say? I don't want to see you. I don't want to see anybody. Even that was no longer wholly true. She was looking forward to seeing Cecile and Helene, when they delivered her furniture.*

Damien O'Conner held out his hand. Instinctively she looked into his eyes. He held her gaze.

He understands how I feel, she thought in surprise. *But why? I don't know him. I don't really remember him from when I was little. But there is definitely some connection here.*

"I would like to come and see you," he was saying. "We could talk over old times." She nodded, quickly, not wanting to commit herself to anything.

It was still raining, a miserable damp drizzle that shrouded the countryside in mist. The kitten waiting on the doorstep was wet and bedraggled. As soon as Jo opened the door he scuttled inside and sat expectantly on the spot on the kitchen floor, where she had fed him the night before. Jo unpacked the car and introduced him to his new bowl. This time he did not stop to investigate, but dived straight into his food; tail in the air like an exclamation mark.

The animal's appetite seemed to stimulate her own. She broke off a hunk of bread, cut a slice of brie and added a tomato to her plate. She ate standing at the kitchen unit waiting for the kettle to boil for coffee. The kitten replete, yawned and stretched.

"What I should do now is to go and do some work," Jo told him. "But you know what, the light's wrong and I don't feel like it. So I'm not going to." The black cat purred as if in agreement and nudged at her legs. "I know. We could both do with a deep squashy sofa to curl up in." The kitten pressed himself against her, leaning hard with all his strength as if directing her towards the stairs. "You want to go and lie on the bed, don't you," Jo smiled at him. "OK, I'll take the iPad up with me. Perhaps we could watch a film, or read a book. No I've got a better idea. It's not exactly work, but who knows I might use it in my next piece."

She picked up her bag, tucked the kitten under her arm and taking her coffee went upstairs to the bedroom. The kitten dived straight under the duvet and Jo made herself comfortable against a pile of pillows. At her feet the kitten purred and slept. Resisting the temptation to cuddle down beside him, she took out "The Antiquities and Curiosities of Kingsfield and Surrounding Parishes," took a sip of coffee and carefully turned over the front cover.

The Reverend Edwin Marriot began with a long-winded account of the area, followed by fulsome praise of the new mansion recently completed at Kingsfield. Jo, her attention wandering, skipped over the text and concentrated on the illustrations. The house had changed very little since it had been built, as had the parish churches. The Stones, however, seemed to have lost their prominence in the succeeding centuries. In his pamphlet the Reverend Marriot had drawn them as two large structures. The first, which he called the King Stone, stood firmly upright thrusting into the sky, the other, the Queen Stone rested beside it. This stone was round with a hole cut through the centre. Both were on a slight incline and an avenue of oaks leading up to the mound gave the whole site the look of an ancient temple.

What Jo had seen from her brief glance was quite different. The Stones, if they were still there, were completely hidden by the trees. They had sunk into obscurity like the religion to which they belonged.

The difference between past and present was something she could explore. Ancient beliefs and superstitions superseded by the rise of the concrete and practical. Factories, facts, something tangible and solid compared to the ethereal, insubstantial, the idea was intriguing.

Grey clouds pressed against the window; she reached up to switch on the light and began to read,

"The Ancient Stones of Kingsfield, called by many of the local inhabitants the Satan Stones, are the subject of various legends and superstitious practices. Some say that they are the Devil's own Ring and Finger wrested from Lucifer the Lord of Darkness by the mighty giant Magog in the course of an epic battle, whereupon falling to the ground they on that instant became petrified into the shapes we see today. Others tell of an ancient race of people building a temple to their heathen gods, of which only these stones and an avenue of lesser stones leading up to them remain.

Whatever the truth in these tales, village maidens still revere the site. When the moon waxes, they come dressed in white garments bringing with them wreathes of flowers and a living offering to the goddess. They believe that the blood of innocents will bring forth new life. To entice back an errant lover, or bind a husband they must crawl, as naked as the day they were born, through the heart of the ring stone. It is also said that any woman who has honoured the stones in this manner will never lack for healthy offspring."

The book fell from Jo's hands, voices rang in her ears, as the memory came flooding back. In the playground of Our Lady of Sorrows' Primary, one summer break time, Bernie O'Callaghan, surrounded by her gang of friends, was boasting about the most evil thing she had ever done.

"I went up there and I did it. I crawled through the stone, just like the big girls said. Then I ran. I didn't look back," she had lowered her voice as the other girls clustered around her. "If you do, you can see the devil himself chasing you."

A collective sigh was followed by a chorus of admiring voices. Jo had hesitated, part of her wanting to join in, but Nan told her that Bernie and the rest of the girls on the estate were common and she was to have nothing to do with them. She had always tried to please Nan, even if it made her different from the other kids, and if Nan had found out she'd be in trouble, so she had walked away.

"Dear God was that what I should have done?" Jo cried. "Would it have made a difference if I'd sneaked up there and crawled through the Queen Stone?" She stared through the rain pitted window, her eyes fixed on the shapes of the trees as she tried to recall that day in the playground, but the memory had gone. Jo swung her legs over the side of the bed. The kitten protested, but she ignored him as she walked up and down the room trying to order her thoughts. Why was all this coming back now? In spite of all the therapy she had undergone since the crash, her childhood remained deeply buried in her sub-conscious. As far as she was concerned it could stay there. So long as it made no difference to her present it wasn't important. Best let sleeping dogs lie, as Nan would have said.

On the other hand, it would be good to be able to tell her baby all about the old days and its family roots. Jo smiled. Was this what had brought schooldays to the surface? Or was it this place? The house she had been compelled to buy, which had led in turn to Richard's purchase of the whole estate.

Jo shook her head. This was stupid, just so much superstition. There was nothing in those old stories, or if there were it was not relevant to her. The Stones were not a fertility symbol, they were... A shudder of unease slipped down her back. The answer was there, like a half seen shadow, or a flicker of light in a dark sky, but before she could grasp it, it melted away.

CHAPTER EIGHT

Jo felt as if her brain was about to burst. Cells had been stretched to the utmost, any more pressure and they would snap. She had to stop trying so hard. If she put the problem of the Stones and what they were to one side, then the answer was bound to come back to her. That's what normally happened when searching for a memory. If it did not, then it was not important. That was how she had justified herself when the psychiatrist had told her she was blanking things out deliberately and so far she had been proved right. If only that niggling feeling of unease would go away.

"We need company," she told the kitten, who promptly jumped from the bed and padded to the top of the stairs. "Great," Jo called after him. "Be like that." The cat miaowed loudly as if in protest and at that moment she heard the sound of a van turning into the drive. "You knew," she cried hurrying down the stairs to open the front door. "You knew someone was coming."

When Helene and Cecile, their boots ringing on the wooden floor, entered they brought with them a sense of warmth and security. Helene flicked a switch and light flooded the downstairs rooms. The late afternoon shadows shrank back into their corners and Jo held out her hand to greet her visitors. Helene's grip was warm and steady. Her skin rough and dry.

"I'm sorry we're late. You must have given up on us. Our last customer was difficult to find," she said.

"Only because you left the map behind and you wouldn't listen to my directions," Cecile said. Helene smiled, her dark, narrow face transformed.

"I should have known better."

"Always go with your instinct. You taught me that," Cecile said.

Helene shrugged and spread out her hands. "Next time I

will take my own advice." She turned to Jo. "It is good to see you."

"And you. You can't imagine how good." Jo wanted to say more but she did not know what or how.

Helene turned to her daughter. "Are we ready?"

"I am as always at your command, ma mere." Cecile gave a mock bow.

"In that case we'll unload the chairs first, then the table."

"Are you coming to help, or do I do it all myself?" Cecile turned towards the door.

"Slave driver," Helene grinned.

"Can I do anything?" Jo asked.

"Just tell us where you want everything Mrs. Docherty and we'll do the rest."

"Please call me Jo. And I'm Mrs. Avery."

"Jo it is then."

The two women worked quickly and efficiently. The table was placed in the middle of the kitchen area with four of the six chairs around it, the other two Jo decided could go in the bedrooms.

"They look as if they've been there for ever. Monty was right again," Cecile said, when they had finished. Jo saw her glance at her mother. Helene lifted an eyebrow. "He was sitting on it all morning," Cecile prompted.

Helene shrugged. "Please do not feel yourself under any obligation," she began, "but my crazy daughter thinks she has found the perfect sofa for your house. Though how she can think that, never having seen the place, I do not know. Nevertheless, guided by instinct,"

"Monty," Cecile interrupted.

Ignoring her Helene continued, "Cecile insisted we load it into the van. Would you like to come out and have a look?"

"No," Jo surprised herself by saying. "Please bring it in."

"You're sure?"

"I trust Monty."

Cecile shot her mother a look.

Helene gave a mock sigh. "In that case more lifting," she

said. The two women went out into the gloom and came back with a sofa, covered in pale velvet, which they placed on the rug.

"I told you so," Cecile said as they stepped back to look. "All it needs now are the cushions and it's perfect." She sat down and gave a little bounce. "It's very comfortable too and clean. It's recently been re-covered and had the springs replaced."

"I don't think you need to sell it to her," Helene said wryly. "I think it's sold."

"It looks good," Jo said.

"Now a mirror in a gold frame, on that wall to reflect back the garden, would be good."

"Cecile," Helene said in a warning tone.

"Sorry. I'm not trying to sell you anything else. I was thinking out loud. This is such a beautiful house and it's crying out to be filled with beautiful things."

"From our stock?" Helene said dryly.

"Not necessarily, though we do have that mirror in the van. No. I think a mixture of old and new would do well here. You're very privileged to be the first person to live here. You can make it truly your own." She came up to Jo and took her hand. "Whatever you do, or say, or feel here will be stamped into the very stone."

"I know," she whispered.

"Every house carries the ghosts of what went on before, but a new one is a like a sheet of blank paper. It's waiting for everything to happen."

"Cecile we really must go. It's getting late and we've taken up far too much of Jo's time already," Helene said.

Jo glanced up. The sky glowered against the windows. Trees stood dark and sodden at the edge of the light. Suddenly, she had no wish to be alone. "No please stay; have some coffee."

Mother and daughter exchanged glances.

"Coffee would be good," Helene said.

They sat around the table drinking from the mugs Jo had

bought that morning. Cecile dreamily cradled her cup between her hands, peering into it like a fortune teller. Helene leaned back in her chair, her dark hair sparking with silver, her narrow eyes amused, yet alert to everything that was going on in the room.

The contrast between them was so vivid, that Jo itched to take up pencil and paper. "I would like to draw you both," she said.

Helene's eyes flickered to the receipt book that lay open in front of her, the page covered with her bold flowing script.

"Jo Docherty, of course, that's who you are. I'm sorry I was so slow getting there. I know your work."

"We've got one of your sketches at home. It hangs on the landing where the moon catches it. It's very powerful," Cecile said softly.

"And now you convert houses?" Helene asked.

"Oh no. My studio is here. It's my husband and his firm that did the conversion."

"You're going to live here?" Cecile looked up sharply.

"Yes," Jo said. "The Granary is mine and it suits me. I don't know if I'll feel the same way once the flats in the main house are occupied."

Helene drew her brows together; her head came up like a dog on point. "The main house is yours as well?"

Something in the atmosphere shifted. An element of danger entered the easy warmth. Cecile let out her breath.

"It's a very fine house," Helene said quickly. There was a pause.

Jo looked away. "I suppose it is, but to be honest I don't really care for it," she murmured.

"Why is that?" Helene's tone was almost too casual.

"I'm not sure. There's something about it that bothers me. I can't explain."

"Something you feel?" Cecile looked at her mother. Helene leaned towards Jo.

"How much do you know about Kingsfield?" she asked.

"Not a lot, which is odd, because I used to live down in

Weston Ridge when I was small. In fact our back garden joined on to the estate, but my nan never let me play up in the woods like the rest of the kids."

"Was that because she didn't trust this place either? Did she feel there was something," Cecile hesitated. "I can't quite think of the right word. Weird, strange?"

"Otherworldly?" Helene suggested.

"You mean supernatural, ghosts and things like that? No except for being a rabid Catholic and thinking the Church had the answer to everything spiritual, Nan was very down to earth."

"And you're the same?" Helene asked.

"Yes," Jo said a little too loudly as Cecile's eyes widened. "I know I had this feeling, but,"

"Don't ever deny what you feel," Cecile interrupted. "You're right about the house. It's a sad place. Built on blood and human suffering."

"I'm not sure Jo wants to know about all that," Helene said carefully.

"I think she does," Cecile's voice was soft and distant.

"I think I need to."

"If you are sure." Helene got up and refilled their cups. Cecile's eyes were turquoise, dreamy, unfocused.

Jo shifted uneasily in her chair. One hand came up and touched the silver cross she wore around her neck.

"There are so many stories about this place that it is difficult to know where to start," Cecile continued. "In the beginning this hill was sacred to the gods. There was a temple up here, where people came to worship and to sacrifice to the moon. A few of the stones are still standing, but there is nothing left of the circle itself. Kingsfield House seems to have been built in its very centre, thus defiling a holy place."

Jo shivered, glancing unconsciously in the direction of the west drive. She was glad of Helene's brief touch on her hand, though Cecile lost in her story did not appear to notice.

"As you can see, this was not a very auspicious beginning, but it gets worse. The man who built the house, Sir William

D'Aubeney made his fortune in the slave trade. Kingsfield was meant to be a home for his family, but his wife died in childbirth, and after that he hated the place and spent as little time as he could there," she paused.

"What about the baby?" Jo prompted.

"He survived."

"Did he live here?"

"I would suppose so," Cecile said. I haven't got that far in my research yet. What I do know is that the sorrow in this house remained. The original family appeared to have died out within a generation and it was subsequently let to a series of tenants. None of them stayed for very long. That is when the rumours began. A pale girl in a blue dress was seen, a baby was heard crying."

"Are you all right?" Helene asked, her face taut with concern as Jo struggled to appear calm.

"How do you know all this?" Jo said.

Cecile hesitated. Once again she looked at her mother, as if waiting for her permission. Helene gave an almost imperceptible nod, which would have been missed by anyone who was not concentrating as hard as Jo and she continued, "I've got a thing about haunted houses, or at least houses that have got a history of supernatural events. A friend of mine is a lecturer and when the university was thinking of buying it I got him to take me round. I …"

You heard things like me, Jo thought. *And you saw things. I think you may be trying to warn me about something, but you don't know how much I know, or more importantly, how much I believe. That is why Helene is being so cautious.*

"Tell me," Jo began. Then a phone rang. Shrilly, persistently. Helene reached for her bag. The call, however, was for Jo. It was Richard.

"Jo are you all right?"

"Yes. I'm fine."

"You said you were going to ring."

"I was. I've got someone here. I'll call you back later." She broke the connection, but Helene was already standing, her bag on her shoulder.

"Please don't mind about us. It's time we went."

"I'd forgotten the time." Cecile glanced at the darkness outside and pushed back her chair.

"There's no hurry, honestly. Richard can wait." *I want to know more. I have to know the rest of it; all the other things I suspect you're not telling me.*

"We can't. Cecile it is Thursday and we have a meeting." Helene was at the door.

"Did you look at the 'Antiquities and Curiosities'?" Cecile said as she followed her mother.

Jo swallowed.

"Old tales," Helene said briefly. She looked back into the lighted kitchen. "May it be a refuge in the darkness," she murmured and rested her hand briefly on Jo's arm.

It feels like a blessing, Jo thought. *Crazy though it sounds, it's like she's making things safe for me.*

Cecile shrugged back her hair. "Who's this?" The kitten padded down the stairs, tail held high and made his way straight to her. Cecile knelt down beside him and stroked his fur. The kitten nuzzled at her legs then turned on his back. Cecile ran her fingers over pink skin studded with tiny black nipples. The kitten curved his claws around her hand. Needle teeth bit into her palm. "Diablo," she murmured. "Little devil."

"I'm sorry. He's got no manners at all. He arrived on the doorstep yesterday and has made himself completely at home."

"He's your familiar," Cecile smiled.

"Familiar?" *Anything to get them to stay a little longer.*

"Guardian, companion, protector. He'll look after you."

"He's a bit small for that," Jo said. The kitten upended himself and looked at her balefully.

"He doesn't think so," Cecile laughed.

Helene had opened the door and was standing with her hand on the frame. "Cecile, now," she said. Cecile straightened up; Helene held out her hand. "Nice doing business with you Jo."

"You know where we are if you need anything," Cecile added. "You can always call. You've got our number."

Jo watched them walk to the van. Cecile took the keys from her pocket and they stood for a moment, heads together, talking in low voices. Then Helene looked back at the house and nodded. Cecile waved her hand and they climbed in. The van revved then drove away, its rear lights disappearing into the tunnel of trees. Jo waited until she could no longer hear the engine, then reluctantly closed the door.

The living room still smelled of their perfume, a mixture of incense and flowers that Jo could not name, but recognised as uniquely theirs. She glanced at the phone where she'd left it on the kitchen counter and thought about ringing Richard, but decided she wasn't ready. He'd quiz her on how she was feeling and his voice would be heavy with concern. He'd try to hide it, but she had become ultra-sensitive to every nuance and her skin would prickle with irritation and she'd have to grit her teeth to stop herself from saying something she would regret and now more than ever it was important that they did not fight.

The irony was she wanted him to care, just not in that overwhelming way. She wanted him to let her do what she must and stop trying to protect her from any more hurt. But if she tried to tell him he wouldn't listen.

He always thinks he knows best, she thought as she started to rinse out the coffee mugs. She had finished and the water was still splashing into the sink, but Jo, her mind distracted, did not immediately turn off the tap. How was she going to draw Helene and Cecile? Not as mother and daughter, that relationship did not define them. There was a deeper layer of meaning to their partnership. Were they symbols of light and dark? Two opposites, or two parts of one whole? The questions demanded pencil and paper. She swept her hand over the surface, knocking the phone and sending it spinning to the edge of the unit. She made no effort to catch it, but it did not fall. Jo sighed. She would have to ring Richard before she started work. He picked up on the first ring.

"Jo." There was a pause. "Have your visitors gone?"

"They were delivering some furniture."

"You've been busy."

"I've been shopping. I went to the supermarket, got some food."

"You sound as if you've settled in."

"Yes," she said briefly. "I'm making the house habitable. You're not coming down tonight are you?" She crossed her fingers.

"No. I've got meetings 'til late. That's why I'm ringing. There's so much to organise for this conference in New York. You don't mind do you?"

"Course not. It's work and I'm busy too." She mouthed a kiss and finished the call.

I didn't tell him I loved him. Did he notice? But then he didn't tell me he loved me either. If this is where we are, what am I going to do? We can't, we mustn't go on like this. For the sake of the baby. Her hand rested lightly on her belly. If only Richard would be as happy as she was, but she knew that when she told him he would be angry and worried. There was, however, time before she had to tell him anything. Time to get him used to the idea that they were finally going to have a child of their own. That this time there would be a strong and healthy baby.

She dried the mugs and put them on the draining board next to the clean bowl marked cat. Where was the kitten? Surely by now he should be demanding supper? Jo opened the front door and stared out into the rain sodden night.

"Diablo," she called softly. No soft little body with its self-important swagger materialised from the shadows. "Kitten," she cried louder, her anxiety growing. Where could he have gone? He'd only just arrived. She couldn't have lost him already. "Where are you, you stupid cat? It's horrible out here and I'm getting wet."

Taking her jacket she set off to look for him. It was gloomy and dark under the trees, but as she turned into the main drive the light faded even further.

Her shoes echoed on the flagstones, rain dripped from the rhododendrons. Patches of lichen and mould on the walls of the old house took on grotesque shapes, shadows lurched from the undergrowth. Where was he? She called his name softly at first, then more loudly, until it echoed around the empty building. The air grew cold, rustled and eddied. The skin at the back of her neck prickled. A soft hand slid into hers, silken skirts rustled against the legs of her jeans. Then came a flash of scarlet, the hand was roughly withdrawn. There was whimper of protest, a rough curse, an overwhelming aura of malice.

He came like a tiger, hissing, spitting, claws scrambling up her legs. The presences faded. The hatred and fear dissolved. Jo held Diablo close, breathing in his kitten smell, as she carried him into the light and warmth of The Granary.

CHAPTER NINE

The house felt safe, a sanctuary against whatever it was out there in the woods. Jo switched on all the lamps, so that every window blazed with light and stood in the kitchen watching as Diablo ate. When he had finished, she picked him up and carried him into the living area. Curling up on the sofa she sat and stroked the little black cat. The action soothed her. Diablo's purrs grew louder, until his whole body vibrated.

"Little devil," Jo murmured affectionately. "Are you my familiar? Do you keep me safe?" She lifted the kitten up and touched her forehead to his. "Or am I adding two and two and making five? That's what Richard would say. He's so practical. He'd tell me it was all in my mind. And maybe it is. When I'm pregnant everything feels different, more extreme. Half the time I just want to cry, or sleep, or both." She put the kitten down on her lap keeping one hand on his soft warm body as he made himself comfortable. "It could be my hormones, except I didn't just hear things, I felt them too. A hand was slipped into mine and what made it real was the pressure of her fingers, the slight dampness of her palm. It wasn't a memory. It wasn't my imagination, Diablo. It happened."

Startled by the vividness of the image, she shivered. The kitten looked up at her crossly and she went back to stroking his fur, drawing comfort from his contented purring.

Had she lived at Kingsfield in a previous life? Some kind of past life regression was a logical idea but completely unrealistic, first because these things didn't happen and secondly because she didn't remember the people she was seeing. The only time anything had seemed familiar was when Richard had shown her around the house and she had had that fleeting image of classical statues, a chandelier and pale green walls. Even that image was easily explained. She could have heard the girls, who had been brave enough to sneak up here and peer through the windows of the empty house, boasting about what they had seen.

Without warning the kitten growled and stretched out his claws, digging sharp points into her thigh. Gently Jo dislodged him.

"Are you telling me not to think about it? I wish I could stop, but I can't leave it like this." The cat stared at her with yellow eyes. "Tell you what, I'll go and see Cecile and Helene. I'm sure they know more than they've said and I've got to get this sorted and soon. It's taking up too much of my time and if I don't get some work done soon I'll have to cancel my exhibition. "

The decision to do something concrete energised her. The next morning as soon as she'd had coffee and fed the kitten, she took her keys and let herself out of the house. As she pulled the door shut, she saw a mark on the frame, which she had not noticed before. At first she thought it was a flaw in the wood, but when she looked closer it appeared to be deliberate as if someone had gauged out a star shape surrounded by a circle. Where had it come from?

If it had been done by the kids from the estate, it would be far cruder, more sexual and explicit. But who else would have gone to the trouble of carving this out? Was it a builders' mark? She ran her fingers along the symbol. It was so deeply scored into the wood that no amount of paint or filler would completely cover it. Yet far from being angry, she felt comforted, as though someone had conferred a blessing on the house.

It was mid-morning by the time she reached Clifton. The sun was shining fitfully from a grey sky, women were loading their cars outside the small supermarket and the bakery was crowded with people enjoying a late breakfast. Most of the exclusive little shops had only just opened and it was easy to find a parking space. She locked the car, slung her bag over her shoulder and experienced a moment of doubt. It was all so ordinary, so safe, how could the answers to Kingsfield lie here? Her stomach fluttered and she knew it was not her rational mind, but fear of what she might learn that tempted her to go back to the relative safety of The Granary.

She hurried down the road to Alice Court before she could change her mind, but when she arrived the wrought iron gate was shut and padlocked. Jo stood and stared at it in disbelief. She grasped the gate and peered through the bars, but all she could see was the empty courtyard. She had been so sure that Helene and Cecile would be there, that she was swamped by irrational disappointment. Telling herself not to be stupid, that she was overacting, she rummaged in her bag for Helene's card. If she had her number she could ring and perhaps they could arrange to meet later in the day. Then she remembered. She had been so confident of finding the two women in the shop, that she had left the card and receipt on the kitchen table. Nor had she put the number in her phone.

She gave the gate another angry shake. As she stepped back she saw on the gatepost, the symbol she had seen on the doorframe of The Granary. She ran her fingers over it reflectively and the thought occurred to her she had not been abandoned.

"Looking for 'elene and Cecile, my lover?" Jo turned to see the woman who had sold her the rug in the antique market.

"I was." Jo shrugged. "It looks as if they've shut up shop."

"Oh they do that from time to time. Off they'll go to some meeting or another. They never say where, but don't you worry they'll be back. Tomorrow maybe, or next week"

The woman smiled and went on her way.

Next week? Is that how long am I going to have to wait? Still there's nothing I can do about it right now so I may as well go home.

The first fat drop of rain splashed on the pavement in front of her. The clouds lowered above the buildings and suddenly she could not bear to go back to Kingsfield. She was not hungry. She did not want a coffee, nor was she in the mood for shopping. She wanted somewhere to go where she could lose herself for a few hours and she knew the very place.

*

Set beside the soaring tower of the Wills Building, the city museum was fronted by a row of heavy arches that concealed its entrance. Jo climbed the shallow marble steps, pushed open the polished doors and made the familiar transition between deep shadow and airy lightness, as she stepped into an entrance gallery that stretched up to the roof. She walked past display cabinets of deep blue Bristol glass and climbed the staircase that circled the core of the building. As she went higher, marble gave way to wood and light streamed into the art galleries.

This was where she used to come after school. Miss Jones, her art teacher, had recommended that she study the work of other artists and she had spent hours first looking, then sketching and copying landscapes, still-lives and drawings. The formal portraits in their thick gilt frames had never appealed. The bland faces painted to their best advantage had always bored her. What excited her was not the surface, but the being beneath the skin.

"You and Kit get to the essence of things in your work. It's like being dissected or skinned alive," the owner of the gallery, where they had first met, had said of their work. "We free the spirit" Kit, her lover and creative partner, had replied.

She was still thinking of him, when she took a wrong turning and found herself in an unfamiliar gallery. Irritated by her absentmindedness, she was about to leave when she saw the portrait of an eighteenth century gentleman. The blood rose to her face when she thought of the last time she had seen him. She had no doubts. It was the man in the barn. The man she had taken so violently, so passionately. She had convinced herself it was a fantasy, born from her desperate need. Circling each other warily, afraid of what they might say or do, she and Richard had not touched each other for months. That night sex with her husband had been wild and strange, almost as if they had been two different people. It was also the night she had conceived.

Hand resting protectively on her stomach. Jo looked at the

face that was at once familiar and unknown. It was strong and vivid, dark brows scowled over eyes that stared into the distance, as if seeking answers beyond the horizon, the nose was straight, the mouth wide and sensual, curved into a half smile. He was dressed informally in an open necked shirt and brown coat, his hair tied back low on his neck, one hand resting on his gun, the other holding the leash of a pair of curly haired dogs. This was a man who was accustomed to having his own way, who could be ruthless, when thwarted, yet charming when indulged.

Not wanting to think what this discovery might mean, she moved swiftly to the next painting. Labelled "Unknown Lady" it showed a woman in a red dress. She had been painted in semi-profile standing on the terrace at Kingsfield, one arm raised to hold back her hair as it blew around her face, the other pushing back her skirts against the wind. Dark curls coiled down her back, her eyes were narrowed, her mouth red as blood, her expression predatory. A powerful and disturbing picture, very different from a conventional portrait, the woman was also unsettlingly familiar.

Jo pressed her hand against her forehead. A sick feeling coiled in the depths of her stomach and to distract herself, she focused on the other paintings in the gallery. They hung in rows set off by deep red wallpaper, which threw into relief their ornate frames. Gentlemen burgesses, country squires, minor gentry and their ladies all gazed blankly across the centuries. None of them were in the least remarkable, except for the painting that hung alone at the furthest end of the room. Knowing this must be the pride of the collection, Jo stopped in front of it and read, "Portrait of a Young Girl, attributed to Thomas Gainsborough."

A girl in a blue silk dress, with a white cat on her lap, looked out of the canvas. The oval face, the pale eyes were as familiar to Jo as her own. This was a face she knew. A face she had sketched only a few days ago, very white and pinched, the eyes demanding yet vulnerable. A face that had pressed against the dark glass of her studio.

Jo crossed herself, instinctively turning to her childhood belief as a form of protection.

What do you want from me? What are you trying to tell me? She stared at the picture willing it to give her some answer. She saw no evil in it and yet the overwhelming feeling she had was one of danger and dread.

"Sweet little thing wasn't she?"

"When she was cleaned up, yes," Jo spoke without thinking.

"Sorry?"

Jo gave a strangled laugh. "I was thinking about something else," she said. She looked at the woman in the long grey coat, who had come to stand beside her and tried to think of a way to change the subject. "Do you think she really is a Gainsborough?" she managed.

"Oh yes," the woman nodded. "There's no record of it, but to my way of thinking there's no doubt about it. If you look at the background, it's very similar to the one in the portrait of his daughters. There's something very far away and otherworldly about it don't you think?"

"No. Yes, maybe," Jo stammered as a chill ran down between her shoulder blades.

"There you are, you can see it too. I've always had a feeling about this one, though truth to tell I don't know anything about her. I like to make up stories about the pictures. To make them seem more real," she smiled at herself. "I have to confess this little girl is one of my favourites. Ever since they did up the gallery and brought these pictures out of storage, I've popped in to see her. It's only been a couple of years, but I've become very fond of her."

"You said these pictures have only been here for two years?" Jo's voice was thin, her hands clammy, her throat tight.

"Yes. There was a lottery grant which paid for their restoration and re-hanging. Are you all right? You look a bit pale." Jo nodded, unable to speak, her last hope of a rational explanation gone. "You could probably do with a cup of tea. There's a very good café on the ground floor. I often treat myself. The woman settled herself comfortably on the bench in front of the Gainsborough, as Jo fled from the gallery.

Far away and otherworldly. The words swirled crazily through her brain. Was that true? Was it all true? What about the man and woman in the barn? He desperate in his need of her, she half naked, hot and feral in her desire. Jo shuddered, her footsteps ringing on the marble staircase as she fled out into street.

CHAPTER TEN

Jo's hands shook. Her heart beat painfully, her breath came in ragged gasps and she had to concentrate hard as she turned out of her parking space and began to drive back to The Granary. The road dipped, then climbed running along the green expanse of The Downs, then back down into the suburbs. Surrounded by neat houses, Jo's breathing calmed, her shoulders relaxed only to tighten again as the road forked and she was faced with the decision whether to go along the golf course, or risk the right turn and drive under the iron bridge.

Jo glanced in the mirror. The car behind her gave her no choice. She had left it too late to turn left. Shutting her eyes she accelerated and shot under the bridge.

The kitten was waiting for her on the front step. He twined around her legs, purring as he escorted her into the house. Once inside, he would not let her pick him up but jumped up on the kitchen unit, swishing his tail in the direction of the kettle.

"OK. OK, I get the message. A hot strong cup of tea to calm the nerves." Jo laughed a little shakily. Diablo opened his mouth wide and gave a huge yawn. "Honestly kitten, if you weren't so sweet and so graceful, I'd think you were Nan come back as a cat."

The kitten gave her a scathing glance and leaping onto the floor, strolled into the living area, where he settled himself on the sofa. Jo poured water onto a tea bag, then added milk and a spoonful of sugar. Holding the mug in both hands she joined Diablo, who nuzzled against her side, twisting and squirming until she let him onto her lap. Jo took a sip of hot tea, put down her mug and one hand on the kitten's reassuring warmth leaned back against the cushions and half shut her eyes.

Like pulling aside one of Nan's net curtains what was vague and indistinct began to come into focus.

She was ten years old, running, scrambling up the garden

path, her sandals slipping on the gravelled surface. Dock and nettles barred her way, but the lash of barbed leaves was nothing compared to the pain of Granddad's words.

"Bad blood," he'd said. "Just like her mother, she has bad blood."

"No. Not our Jo," Nan pleaded. "How can you say that? She's only a little girl."

"She was fighting." He pushed at the letter from the school, sending it to the edge of the kitchen table. "It's not the first time."

"Patrick," Nan's voice dipped into a placatory whine.

Jo, caught in the doorway like a fly in amber, drew in her breath. Surely Granddad would say he didn't mean it, would say he was only joking, that she wasn't really such a bad little girl. Listening so hard that she could hear the blood pounding in her ears, she waited. There was no reprieve. Granddad reached for his packet of fags and ignoring Nan's disapproving glance lit up. As the smoke from the Marlborough rose into the still summer air Jo fled. Out into the garden she went, stumbling up the steps and across the ragged grass, biting her lip as she tried to hold back her tears.

She was bad, bad. That's what the teacher had said when she punched Maureen Arscott. But Maureen had been picking on the little ones and no one else had tried to stop her. It wasn't fair. She was only trying to help. Jo skittered to a halt at the boundary fence. Clenching her fists, she rubbed her eyes hard. She hated Maureen. She was mean and sneaky and got other people into trouble. And now all because of her, Granddad said she was bad too and Nan hadn't stopped him…

They didn't love her. They never had. That's why they kept her in and wouldn't let her play in the street with the other kids. But she didn't care. Jo sniffed and rubbed her arm over her face, streaking her cheeks with dirt and tears. She'd show them. If they thought she was bad like her mum, then she would be. She'd do something she mustn't. Something she knew was wrong. She'd sneak out of the garden. She'd go up the hill to the big house and if something bad happened to her up there, then they'd be sorry. Lifting the wire at the bottom of the garden, she squeezed under the fence. At the base of the hill there were few trees, just tangles of brambles and banks of fern, criss-crossed by well trampled paths, littered with crisp packets, cans and sweet wrappers. Higher up the slope grew ancient oaks, ash trees with feathery leaves and a few sturdy beeches, their branches sheltering dry hollows and leaf filled dips.

Chest heaving with sobs, Jo clambered upwards. Within a few yards the path petered out. The trees became dense. It was cooler and quieter. Jo kept going. What she was doing was wrong, but she did not care. Nan had said she was never, ever to go up there. The land was private. It belonged to the big house, where once not so long ago the bad girls went and sometimes never came back.

It was hard going up the steep bank. She couldn't stop crying and it hurt when she tried to catch her breath. If she stopped, her feet slid backwards and she had to grab hold of a tuft of grass to keep herself from falling. It was as if the land itself wouldn't let her go on and this in itself spurred her on. Fighting the pain in her side, head spinning, gulping and gasping she clawed her way upwards until finally she half fell out of the wood.

As she stumbled over her feet, the world tilted. Sick and dizzy, she closed her eyes. There was an intense silence, then nothing. The hum of bees and the heavy scent of lavender brought her to her senses. In front of her rose the façade of Kingsfield House, its golden stone glowing in the sunlight. At the top of a shallow flight of stairs, double doors stood open offering a glimpse of the entrance hall, where marble statues of half-naked gods and goddesses stood white against the pale walls.

Jo stared fascinated. It was like being in the museum. Even the light was the same, cool and elegant, then the silence was broken by the swish of skirts and a woman in a long red dress appeared, dragging a small girl by the arm.

"How dare you," she screamed. "How dare you address me

in that manner?"

"I shall do as I please," the girl spat. She kicked and clawed at the woman, who seized her hair and jerking back her head, lifted her hand to strike the child across the face.

"Stop it," Jo screamed.

Startled, the woman turned. The girl arched her back, thrusting the whole weight of her body into her captor's stomach. Winded, the woman let go and the child ran through the open doors down the steps, past Jo and into the woods.

For a moment Jo hesitated, then terrified that the woman had seen her, she followed the girl into the trees.

She had to get home, but the path was gone. Instead of beaten earth, cracked by the summer drought, there was grass running through a copse of saplings. Bewildered, Jo looked back at the house. This was where she had come out, so it must be the way home. All she had to do was to go through the trees, down over the ridge and she would be in Granddad's garden.

Without being aware of it, her ears strained to hear the usual sounds of summer, the distant rumble of traffic on the main road, the shouts of kids playing in the street, the metallic tune of the ice cream van. All she could hear was her heart beating faster than usual and someone crying.

What should she do? At any moment the woman in the red dress might come out of the house. Even if the path was not the right one at least she would be hidden by the trees. With a swift backward glance Jo plunged into the copse. The grass curved, then broadened out in front of a small, white building that looked like one of the Greek temples they had learned about in school. On the steps, her head in her hands, was the girl, her body shaking with sharp, angry sobs. Her thin hair, greasy and knotted, straggled down her back. Her long blue dress was torn and stained, but when she glanced up Jo could have been looking at her own image. The girl's skin was as white as hers; the shape of her nose and mouth similar, only her eyes were a pale blue version of Jo's blue green. It was so weird Jo wanted to run back down the hill, but something held her.

"You helped me," the girl said. "I must thank you for that." She reached up and seized Jo by the wrist. Her nails were bitten and ragged, her skin filthy. She lifted her skirt and wiped her eyes, then she blew her nose into her fingers and wiped them on the grass.

"She locks me in the attic," she whispered. "But she won't get the better of me." The girl was defiant. "Sophia thinks she can treat me as she pleases, but one day I will show her."

"Is she your mum?" Jo was puzzled. She had always thought that now the nuns had gone the house was empty. So who were these people?

"My mum?" The girl frowned as if she did not understand.

"Or is she your sister?" Jo prompted. The girl's face tightened.

"I have no mother or sister. There is only my guardian, Cousin Nicholas." As she said his name, her face changed. The narrow pinched look softened, her cheeks flushed and her pale eyes darkened. Clasping her hands to her chest she continued,

"He is so tall and handsome. His eyes are like velvet. His voice is so warm and kind, though sometimes he teases and pretends to pay her more attention than he does me. But it is only pretence, for when I grow up we shall marry. Come. Come with me and I will show you his portrait." The girl jumped to her feet, quivering with such intensity that she frightened Jo.

"I don't want to play anymore." Jo started to back away.

"No please stay. No one ever comes to see me. I am always alone," the girl cried and Jo who was never allowed to play out like the other kids in the street, felt sorry for her.

"I've got to go now, but I could come back tomorrow," she offered.

"No," the girl drew out the word like a long sigh. Jo bit her lip.

"I know," she said struck by a sudden thought. "If you like, we can be friends. Best friends even." The girl looked at her blankly, as if she had never heard the expression before. "You know, we have to tell each other everything and never break our secrets."

The girl smiled a bitter smile.

"I'm good at keeping secrets. I see much, but I say nothing. Otherwise they would think me mad."

"I'm good at keeping secrets too." Jo held out her hand. The girl stared at her palm and frowned.

"What is it?" she said.

"It's my fingers. See. When I put out my hand my fingers stay curled up. Nan says that means I can keep a secret. If your hand lies flat then you can't keep your mouth shut and you tell everyone everything."

The girl copied Jo's gesture. Her fingers curled around her palm tight as a knot.

"You see. I will never tell. Never ever."

"Nor will I," Jo breathed. "Never. And–" a wonderful, idea occurred to her, "–to make it really, really good, we could be blood sisters."

"Yes!" the girl breathed. "You shall be my sister. Then I, Ann Georgiana Hamilton, will never be alone again."

"Nor me, Joanna Mary Docherty!" Jo cried grinning. The pain of Granddad's words forgotten, happiness welled up inside her. "We'll help each other. Always." This was getting better and better.

"As you helped me today." Ann's face glowed.

"Of course. We've got to be there for each other. Now we need something sharp. You've got to cut yourself and rub the blood together for it to work."

"Like so?" Ann took the scissors that hung from a chain around her waist and dug the point hard into her finger. Blood bubbled to the surface. Jo swallowed and stretched out her hand. Swift as a snake, Ann stabbed at Jo's forefinger. There was a moment of intense pain then a single drop of blood stood on her skin.

"Now and forever," she said.

"Now and forever," Jo echoed.

Both girls sighed. They pressed their hands together and rubbed their palms, one against the other. Closer and closer they leaned, their breath mingling, their faces almost touching. Ann's eyes were pale as water. Looking into them, Jo's head spun. A cloud crossed the sun and everything went dark. She put out a hand to steady herself and she was standing at the edge of the wood looking down into her back garden.

"Joanna Mary Docherty, where on earth have you been?" Nan's voice was sharp with anxiety.

"Nowhere," Jo lied defiantly.

"You've not been up there?" Nan glanced swiftly up the hill and crossed herself.

"No," Jo held her head high and looked her grandmother straight in the eye. "I haven't."

"That's all right then," Nan heaved a sigh of relief. "So long as you stay away from those woods and that place. And go on being my good little girl, like you always are."

"I am good, aren't I Nan?" Jo needed it confirmed after her terrible fear of not being loved by Nan or Granddad. "I'm not like my…"

"Shh," Nan put her finger to Jo's lips. "We don't talk about that. Remember. You're a good girl and you do as you're told."

And I did. Didn't I, Jo thought twenty-five years later.

CHAPTER ELEVEN

It was clear that Ann was the girl in the blue dress, the girl whose face had appeared in her drawing. She was also the girl in the Gainsborough portrait in the museum. She was real; there was no longer any doubt about that. She had lived in Kingsfield House two hundred years ago and Jo had met her. In a slideshow of images the memories triggered by the painting were coming back. Jo bit her lip. It had all seemed so innocent, so easy, nothing more than a game, when it first started.

At the time, the best thing about Ann was that she was Jo's secret. Something only she knew and she wasn't going to share it with anyone. It made her feel special and important, even if the other girls didn't want to have anything to do with her.

She hugged the thought close, as she scrambled up the hill, after school that next afternoon. It was hot and sticky, but when she reached the top the blazing heat gave way to the warm stillness of that other time. She ran as fast as she could along the path to the summerhouse, then stopped, almost winded by disappointment when she saw that there was no one there.

She sat down on the steps and waited. Midges danced in a shaft of sun. The sky was blue, dotted with puffy, white clouds. Jo rested her elbows on her knees and stared through the trees. There was a whisper of breath on her cheek then a pair of soft hands covered her eyes. Jo grabbed at the wrists and pulled them away.

"Where have you been? I was waiting," Jo said.

"I was here all the time. I wanted you to come so I did some magic and you did."

"I nearly didn't," Jo lied, having learned from the girls at school never to make herself too easy, too accommodating.

"But you had to, you're my sister, my best friend," the girl said the last two words as if they were still unfamiliar. She stood up and held out her hand. "I want to show you something. Please," she added as Jo refused to move. "Please," she wheedled, head on one side, her eyes anxious.

"OK," Jo relented. "Where are we going?"

"To the house." Ann ran down the steps then stopped. "I never asked you where you live."

"Down there." Jo pointed in the general direction of Weston Ridge.

"In the village?"

Jo hesitated, no one could call the council estate a village.

"Arnold Grove," she said.

Ann smiled, a superior, triumphant sort of smile.

"I have never heard of it, so it cannot be of consequence, but I can show you something quite magnificent. Come. We will pretend we are great ladies come to view the treasures of Kingsfield."

Linking arms with Jo, she led her to the front of the house and up the steps to the main entrance. When Jo saw the footmen waiting to hold open the doors, she hung back, afraid that two scruffy little girls would be turned away. As if Ann knew what she was thinking, she dug her nails into Jo's forearm and winked. Then, head held high, she sailed past sweeping Jo, who expected at any moment to feel a restraining hand on her shoulder, in her wake. The footmen, however, inclined their heads towards Ann then stared straight in front as Jo stumbled after her.

It's as if they don't see me, Jo thought and the skin rose in goose bumps on her arms. In the entrance hall a marble staircase curved gracefully upwards. The walls had been painted a pale green and statues of naked men and half dressed woman stood in niches around the entrance hall. Seeing her amazement, Ann slipped her arm around Jo's waist.

"Is this not very fine, my dear Madam?" she said in a mock grown up voice. "Consider the plasterwork. As for the statues, they are from Italy, brought home after the Grand Tour."

Jo looked up and a shaft of sunlight caught the crystals of the chandelier. Her head spun, she felt sick and dizzy.

"I've got to go," she said, tearing herself free. The footmen at the door did not react as she fumbled with the doorknob. It was like being in a dream except for the smooth roundness of the brass beneath her hand, the warmth of the sun on her shoulders, the sharp pain in her side as she ran through the bushes and scrambled out into the harsher light of a newer day.

In the kitchen, Nan was at the sink wringing out some floor cloths. Without waiting for her to turn around, Jo flung herself at the familiar solid body.

"Whatever is it? You look as if the devil himself were after you?" Nan cried. Jo breathed in her scent of carbolic soap and washing powder. She held on tight and began to feel real again. Nan turned and stroked her hair with slightly damp hands. "It's all right," she said.

"I thought I was late. I thought you would be worried."

"I might well be if you're going to come back in this state. Playing outside in this heat isn't good for you. I'll have to keep you indoors in the cool, if the weather doesn't break. I know, tomorrow's Saturday, so we'll go into town to do a bit of shopping. We'll go early before it gets too hot and who knows, if you're a good girl, I might treat you to one of those big tall ice creams. You'd like that wouldn't you?"

Jo nodded, her face buried in Nan's hard breast.

For the next few weeks, she stayed close to home. Then school finished and she grew bored. It was still unusually hot. During the day the streets were deserted, but in the evenings she could hear the sound of other children and began to forget how frightened she had been. After all, nothing bad had happened to her. Ann did not want to hurt her, she just wanted to be friends. And she was her friend. Her very special friend. The sort of friend that no one else she knew could possibly have.

Ann had been a bit mean, but that's what friends were sometimes and now Jo was being just as mean by not going to see her. She ought to go up to the house, she had to, otherwise they might not be friends anymore and then she'd have the long summer holidays all on her own with no one to play with.

Jo waited until it was cooler, then climbed the hill. The ground was baked hard, riddled with cracks, the grass bleached, the leaves on the trees withering from lack of water. A Pepsi can glinted in the sun, a fish and chip wrapper lay beneath a shrub. The windows of Kingsfield were crusted with cobwebs and when Jo peered into one of the back rooms, it was empty.

She should have come earlier. Ann had given up on her and was no longer her friend. Furiously Jo blinked away tears. If that was the way she wanted it, well she didn't care. Rubbing her nose with the back of her hand, she stalked back through the trees, crawled under the fence and into the garden. She sat for a bit on the scrubby piece of lawn pretending to be at the beach, but it was no fun on her own and she was glad when Nan rapped at the kitchen window and called her in to the shade.

It wasn't quite time for tea and Granddad was in the front room with the television blaring away. Jo stamped her way up to her bedroom. Now that Ann had gone there was nothing to do. She sat on the bed for a while glaring at the sweep of the hill beyond the garden. Then a flicker of colour caught her eye as next door's cat, a huge fat ginger tom, heaved himself onto the top of the fence. For a moment, she thought he was going to topple over, but he balanced his bulk and lifted his face contentedly to the sun. He looked so funny with his tail curled around his paws and his body spilling over on either side of his perch that Jo reached for her sketchpad and began to draw.

The rounded shape of the cat's body elongated itself into an oval. The wooden slats of the fence became a neck, then shoulders. Jo scribbled out her drawing, sucked at her pencil, tried again and once again Ann's face took shape on the paper.

"Go away," Jo scored deep lines across the page. "I don't want you. You didn't come when I went up to see you. I don't want you here." She ripped out the page, tore the paper into tiny strips, then even smaller pieces and flushed them down the toilet. She shoved her sketchbook deep into the back of a drawer and she ran downstairs for tea.

For the rest of the summer, she did what she was told, helping Nan around the house and going with her when she cleaned the church. Sometimes she wondered if she'd seen Ann because she was bad. Was the way she treated Jo, one moment pretending to be her friend, then scaring her, a sort of punishment? Mostly, however, she tried not to think about her. As the holidays dragged on, Nan finally relented and she was allowed to play with some of the other girls, so long as she was home early and didn't hang around by the pub or beg rides on the older boys' bikes like Maureen and the really wild girls did.

What Jo did and what she told Nan was not always the same and although she was never fully accepted she did find her place on the edge of the tribal culture that ruled in Weston Ridge. Gradually, she managed to push the girl in the blue dress to the back of her mind. The sketchpad however stayed in the back of the drawer.

Back to school in September, everything changed. Some of the girls she'd been playing with went up to senior school. Jo was in the top class and friendship patterns had to be redrawn. At home, Granddad's cough, which had plagued him for years, got steadily worse. Nan kept the heating on all the time, but he still complained of the cold and the pain in his chest. It did not stop him smoking. The day it happened he had run out of cigarettes.

"I'll have to nip down to the shop. I'd send you, but the new owners have gone all funny about serving kids," Nan said. "You know what your Granddad gets like if he hasn't got his fags." She looked pleadingly at Jo. "I won't be more than a minute or two so keep an ear out for him like a good girl. You can do your homework in the kitchen."

Obediently, Jo went to fetch her books. The door of the front room was ajar and as she came back downstairs she heard Granddad shifting in his chair.

"Noreen," he wheezed.

Jo stood on the bottom step and waited. Perhaps he'd stop. Then when Nan came back, she could say she'd looked in and Granddad had been all right.

"Noreen." He was louder this time; an edge of discomfort in his voice. It was no longer possible to pretend she had not heard. Jo took a deep breath.

"I'm coming Granddad."

"Noreen?"

"Nan's gone out."

"I need the toilet," he whined.

"Nan will be back in a minute," Jo said desperately, but Granddad's need was too great.

"Help me up," he demanded. Reluctantly she went to take his arm, but he drew back. "No, no. That's no good. Stand still and let me lean on you." Steadying himself on the arms of his chair, he began to push himself to his feet, but half way up he got stuck and Jo had to move closer, breathing in his old man's smell, as she stood next to him. "No. Not like that, you stupid girl."

The sweat stood on his forehead. His skin was clammy, his hand as he squeezed her shoulder nothing but bone. The granddad who had once carried her on his shoulders had shrivelled inside his clothes, even so it was hard for her to bear his weight.

They shuffled along the corridor. At the kitchen door, he stopped with such a look of distaste on his face, that Jo was terrified he had wet himself.

"Come on Granddad. Nearly there," she coaxed.

"I know," he snapped.

The down stairs toilet smelled of Dettol. There were lace curtains at the window and a pot of plastic flowers on the sill. Jo guided Granddad inside then backed away into the kitchen, trying not to hear the sounds that came through the half open door. First the noise of Granddad's pee, then a bout of coughing, followed by hawking and spitting. Finally the flush and his voice, querulous and demanding,

"Well get me back, then."

Dutifully, she braced herself against his weight. Half way across the kitchen, he slumped against the table, the cough bubbling up in his lungs and spurting out of his mouth. Phlegm, flecked with blood, dribbled down his chin. Jo looked steadily out of the window, until the fit had passed.

"All right Granddad?" she asked anxiously.

"All right." His voice was barely a whisper.

"Just a bit further," Jo said.

"I know, I know." They were in the hall now. Through the open door of the front room Jo could see Granddad's chair. As if spurred on by the sight, he jerked forward. His hand slid from her shoulder, he gave a strangled cry and his legs gave way. The force of his fall knocked her sideways. Getting up on her hands and knees, she crawled over to where he lay, his breath rasping in his throat, his hands flailing as he struggled for air.

"Granddad," she wailed. "Granddad get up." Another strangled gasp was the only reply. Jo knew she had to get help. She looked at the phone that stood on the hall table under the picture of The Scared Heart. If she could reach it then she could ring for an ambulance, but Granddad was blocking her way and she could not make herself push past him.

She'd have to run to the neighbours' but Nan didn't like her having anything to do with them and she'd told her to stay and look after her granddad. If only Nan would come home. A sob rose in her throat. Granddad's face was turning dark red. Jo backed away down towards the kitchen. She'd go next door, she'd tell them what had happened. It was an emergency. Or maybe she should wait. Nan had only gone to the newsagents. She had to be back soon. Before she could make up her mind, the back door opened.

"Nan," she cried. "I couldn't help it. Granddad fell over and he's not moving."

Nan knelt beside Granddad and put her head to his chest.

Then she looked up at Jo and her eyes were afraid and her mouth shook,

"Ring nine, nine, nine, love," she said.

*

It was her first death. There were so many to follow. Remembering, Jo mimicked her childhood self and wrapped her arms around herself. Diablo snuggled closer, butting at her with his head until she stroked his fur. Her hand moving backwards and forwards calmed and soothed them both and with the release of tension came the tears. She wept for her family, for Kit, her partner and her lover, and for all those children that should have been. The tears turned to sobs, great shuddering sobs that shook her whole body, until finally, exhausted both physically and emotionally, she leaned her head against the cushions, closed her eyes and slept.

CHAPTER TWELVE

In Jo's dream it was dusk and she was sitting on her bed in her room in Arnold Grove, waiting. The ambulance had come and gone, taking Granddad to the hospital. While they were putting him into the vehicle she had been sent up stairs and told to keep out of the way. Nan had gone with him and none of the neighbours had remembered her granddaughter. Jo put her thumb in her mouth, but it did not help. She was frightened and anxious and she did not want to be alone.

From her window, she could see the rise of the hill at the end of the garden. Up there in the old house, her best friend was waiting. She took her coat and went outside. She could see the glow of the lamps along the main road that ran through the estate. In the wood the trees stood bare against the orange sky and the paths ran pale through the undergrowth, but as she scrambled upwards the light changed. It grew darker, deeper, denser and when she reached the top of the hill, the air was crisp with frost and the sky glittered with stars. A thin moon hung over the house and the windows shone gold against the night.

She ran across the terrace and into the house, up the back stairs and along the first floor corridor where she found Ann sitting on the top step of the marble staircase. She was as thin and pale as before, but she wore a fine gown of deep blue velvet trimmed with falls of lace at the neck and the wrists. Her face and hands were scrubbed clean, her hair was curled and pinned on the top of her head and dressed with a velvet ribbon to match her gown. Around her neck she wore a silver locket. She moved her skirts aside to make room for Jo, then put her arm around her shoulders and whispered,

"I am so glad you are here. My best friend, my sister." Jo leaned her cheek against Ann's and half closed her eyes. "I have been so ill. They thought I would die, but I would not. I was waiting for you," Ann murmured. "It has been so long."

She turned her face to Jo's. "You look so unhappy. Please do not be sad." She leaned forward and kissed Jo lightly on the lips. Her breath smelled of wine and cinnamon. Jo felt tears sting her eyes, then roll down her cheeks.

They sat there for a long time. Ann murmuring endearments, Jo her thumb in her mouth, gradually drifting into a warm half sleep.

"He is returned!" Ann's fierce cry woke her. Her head jerked forward as Ann pushed her away and she fell sideways against the banister knocking her forehead on the cold stone. Ann scrambled to her feet, Jo completely forgotten, as she stood transfixed, her eyes fastened on the man who strode into the entrance hall.

She waited, quivering as he flung back his cloak, tossed his hat to the waiting footman and called for something to take away the chill of the journey. Then she started down the stairs, her feet flying, her face flushed. She was half way down, when a fit of coughing seized her. She pressed one hand to her side, the other over her mouth.

"Annabel!" he cried and taking the stairs two at a time he was at her side. "Little coz, I thought you were recovered," he said, as he scooped her up into his arms and carried her tenderly down the stairs. "I have gifts and all manner of pretty things for you, but you must wait until I have washed away the dust." He set her on her feet. She swayed a little and stretched out her hand towards him, but he had already turned from her, his eyes on the woman who had just entered.

"Come to the fire and warm yourself." Her voice was low and husky. She held a glass of claret in her hand, the red wine glowing in the light of the candles, echoing the scarlet velvet of her dress.

Jo stared at the couple. They were both beautiful. He was tall and slim with dark hair, which was tied back in a sort of ponytail. She was only a little smaller, her skin was the colour of coffee and her hair tumbled in dark curls over her shoulders.

A footman took the empty glass. Nicholas offered his arm

to Sophia and led her away. Forgotten by them both, Ann trailed disconsolately behind. Jo put her head on her arms and cried.

Her cheeks were still wet when she woke. It was growing late. The arched window framed a darkening sky and the room was full of shadows. Stretching out her legs, she dislodged the kitten which leapt to the floor and stood looking at her accusingly.

"OK you need feeding," Jo muttered getting up from the sofa. She moved stiffly into the kitchen, her mind half lost in her dream. Scooping out food into Diablo's dish, she did her best to shake off the feelings of grief and longing and tried to concentrate on what she had learned about the people who once lived at Kingsfield. The man in the portrait in the museum was Nicholas D'Aubeney, the woman in the red dress Sophia. Sophia was his lover, while Ann, Jo's best friend and blood sister, loved Nicholas with a passionate and frightening intensity. The desperation and longing was in her eyes, in the way her face softened at the mention of his name. Her whole body trembled when she saw him, as if she could hardly hold back from flinging herself into his arms.

Poor kid. With the wisdom of her thirty-five years Jo shook her head. It was hard loving someone so much that you made them the centre of your universe. No one could sustain such an emotion. At some point, since he was only human, Nicholas was bound to let her down and Ann would have to face the fact that he was not perfect. The best Jo could hope for was that Ann had been older when it had happened, or that as she grew up her own feelings had become less intense. She doubted it however. There was nothing to suggest that Ann would grow any more calm and rational. If anything it was likely that her emotions would become more violent, more unbalanced as she was forced to witness the bond between Nicholas and Sophia. Whichever way Ann's feelings took her, Jo was sure that at some point she would be able to remember.

In the past her mind had blanked out what it could not bear. Now, whatever had held the memories at bay had gone.

Inevitably she was going to have to face up to what had happened; beginning with the growing conviction that she was somehow to blame.

"It was my fault," she whispered. "The crash, it was all because of me."

*

It rained on the day of Patrick Docherty' funeral. A nonstop drizzle blurred the window of the front bedroom where Jo stood waiting. Her stomach felt tight and hard. Her mouth tasted of acid and the horrible furry white stuff Nan had made her drink. Her tights were scratchy, her new shoes stiff, her hair pulled too tightly back under her head band. Jo leaned her forehead against the glass and peered down the street.

At long last she was going to meet her mum. The mother who had abandoned her as a baby, who Granddad had always said had bad blood.

As the Jaguar turned into Arnold Grove, her stomach twisted and when the car pulled up in front of the house, she had to swallow hard to stop herself from being sick. Biting her lip, she watched as the driver's door opened and a large, red-faced man got out. He wore a dark suit and black tie and his hair was sleeked over his balding head. Ray Harris, her step-dad.

Ray walked around to the passenger side and opened the door. As Melinda Harris slid out of the car with all the elegance of a top class model, Jo drew in her breath. It was like a fairy tale come true. Her mum wasn't bad. She was beautiful. She was slim, fine boned with silver blonde hair that fell to her shoulders, and in her trouser suit and heels she looked like something out of one of those glossy fashion magazines Nan read in the dentist's waiting room.

Without looking at her husband, Melinda strode up to the front door. Jo tensed, ears straining for the sound of the doorbell. It did not ring. Nan, who must have been watching from the lounge, had already opened the door. Jo crept to the top of the stairs. She had not seen her mother since she was six months old and had no idea what to expect. There were no photographs, no letters, no trace of her in the house. Except for a few comments from her grandparents, it was as if Melinda had ceased to exist and now she was here. Holding onto the banister to steady herself Jo looked down into the hall.

"I suppose you'd better come in," Nan said stiffly, turning her face away to avoid the possibility of a kiss.

"It's been a long time," Melinda said coolly. Nan nodded.

"Nearly eleven years."

"Too long Mother-in-law." Ray arrived face flushed, sweating slightly.

"You'll be wanting a cup of tea," Nan said.

"Ta," Ray said.

He's common, Jo thought hearing her Nan's sniff of disgust. *And fat.* At which point Ray looked up and saw her.

"Hullo little girl. You must be Joanna," he boomed. "Come on down and say hello to your Uncle Ray."

Jo let go of the banister rail she had been clutching. Step by careful step she made her way down the stairs. Nan and Melinda had already gone into the kitchen and Jo could hear their voices strained and cold above the sound of the kettle boiling on the gas.

"She's got your eyes and your colouring," Nan was saying. "And your sensitive stomach. Always being sick you were when you were her age. This has all been very upsetting for her you know. First her Granddad going and now…"

"And now her long lost mother turning up." There was a pause, then Melinda said her voice almost pleading, "I had to come. I had to see her. She's my child after all, but if you and Dad had had your way, you'd have shipped me off to the mother and baby home."

"We thought it would be for the best. The baby adopted by a good Catholic couple, you going back to school and the rest of us getting on with our lives."

"As if nothing had happened?" Melinda cried.

"As if nothing had happened," Nan's voice was firm.

"You don't honestly believe that, do you Mum? Dad

would never have forgiven me. He'd have always held it over my head. I let him down and there's no going back from that."

Jo's foot was on the bottom step. Her insides were jumping like a bag of frogs and there was that warning wet feeling in her mouth that happened just before she threw up.

"Hey little one. Pleased to meet you." Ray put out a large red hand. Jo gulped. Ray smiled and his face was kind and welcoming. "It will be all right, you know. Worse things happen at sea and all that. I know you've lost your granddad and you must be feeling more than a little bit sad, but maybe I can help. In the meantime we'd better go and join the ladies. It's not too easy for them either and it sounds as if they could do with a break from all that heavy talk. All right?"

Jo hesitated then she took his hand. It was warm and firm, curling around hers protectively and she felt much better as they walked into the kitchen together.

*

The funeral was held at Our Lady of Sorrows. Built in the fifties for a growing Catholic population, which had since moved on, it was too large for its congregation. In spite of the electric heaters glowing fitfully on the walls, it was cold and its empty spaces rang with the sound of feet, as the pews filled with Nan's friends from the church cleaning rota and the Catholic Women's Guild. Granddad's friends from the pub had come too and some of the men he had worked with on the docks.

Afterwards people came to the house for tea and sandwiches and fancies from the local cake shop. Jo could not eat. She drank a little of the lemonade Nan had bought for her then found a place in a corner of the front room from where she could watch Melinda. Her Mum was so different from anyone she had ever met. She was sophisticated and glamorous. She talked easily to everyone, although Jo, straining to hear every word in the hope that she would learn more about her past, found that she told them very little.

Nan poured tea and urged everyone to eat. One or two of her friends came and asked Jo if she was all right, but to her relief most people ignored her.

Melinda and Ray were the last to leave. Melinda kissed her very lightly, just brushing her forehead with her lips. Jo wanted to grab hold of her mum, squeeze her tight and breathe in the lovely cool scent that she wore, but she did not dare. Nan shut the door behind them, kicked off her shoes and reached for her cigarettes.

"Well that's that then," she said.

It was over. Her mum had come and gone, leaving behind her a trace of a world far more beautiful and exciting than anything to be found in Weston Ridge.

Two days later, however, Melinda Harris was back. When Jo came home from school she was sitting at the kitchen table with Nan. The teapot was set like a barrier between them, the tea in their cups left to go cold. The room smelled of her perfume, clear and cool, lemons and pale sunlight fighting against the ever-present smell of Nan's bleach and blue soap.

Nan fingering her cigarette packet looked grim. Melinda's face was set but when she saw Jo her features relaxed, her whole face lit up and she smiled so radiantly that Jo stood in the doorway unable to move. No one had ever looked at her like that. Her legs were all wobbly, her eyes prickled but she didn't want to cry, part of her wanted to run and throw herself into Melinda's arms, another part was too scared to move in case her mum was just being nice like she was to everyone and if she tried to hug her she'd give her a quick pat and put her to one side, like Nan did.

"We've been talking about you," Melinda said. "Your nan and I. We were saying, weren't we," she glanced sharply at Nan whose mouth was set in the thin line she used when she simply didn't trust herself to speak. "That it would be best if you come and live with me and Ray." Nan jerked her head in a brief sharp gesture that might, or might not, mean that she agreed. "You're my little girl and it's time we got to know each other." Melinda looked at Jo, who nodded scarcely able to believe what she was hearing. "In lots of ways too, it's the best time to make the move as you'll be going up to senior school next year and we can't have you going to St. Thomas Aquinas."

"There's nothing wrong with St. Thomas," Nan said through gritted teeth. Melinda ignored her. Focusing totally on Jo she continued, "We'll send you to a really good school, Redland or St. Dominic's. You'll love it there and you'll love living with me and Ray. It will be such fun." Jo heard Nan snort but she didn't care. Her Mum wanted her, loved her even. Living with Melinda was beyond anything she had ever dreamed of. "You'll have everything you want and you can see your Nan whenever you like. Either she'll come to us, or Ray can drive you over here. How does that sound? OK?"

"She can come on the bus," Nan said before Jo could speak. "And you'll send her to a convent school and since I don't suppose you go to church any more, every Sunday she'll come back here and go to Mass with me."

"Fine. That's sorted then. Oh Jo I can hardly wait. You'll be coming to us after Christmas. I'll have my own little girl back, just as I've always wanted. Come here my darling." Melinda held out her arms and Jo ran into them. They hugged each other tight. Melinda's lips moving against her daughter's cheek, her breath delicate as butterflies' wings. "You'll love it, you'll see," she whispered and not even the sight of Nan standing straight backed at the sink could spoil the wave of happiness that swept over Jo.

After Melinda had left, an awkward silence filled with hurt and unspoken recriminations hung over the kitchen. Jo didn't know what to say. How could she tell Nan she was glad she was going to live with her Mum and Ray? The whole idea made her so happy she could burst. The only thing that spoiled it was that she didn't want Nan to be sad. Once or twice Nan looked as if she might be the first to speak, but she didn't. Eventually, she lit a cigarette and went into the front room to watch her favourite soap.

Jo, however, could not settle. Restless and bubbling with joy, she wanted to tell her friends that she was going to live with her mum and step-dad; that they had always wanted her.

It hadn't been right for her to go while Granddad was alive, but now she was going to join them and live in a posh house in Stoke Bishop and go to a private school.

Even as the thoughts whirled deliciously through her mind, Jo knew that there was no one in Weston Ridge she could share them with. The girls at school would think she was boasting, that she was getting too stuck up and it was up to them to put her well and truly in here place. She had weeks to go at Our Lady of Sorrows Primary and if they thought she was lording it over them her life would not be worth living.

There was one person who wouldn't look at it like that. What did it matter if she was a ghost or something? Ann would understand about being left out, about being different. Now Jo had found her mum again, she'd be pleased for her. Besides, since she was leaving Weston Ridge, this would be the very last time she'd ever see her and it was only fair to her blood sister, her best friend to say goodbye.

Jo took her anorak and went up the hill. It was dark and cold and as she neared the house the darkness grew deeper.

Ann was sitting by the fire reading a book.

"Where have you been? Why have you not been to see me?" she demanded so petulantly that Jo's happiness deflated.

"I don't know," she muttered. "I'm here now, aren't I?"

"I missed you." Ann's voice trembled. Her pale blue eyes filled with tears and Jo felt horrible.

"I wish I hadn't come now," she muttered. "I only wanted to tell you I was going to live with my mum."

"Your mum, who or what is that?" Ann's voice grew shrill.

"My mother," Jo growled. "Don't you know anything?"

"Your mother!" Flinging her book across the room, Ann leapt to her feet. "You said you were an orphan like me."

"No I didn't. I said I live with my nan, my grandmother I mean."

"You can't leave me. You can't." Ann's voice rose to a shriek, then descended into a whine, "I will be so lonely without you."

"I've got to. I want to. But I can always visit," Jo offered.

"That's no good." Ann's eyes were narrow with rage. "I want you here always."

"That's too bad, 'cos I can't be here. My mother," Jo drawled out the word to make it more hurtful. "My mother wants me with her."

Ann's whole body shook. She grasped Jo's wrist, digging her nails into the flesh as she hissed,

"You can be here and you will be. You'll come back and I will be waiting."

CHAPTER THIRTEEN

Ann won't let me go. She's always had this hold over me and she still does. Jo closed her eyes against the image of Ann's fury when she had told her that she was leaving Weston Ridge. Then she opened them again. This time she was not going to escape her memories. Whatever it took, she was going to go on to the end of the story.

She had always known that she had, in some way, been responsible for what had happened, but she didn't know exactly how. The counsellor she had seen after the accident had told her that her guilt had been so deeply buried that it would take a long time before the truth would surface. As the years had gone by, Jo had accepted that it never would. She had almost managed to convince herself that it didn't matter. There was no point in dredging up the past, because living in the present moment was what mattered. Then twenty-five years later it had all come flooding back. The chilling fact was that Ann had a long reach and she was prepared to wait. The question was what was she waiting for?

*

The year Granddad died was Jo's last Christmas at Nan's. As the condensation caused by steaming the pudding streamed down the windows, the four of them, Nan, Melinda, Ray and Jo crammed into the kitchen. Ray settled himself on a chair, his huge bulk taking up most of the space and Nan carefully working her way round him, served out dry turkey and hard roast potatoes. The pudding was thick and black, the custard lumpy and afterwards Nan switched the lights on the silver Christmas tree in the front room and they watched television until it was time to leave.

The Christmas tree in Stoke Bishop was real. It stood in the hall and its scent filled the whole house. Swags of ivy twisted up the banister, bowls of scarlet apples spiked with holly and clusters of fat red candles stood on tables and sideboards. Jo had never seen anything so beautiful. The whole house was more wonderful than she could have imagined. Her own room had a small four-poster bed with brass rails and frilly white curtains, a deep pink carpet, built-in cupboards and a desk on which stood a portable television.

"That's your present from Ray. He's so happy you've come to live with us. Do you like the room darling? If you don't, we can change it. You can have anything you want. You know that don't you?" Melinda put her arm around her daughter's shoulders. Her touch was as light as the silk scarf she wore around her neck. She led Jo to the mirror beside the bed and bending down rested her cheek against hers. Their faces, two pale ovals were reflected in the glass. Hair silver blonde, eyes green. The smaller face less defined.

"We look like sisters," Melinda breathed.

"Girls are you coming down? There's a great pile of turkey sandwiches waiting here and I've cut up some of that Christmas cake Frieda made."

Melinda pulled a face.

"We'd better go. Ray gets so bothered about food. After that dinner at Mum's I don't think I could ever eat another thing, but he'll fuss so if I don't. He's been very good to me Jo. I don't know what would have happened to me if I hadn't met Ray."

Next morning Jo woke disorientated. Looking for the toilet, she opened the wrong door and stepped into the corridor. From across the landing she heard Melinda say,

"I'm not going."

"But we always go to Don and Frieda's. They're our oldest friends."

"Then you go. I told you, I'm staying at home with Jo."

"Can't you get your mum over?"

"After all the damage she's done? God only knows what she'd be telling her while we're out. Oh don't look like that. It's only for a little while. Once she's settled in, I'll get a regular baby sitter, until she's old enough to come out with us."

"It won't be the same without you."

"There will be plenty of luscious lovelies for you to flirt with."

"No one as luscious as you."

"Ray don't."

"Why not? I'm not going to work."

"I just…"

"It's not the little 'un is it?"

"Of course not. Come here."

"That's more like it."

*

Jo heard Ray whistling as he lumbered down the stairs. She pulled on her clothes and followed, hoping that someone would be making breakfast. In the kitchen Ray was feeding bread into the toaster; his silk dressing gown stretched tight did not quite meet over his bulging stomach.

"Toast?"

Jo averted her eyes from the white skin matted with dark hair.

"I usually have cereal," she said.

"Let's see what we've got then." Ray opened a cupboard and pulled out a box of cornflakes. "These any good?"

Jo nodded. He took milk from the fridge and poured it over the cereal. Jo watched anxiously. Nan always heated the milk, turning cornflakes into a warm mush liberally covered with sugar. She dipped in her spoon and raised it to her mouth.

"All right then?"

Jo pulled a face as her throat closed against the taste of cold milk.

"Yuk," she dared, lowering her spoon. Unlike Nan Ray did not tell her to stop her nonsense and think of the starving millions.

"Always thought they tasted of cardboard myself," he beamed and leaning forward tousled her hair. Jo smelled sweat and a kind of swimming bath smell.

"I'll have toast please and," she hesitated "jam."

"Anything for you little 'un," Ray said putting another

slice of bread in the toaster.

Later that day, when Ray had gone to Don and Frieda's, she sat on the big leather sofa in the lounge and Melinda reached behind the art books in the bookcase and pulled out a scrapbook. The cheap paper cover was pasted over with pictures of flowers, except for a circle in the middle, where the initials M and J had been drawn in thick black ink, then repeated around the border in fanciful curlicues. Melinda hugged the book to her breast before laying it gently on the coffee table. Kneeling down beside it she said,

"Come here Jo. You want to know who your dad was, don't you?" She reached up and gently pulled her daughter down beside her. Jo chewed her lip. Pleasing Melinda meant betraying Nan and possibly Ray too, but she did want to know. More than anything she wanted to know why her mum and dad had left her.

"Don't worry. Your Nan won't know I've told you and Ray knows all about it," Melinda said carelessly, as if he did not matter. She sighed and stroked the scrapbook, her fingers following the outlines of the letters as she stared into her past. Jo felt the warmth of her mother's body next to hers, smelled the cool scent of her perfume, the taint of the wine she had been drinking on her breath.

"This is where we lived." Melinda opened the book at a photograph of a tall thin house, with boarded up windows and a small front garden full of rubbish. "And this is us." A young couple, he tall and dark, she small and white blonde; both with long flowing hair held back by a band of material tied around the head, wide legged trousers and embroidered shirts. He wore a single earring, she had gold hoops in her ears. These were her parents.

"James Barrington-Stuart. Isn't he gorgeous? And so young, so alive. He would try anything. 'Life is for the experience,' he always said. 'Go with it and live.' We were going to travel. India first, then San Francisco. We had it all planned, until your Nan shopped us. I'm sure she thought it was for the best. She said it was no way to bring up a child, but we loved you, we really did. We just wanted to do it our way." Her hand searched blindly for her glass. Jo reached up and took it from the side table, where Melinda had left it and handed it to her. Melinda took a gulp.

"He was never the same afterwards. He came out of prison with a habit and it killed him." Eyes full of tears she turned passionately to her daughter. "He was so beautiful, so good and so much fun."

And dead Jo thought staring at the flames flickering behind the bars of the gas fire

*

After the Christmas holidays, Jo went to her new school. The nuns at St. Dominic's were strict but fair. They demanded the best from their girls and Jo thrived. She loved the discipline, the uniform and especially the time spent in the art room. Miss Jones was young and pretty, she painted canvases flowing with colour and movement and she did everything she could to encourage and nurture Jo's talent.

*

"I'm going to be an artist, when I grow up," Jo announced in the middle of her first year.

"It runs in the family," Melinda said.

"Not Nan and Granddad?" Jo was surprised.

"No silly, your father."

Jo looked across at Ray to gage his reaction.

"Your real dad, little 'un. Never me. I'm no Picasso. Your mum, now, she's a real work of art." Melinda flicked back her hair.

"It's true I've always been interested in art. Before I had you, I was going to be a designer. Perhaps I'll take a course when you go to college. We could study together."

"You'd be brilliant. Both of you," Ray beamed. "Go on little 'un show us what you can do."

Jo hesitated. Melinda clicked her tongue.

"Don't press her Ray. Creative people can't do it to order like you can tune an engine."

"I can do people," Jo said quickly. "I can do you if you

like."

"Me?" Ray flushed with pleasure. Jo nodded. She fetched her sketchpad and began to draw. Ray was so big and uncomplicated, it was easy.

"It's not quite right," she said when she'd finished. "You're nicer than that."

He took the paper gingerly as if afraid of what it might show.

"Well," he said. "Well." He put the drawing down and gazed at his stepdaughter. "I'm having that framed."

"You like it?"

"It's…" Suddenly his eyes were full of water. "Whatever you need little 'un you'll have it. Paint, paper, crayons you name it and you'll have the best."

The following morning, Melinda took her to the art shop on Black Boy Hill and bought her everything she asked for. In the years that followed she took Jo to galleries and exhibitions and to London if there was an important show on at the Tate or the National Gallery. When Jo was a little older, they went to Paris, Florence, Rome, Milan, Madrid, New York and Venice for the Biennale. Ray paid for everything but he never went with them.

*

On Sundays, Jo went to Mass with Nan, but as she got into her teens she spent less and less time in Weston Ridge nor did she ever take her sketchbook with her. Although art was the most important thing in her life, after her family, she only drew at school, or in the house in Stoke Bishop, which she now looked on as home.

Her last picture of Melinda was that night, the night of the party. Her mother was getting ready to go out and Jo sat on the side of the bath sketching Melinda soaking in scented water.

"I wish you were coming tonight," Melinda said.

"I don't. It will be boring. We do the same old things, see the same old people every Boxing Day."

"You're right. We should be at a nightclub, somewhere

sophisticated and exciting," Melinda sighed.

"Rather you than me."

"I know it's not your thing Jo, but going to Don and Frieda's isn't mine either. I don't know how I'll stand it. I'll be on the G and Ts before I leave the house. Oh well. It'll keep Ray happy I suppose. He's such a creature of habit it would kill him to do anything out of the ordinary at Christmas. Anyway since I can't persuade you to share my suffering what will you do with yourself tonight?"

"Draw, watch TV. Go to bed early."

"Boring!" Melinda waved a languid hand. "Tell you what, why don't you sleep in here with me tonight? Then, when I get back, I can give you all the gory details."

"You mean what everyone wore and what they said and who got drunk and who threw up on the carpet."

"Or in the pot plant, like last year."

"Disgusting."

"I know, but it's got to be done." Melinda rose slowly letting the water run from her shoulders, down her firm white body, with its tight hard breasts and narrow hips. She stretched out her arms and Jo wrapped her in a soft, warm towel.

"Look," she said, stepping out of the bath and leaning back against her daughter. "We could be sisters." Jo looked at their two faces reflected in the misty surface of the full-length bathroom mirror. Melinda was right. The older she got the more like her mother Jo looked. They had the same silver gilt hair, green eyes and pale skin. Side by side they were the same height and build.

Blood sisters, the thought chilled her. Dropping her arms Jo stepped back. She did not want to think of Ann, of that other time, of that garden where the girl with the hair like hers, but with pale blue eyes, had taken out her scissors and they had cut through their flesh and mingled their blood.

"No," she said out loud.

"No what?" Melinda dropped the towel on the floor. "Come on Jo, time to zip me into that figure hugging

- 102 -

number."

Jo waved her mother and Ray off, shut the front door behind them and went upstairs to Melinda's room. She and Ray no longer slept together. A few years ago, he had been banished to the spare room, supposedly because he snored and kept Melinda awake. Sitting on the big wide bed, propped up against feather soft pillows, her sketchpad on her knee, Jo felt far away from that strange time at Kingsfield. It was like something that had happened to someone else. Or a picture seen down the end of a telescope, tiny, but perfect in all its detail and totally irrelevant.

She did not, however, risk drawing anything new, but shaded her sketch of Melinda in the bath, then doodled some abstract patterns, before hastily putting the book to one side and reaching for the remote. The room was warm, the film unexciting and Jo soon found herself yawning. Looking at the clock, she saw that there were hours before Ray and Melinda would be back. Feeling too lazy to go into her own room, she slipped off her clothes and, as she often did, took a pair of her mother's silk pyjamas and snuggled down under the duvet.

Relaxing in the scent of her mother's perfume, she slept. The hand clamped around her breast jerked her awake. Thick fingers pulled at her nipple, hot alcohol fumed breath panted against her neck followed by wet slobbering lips, heavy groans and a knee forcing her legs apart.

"Get off me." Jo fought and struggled against the encircling arms. Shoving her elbow into his stomach, she screamed and rolled off the bed, stumbling across the room as Melinda flung open the bedroom door.

"What the hell's going on?" Melinda slurred. Her face was flushed, her hair disordered. One strap had slipped off her shoulder and she put a hand on the doorframe to balance herself when she saw the rumpled bed and Ray, sitting there, hands hanging between his thighs, his trousers and underpants on the floor.

"Mum." Sobbing Jo threw herself into her mother's arms.

"It's all right. I'm here. Dear God what has he done to

you?" Melinda wrapped her arms around her daughter. "Come on darling, come with me. Let's get out of here. Oh how could I have left you with him? It will be OK. Don't worry. I'll look after you." Leaning against her mother, hardly able to walk, Jo let Melinda lead her away. At the door Melinda turned and hissed at Ray,

"You disgusting piece of shit, how could you? How could you do this to her?"

"Jo," Ray lumbered to his feet. "Jo I didn't mean it. I didn't know it was you. It was her bed. Dear God what have I done? What have I done?"

"Mum I'm sorry, I'm sorry," Jo sobbed.

"Oh darling you've got nothing to be sorry about. It's him. He's vile. God, I never thought he would do anything like this, but don't worry, we're getting out of here. We're going and I promise you will never see him again. Never. I'll look after you, I will." She hurried Jo into the bathroom, where she undressed her and wrapped her in a clean towel while she ran a bath and filled it with sweet scented essence. She helped Jo into the steaming water and gently sponged her clean.

"It's all right. We're not staying. We're getting out of here," she kept repeating as Ray hammered at the door begging and pleading to be let in. He had to explain. He didn't mean to do anything. He loved Jo, he always had, but only as a daughter, his own little stepdaughter.

"Take no notice, don't listen. It's all lies." Melinda poured more water over Jo's head. "There now, isn't that better. Or at least as better as it can be," her voice broke. From outside the door came the sound of Ray's sobs.

"Oh get lost," Melinda snarled. She got to her feet and banged on the locked door. I'm taking her away. If you so much as look at us when we come out of here, then I'm sending for the police. Got it?"

There was the sound of some incoherent reply followed by shambling footsteps and the banging of a door.

"Where are we going?" Jo asked as dressed and washed, she followed Melinda to the car.

"To your Nan's of course. Blast this key, why won't it fit in the bloody lock." Melinda swayed a little as she struggled to open the car door. "We'll be safe there. Both of us. God knows I should have listened to her. She never trusted him. Never. Once she knew he'd been divorced she told me. I should have known. Oh Jo I'm so, so sorry, but don't worry. I'll make it up to you. I promise I will."

Melinda drove fast. Her hands gripping the wheel hard as she peered through the ice that formed and re-formed over the windscreen. Beside her, Jo huddled in her seat, hands clenched against her lips, trying to hold back the small animal whimpers that rose from the back of her throat.

Ray hadn't meant it. He was drunk and he'd thought she was Melinda. But she shouldn't have been in her mother's bed. It was all her fault. She'd ruined everything.

"Bastard," Melinda snarled and accelerated. Jo swallowed. Not far to go now. Up the hill, round the corner, then under the iron footbridge that spanned the road leading past the big house and into Weston Ridge.

She was standing there, her dress pale against the dark sky, her arms outstretched. Her voice in Jo's ear, insistent, reproachful.

"You said you were an orphan like me."

"No," Jo cried lifting her arms to shield her eyes.

"Darling what is it?"

"Mum don't."

It was too late. Melinda glanced up.

"What the hell!" She brought her food down hard on the brake. The car hit a patch of ice and slid straight into the base of the wall.

CHAPTER FOURTEEN

"It was my fault. It was all my fault." Jo stared out of the window at the impenetrable night that surrounded The Granary. If she hadn't been in Melinda's bed that night. If she had agreed to go to the party, however boring it was going to be, then they would have all come home together. Neither Ray nor Melinda would have been so drunk. Jo closed her eyes momentarily at the memory of Melinda at the doorway of her bedroom, one strap of her dress sliding from her shoulder, her hair so carefully put up only a few hours ago, wild and tangled. She was carrying her sandals and swaying slightly as she screamed abuse at Ray for raping her daughter.

But he didn't, Jo thought. *He didn't do anything. Except kill himself, slitting his throat after we'd left, unable to live with the thought that he had driven away the two people he loved most in the world. I should have stopped him. I should have stopped her too. She reeked of gin. Even when she was holding me and sponging my back and drying my hair and helping me on with my clothes, she reeked of it. And then she got in the car.*

Tears slid down her cheeks as she remembered lying in her hospital bed, Nan sitting beside her, her work worn hand hard on hers as she told her that Melinda had been killed in the crash. The car had skidded on a patch of black ice. She hadn't stood a chance.

"Our Lady was looking after you my love." Nan squeezed Jo's fingers. "For that we must be grateful." Jo who could not remember any of what had happened during the crash, or much of what had happened before the accident, nodded.

As the years went by and they kept telling her that she must not feel guilty, that there was nothing to feel guilty about, she did wonder what it was that she was hiding so successfully from herself, but no counsellor or psychologist had ever been able to prise it from her. Now, however, she knew.

The crash, her mother and her stepfather's death were all tied up with the figure on the bridge. Ann, the girl in the blue dress, her blood sister, who would not let her go.

But what was Ann? Was she simply a manifestation of subconscious guilt? If so why was she suffering from it now? Or could it be that being back here at Kingsfield, she needed to sort out her past so that she could concentrate on her future. Jo cupped her hands around her belly. Early pregnancy sent hormones into overdrive. Emotions veered wildly from elation to despair. Could this have been the trigger? For a moment she almost managed to convince herself that this indeed was the explanation, because this time she was going to carry her baby to term. She was going to give birth to a strong and healthy child.

Except that she'd been here many times before, and nothing like this had ever happened. Nor were hallucinations one of the symptoms of early pregnancy, however much she might want to convince herself they were.

That left only one explanation. If Ann was not a product of her imagination, if she had lived at Kingsfield two hundred years ago then what she was seeing was a ghost.

"I don't believe in ghosts. I don't," she said out loud. "Nor any of that paranormal stuff." She glared at the kitten, which looked back at her with unblinking eyes. "OK. You may have a point. There are more things in heaven and earth. Maybe there is something here. But who would know?"

*

In the brightness of an early summer morning, Jo weighed out sultanas, raisins and oat flakes. She chopped glace cherries and licked the sweet redness from her fingers. She mixed in plump hazelnuts and nibbed almonds and measured out two tablespoons of butter, which she heated in a pan. Warming a spoon in hot water, she dipped it into the tin of golden syrup and watched as it slid slowly and sensuously to join the melting butter. Yellow became gold, gold became brown. She tipped the warm liquid into the dry ingredients and stirred.

Wrinkled fruit glistened, oats took on a glossy sheen, the rich smell of syrup rose to her mouth. The cherries glowed like rubies in amber. Humming tunelessly under her breath, she smoothed the mixture into the baking trays and reached for the phone. She'd try Helene and Cecile again. She'd found their numbers before she'd finally gone to bed in the early hours and if they didn't answer she'd text. If they replied then she'd ask them round for coffee and cake and ask their advice as to what she should do.

Looking back on their conversations, she was sure that Cecile was trying to tell her something, or at least find out what, if anything, Jo had experienced. Helene, moreover, had been trying to warn her off, but she had been too obtuse to pick up their subtle hints about the house and the estate. Now, however, the situation had changed.

The phone rang and rang in Alice Court. No one answered, so Jo tried the mobile number, again there was no response so she left a message, then sent a text. Reassuring herself that they could be serving customers, or out on a delivery and that she could try again later, she took bars of dark chocolate, broke them into squares, set them in a bowl over bubbling water and stirred. Diablo sauntered down the stairs and nudged against her legs.

"Later," she told him. "If I stop to stroke you now, this will go into lumps."

The kitten tensed his muscles, waggled his bottom and leapt onto the draining board. On the other side of the glass, a blue tit pecked seed from the terracotta feeder, Jo had hung at the window. Diablo batted the glass, the bird cocked its head and continued to feed. The cat crouched, his tail lashed, as he jumped at the bird.

"Don't," Jo cried, but she was too late. The kitten banged his head against the glass and the startled blue tit flew off. Instantly, Diablo pretended nothing had happened and after a sideways glance at Jo, stretched out on the window sill, yawned and fell asleep, his face pressed to the glass.

"Silly thing. Next time listen to me," Jo muttered fondly as she spread the topping over the biscuit base.

The kitchen was full of sunlight, the smell of chocolate and warm syrup. The knock on the door was firm, but undemanding. Jo rubbed sticky hands down the front of her jeans and pushed her hair behind her ears. Because she had been thinking of them, she half expected Helene and Cecile, and was taken aback when it was Damien, dressed in old jeans and a faded sweatshirt, leaning against the doorjamb. Seeing her, he smiled, the smile fading quickly, when he saw her frown.

"Have I come at the wrong time?"

Jo shook her head. Her hair swung back from behind her ears and she held out her hands.

"I was making Florentines."

"They smell wonderful."

"Oh, come in please," she cried, still flustered by his unexpected arrival. He followed her into the kitchen and she waved him towards a chair. "Coffee?"

"If you're not too busy."

"No, I've finished the baking. If we wait a minute or two they will be cool enough to cut." Jo busied herself with mugs and plates.

"I was doing my parish rounds. You are the last of my calls," Damien said.

"Do I count as one of your parishioners then?"

"Oh I think so. Yes definitely. I need as many as I can get."

"So you go out into the highways and byways to find them"

He grinned.

"Not exactly. I rather think you came to me."

It was Jo's turn to smile.

"I suppose that's true." She flicked her hair back from her face. "I have to tell you, I don't feel like a parishioner, yours or anyone else's."

"An old friend then," he said.

But I didn't know you. You were just one of the lads who

hung around with the Callaghan boys, the one Bernie told everyone she fancied. I thought all boys were loud and boring.

"A friend from *the past*," Jo conceded.

"Are you always that precise?"

Jo considered. *Only recently when I seem to be constantly probing beneath the surface, trying to see what is beyond the obvious,* she thought. "Would you like a Florentine?" she said, needing to lighten the conversation.

"I thought you'd never ask."

Cracking the rich, sweet covering, sinking the knife into the slightly gooey base, she cut two squares. She poured coffee. From his sun bed on the windowsill the kitten stretched against the glass, then rolled over onto his stomach and got to his feet. Stepping delicately around the edge of the sink, he leapt onto the table.

"Diablo!" Jo cried. The kitten ignored her. Threading his way between their mugs and plates, he scrambled up Damien's arm and spread himself across his shoulders.

"Put him down if he annoys you."

Damien sunk his teeth into his Florentine.

"Don't worry. He's fine. I like cats. Anyway it's rather appropriate, the devil on my shoulder."

"Tempting you?" again she had spoken without thinking.

"Only to another piece."

"Sorry, that sounded very personal. I didn't mean to..."

"I'm quite normal you know." He seemed to understand her confusion.

"Oh yes?" Jo lifted an eyebrow.

"Well perhaps not."

"Definitely not. No other priest I've ever known has a ponytail."

"Is that the total sum of my strangeness?"

"You are teasing me."

"Yes. But you rather let yourself in for that. "

"OK. I did rather, but I still have a point. You're no Father Egan."

"No, thank God and yes you do have a point. In fact that's

why I'm here." Jo raised an eyebrow. "At Weston Ridge. When I got sent to this diocese I don't think the Bishop knew what to do with me, so he put me here in the hope that I'll rejuvenate the parish, but to be honest all I seem to be doing is annoying all the old ladies."

Jo nodded.

"Nan would never have forgiven you for not wearing a dog collar."

Damien gave an exaggerated sigh.

"If that were my only crime! Here they like it as it always was. They'd have the Latin Mass back if they could. But who can blame them? For the most part they are old and come from relatively unsophisticated backgrounds."

"The Micks and the Polacks. To put it crudely."

"Jo!"

She laughed,

"Bless me Father for I have sinned."

"Absolved. We don't do much of that any more either."

"What? Absolution?"

He nodded.

"Not many young people go to Confession anymore."

"Then I really am out of date."

"Let's say you have a refreshingly irreverent attitude."

"And you?"

"My parishioners would probably not think of me as refreshing," Damien said dryly.

"Sorry. I seem to be putting my foot in it again."

"Being with a priest makes you nervous?"

"No. Not at all. No," Jo protested, then smiled ruefully as she saw his grin. "Perhaps it does a little. I can't get used to the idea, that someone I was at school with is now my parish priest."

"School was a long time ago."

"Our Lady of Sorrows Primary. You must have been in Top Juniors when I started."

"After that I went to St. Thomas Aquinas, but you didn't go there, did you?"

"No. When I went to live with my mum they sent me to St. Dominic's. She thought a private, convent education would give me a better start in life."

"Did it?"

"I don't know. I think I most probably would have gone to Art College in any event."

"And after Art College?"

He doesn't know. He's never heard of my work. "Two of the most promising young artists of our generation." That's what they said about me and Kit. We were considered for the Turner prize and featured in all the Sunday supplements. How could he not have heard? This is stupid. He's a priest. Why should he know about me and Kit? And why do I care? Why do I want him to know that I was successful and famous? But I do. Jo took a breath, trying to decide how much to say.

"I worked with someone called Kit Howard. We did quite well." *How stupid, how patronising, that sounded.* ."No," she paused. "We did very well."

"And now?"

"Kit died. He had pneumonia. He was HIV positive."

"I'm sorry." He showed no disgust, however well-disguised. He leaned towards her, as if he wanted to take one of the hands she had clamped around her mug. He waited to give her time, then said, "And after Kit died, what happened then?"

"Then I got married." *How pathetic. Nothing about my work, just my marriage. As if that had been an end in itself.* Angry with herself, she was filled with a wicked need to shock. "I'm Richard's third wife."

Damien looked at her. His eyes, quite dark in some lights, were flecked with specks of hazel and green. She could see him as a green god. A symbol of something wild, yet sacred. She wanted to paint him, as Herne the Hunter, or Cernennus, half naked, his body wreathed in vines.

"More coffee?" she said to distract herself. He ignored the question and still holding her gaze said,

"I led a pretty rackety life 'til God caught up with me."

"I don't believe in God," Jo said flatly.

"How can you be so sure? When things go wrong, or when you're scared don't you sometimes send up a quick prayer, just in case? I know I do."

"You have to believe. You're a priest."

"So? I'm human too."

"You mean sometimes, you don't believe?"

"Doubt is part of the human condition. Most of the time, I do believe, but sometimes I find myself overwhelmed by the impossibility of it all."

Jo poured coffee and cut more cake. They ate and drank in silence, somewhat surprised by the direction the conversation had taken. Diablo woke, stretched out his legs and nibbled Damien's ear. Jo went over and lifted him gently from the priest's shoulder.

"Wicked creature. That's no way to treat a guest."

Damien reached up and stroked the kitten and when Jo put him down, Diablo settled at the priest's feet.

"He's living up to his name. Was that your idea? "

"No. Someone else called him that." *Someone who believes in the supernatural side of life, in the power of things and places. In our power to affect the things around us. Someone I urgently need to contact.* "What about ghosts?" she said.

Damien looked surprised.

"Are you saying you believe in them, or you don't? Or are you asking me what I think?"

"I'm sorry, I was thinking aloud. If you believe in God, then surely you must believe in the supernatural?"

"That doesn't necessarily encompass ghosts," he said cautiously.

"You don't think they exist?"

He shrugged.

"I've not given it much thought."

"Oh," Jo said briefly. He seemed to sense her disappointment and continued,

"There are people in the Church who are convinced that

the dead don't leave us."

"You mean that they are still here? That this is the afterlife?"

"No. This isn't what happens to you after death. There is another dimension, the state people call heaven and hell, but not everyone has got there yet. After death some are trapped on earth and that's why the Church has powers of exorcism. To send spirits on their way."

"I thought exorcism was to get rid of evil spirits, like poltergeists and things," Jo said.

"They are not necessarily evil. Apparently one theory goes that some restless spirits stay here simply because they don't understand that they are dead."

Jo shivered.

"They have to be convinced that they've died?"

"You could put it like that. Why did you want to know?"

I hoped you might be able to help me sort out what is going on here. But if you don't believe then there's no point.

"I'm interested, that's all."

"Most people are. I sometimes think that an interest in the supernatural is the first step on the path back to some sort of belief in a higher power, because all of us need a spiritual dimension to our lives. You have it with your work, I would guess. I have it with mine. It goes with the job. As for ghosts, I like to keep an open mind. There are all sorts of stories about this place."

"People have seen and heard things?"

"So they say."

"And you believe them?"

"Who am I to doubt? After all 'There are more things in heaven and earth. Horatio.'"

"Bloody Hamlet," Jo smiled.

"OK it's an over rated quote, but it's probably used so often because it does sum things up rather well. Besides I take it as part of the job description to believe in things that have no logical explanation."

"So if I were to tell you I'd seen a white lady with her head tucked under her arm, you would believe me?"

"Not a headless lady, I wouldn't. She's not part of local legend."

"Then what is?"

Damien looked around the kitchen, as if wanting to avoid giving her an answer. Finally he said,

"There are always stories about a place like Kingsfield. Don't you remember them as a kid?"

You're not going to say any more. You'll think I'm stupid going on about ghosts when there are deeper things to talk and think about. Or perhaps you don't want to frighten me.

"I don't know any local stuff. Nan never let me mix. I left Weston Ridge when I was ten and when I came back I didn't fit in."

"That must have been hard."

Jo shrugged, dismissing years of being made to feel like an outsider, both by Nan's snobbery and the neighbours, who considered Noreen Docherty and her granddaughter too stuck up for their liking.

"I wasn't here for long. Once I was old enough, I persuaded Nan to let me have a flat of my own, but you must have left by then."

"I went to university," he said abruptly.

And what happened then? She wanted to ask. There was something about the way in which he had spoken which warned her not to pursue the subject of Damien's past.

"Most of us left the estate. That's part of the problem here, an aging congregation and an influx of people from different cultures. There are very few of us left from the old days. There are still some of the Callaghans around. The parents of course and Bernie and her brood." Damien smiled and seemed to relax. Jo tried to think of other people they might have in common.

"Maureen Arscott is she still here?" she managed finally.

"Did you know her well?" Damien's voice was cautious.

Oh God I've asked the wrong question.

"Not very. I remember her from when we were in Top

Juniors. She was part of Bernie's gang, not really a friend."

"She killed herself about three years ago. She'd been depressed for years and spent a lot of time in and out of hospital, but in the end I suppose she felt there was nothing anyone could do to make it better."

Jo felt as if she had been punched in the stomach.

"What about her family?" she asked.

Damien looked sad.

"There was only the little girl."

She had a child and she killed herself; left a little girl to deal with the world on her own. How could she have been so selfish? Didn't she know there are women who would do anything to have a child to love and protect? Jo bit hard on her lip, fighting back the anger, which threatened to dissolve into tears.

"Are you OK?"

"I'm fine," she lied furiously.

"No you're not. But you don't want to talk about it."

"How did you know?"

He shrugged.

"I've been there," he said simply. "Everyone tells you to talk it through, to get it out of your system, but for some of us it doesn't work that way." He smiled ruefully at her and she found herself able to smile back. He got up and held out his hand. His grip was firm and warm.

"Thanks for the chat. I must go and minister to my old ladies. If you feel like another session, give me a ring." He reached into his pocket and pulled out a used envelope and a chewed biro. "Here's the number of the presbytery. Phone any time. I'm always on call." He glanced at it apologetically. "I'd give you my mobile number, but I can never remember it and besides I always have it switched off."

Diablo trotted after them to the car. He twisted round Damien's legs, arching his tail and purring and when the priest opened the door, the kitten jumped in and settled himself on the passenger seat. Damien leaned inside and picked him up and handed him to Jo.

"Keep him safe. If I squashed him under my wheels, I don't think you would ever forgive me."

The kitten wriggled frantically against her chest and as soon as Jo heard the car turn into the road she dropped him on the cobbles.

"Keep your claws to yourself, you horrid creature," she scolded affectionately. "What's all this about trying to leave home? I know he's nice but this is where you belong. Or isn't the brand of cat food you get here good enough for you?"

The kitten stared at her disdainfully and stalked off up the stairs.

CHAPTER FIFTEEN

When Damien had gone, Jo tried Helene and Cecile again. There was no reply either from landline or mobile, not even a text. Jo stared at the screen with incomprehension. She had been so sure that they would be with her as soon as they understood how much she needed to talk to them. Where were they? Why weren't they replying? How could they leave her here at Kingsfield all on her own?

She scrolled down her messages again. There were a few business ones, requests from buyers or galleries, which she ignored and a text from Richard asking her to ring. She hesitated. Her finger hovered over the delete key, but since Damien had gone there was an empty hollow feel to the house she had not experienced before. She needed human company or at least the reassurance of a human voice.

"Darling, Jo. How are you? How's it going? Have you been sleeping? Eating?" For once she was grateful for Richard's overzealous concern.

"I'm fine," she told him more warmly than she had intended. "In fact I've been baking. Your favourites. Florentines."

"Mmm," he sighed. "Wish I was there to share them."

"Me too," Jo responded, her body stirring with an unexpected pang of desire.

"If I could, I'd be right there." There was a significant pause, then a quick in-drawing of breath. "Unfortunately I have a meeting in about twenty minutes and another later this evening. I wanted to remind you that I'm off to New York at the weekend, but I can be with you tonight."

"Yes," Jo said. "That would be good." Even though she was sure he would not believe her if she talked about what she had seen and felt, Richard's practical common sense would help banish the ghosts if only for a little while. What would happen when he was away, Jo did not want to think about.

In the meantime, she had work to do. Somewhat reluctantly, she went into the studio. Sunlight flooded in through the glass walls and ceiling; a blackbird hunted for worms on the lawn and seeing it Diablo pressed his nose against the glass and made an odd chittering sound at the back of his throat.

"You're not having it. Cat food is the only thing on offer in this establishment," Jo laughed. The bright day, the cat, the bird it was all so ordinary, so far away from the fears and shadows of the night. Reassured she turned to her work.

Blue, grey, green, gold, black lines, smudged shapes, bit by bit the painting came together. It was abstract, but using brushes and fingers she gave it texture and depth. There was nothing untoward, no unwanted figure or building, nothing but her concept of the landscape of Kingsfield and beyond.

By late afternoon she had finished. She made herself a sandwich and a coffee, fed the kitten, which scoffed everything in his dish as if he had been starved for weeks, then demanded to be let out. The late afternoon sun filled the courtyard with warmth. Trees rustled in the faint breeze. Jo breathed in the freshness of the air, enjoying the feel of it on her skin. Soon Richard would be here and she ought to think about what she was going to cook. Or perhaps they could go out for a meal, or have a takeaway? She might even tell him. Jo's hands strayed to her stomach. She smiled dreamily then shook her head. Perhaps not yet. Perhaps she would keep her secret to herself for a little longer.

When this baby was born they would go for walks in the woods. Strapped onto her back, she would show her child the light on the trees, the clouds chasing across the sky.

"When you're older you can play in the garden, but you're not to go too far without me," Jo murmured. "I'll keep you safe. I'll always keep you safe. Shh, don't cry." Cry? Jolted back into the present Jo stiffened. Scarcely daring to breathe she listened, until ears straining for every sound, she heard it again, a faint wail that seemed to drift in from somewhere beyond the trees. Jo ran to the bottom of The Granary's drive.

There was no one there, but the crying was louder now.

"Hello," she called. "Where are you? Are you OK? Has something happened?" She stepped out into the main drive, glancing from side to side, telling herself that at any moment she would see a mum with a screaming baby in its buggy. It was probably some young girl from Weston Ridge who wouldn't need or want her help, but as the crying increased in intensity Jo couldn't go back into the house. Suppose there had been an accident. Suppose the girl had collapsed. She couldn't leave her, not without making sure.

She began to run. Over rough ground at first, then her feet meet smooth flagstone and with a sudden dimming of the light she slid into her teenage self. A hand slipped into hers pulling her on and on. There was a mist around her, the air was cold and damp. The windows of the house glowed with candlelight, but Ann would not let her stop.

"Hurry, there is no time," she hissed, her nails digging into Jo's wrist as they raced past the house and along the west drive. Ancient oaks loomed over their heads, shutting out what light there was, tunnelling their vision so that all Jo could see were the Satan Stones silhouetted against the moon.

The King Stone stood straight and proud, beside it the Queen Stone, a perfect circle, its centre smoothed by centuries of ritual. In front of them was a figure of a woman. Her dark curls tumbled to her shoulders, her head was wreathed with flowers and there were more flowers in the basket at her feet. In one hand she held a knife and in the other a small, struggling, furry creature.

"Sophia," Ann hissed, coming to a halt.

"What's she doing?" Jo gasped.

"Her sacrifice. Her sacrifice to the goddess. She'll spill the blood and mutter the charms, but to no avail. She's lost him. He's not hers anymore, if he ever were. He's mine and all the spells and incantations in the world won't bring him back."

A flash of silver in the moonlight. A small dark body held up to the stone, the drip of warm blood, a cry of intercession then raising her arms high Sophia began to sway and chant.

"Look at her. She thinks she has power, but she will not withstand us. Come, now is the time. There are two of us. We are bound by blood, you are my sister, my kin, you will save me from her. You will send her far from me, far away to a place where she cannot hurt me, to the place where you came from."

"No. I don't understand," Jo tried to protest, but Ann's grip was firm.

"You promised. You promised to help me," Ann cried and began to chant. The words were archaic, some were in Latin which Jo recognised from school, others in a language she had never heard. They rose and dipped and Ann stamped out their rhythm with her feet, holding Jo's arm so that she was made to move with her, until she too was taken over by the beat of the incantation, swaying and moaning and crying out words she did not understand. But it no longer mattered. As Ann's spell rose to its crescendo the light began to change. While around them the night darkened, the centre of the Queen Stone began to glow, palely at first as if a sickly moon was trapped within its hub then more and more strongly. Silver giving way to white gold, flecked with an electric blue and shimmering emerald the colours flowed down onto the mound. They pulsated throbbed, swirling into a vortex of power.

Like a whirlpool sucking her down, Jo felt the energy reaching out to her. She stumbled, she leaned, but Ann held her firm. Her voice was growing hoarser, her body shook, but nothing could deflect her from her course.

Sophia screamed. Stretching out her arms towards them she tried to run.

"Help me." The cry echoed around the Stones, then her body crumpled and she was dragged screaming into the centre of the Queen Stone.

"Gone," Ann spoke into total darkness. "My sister," she murmured. Her hand fell away, her lips touched Jo's cheek.

Jo turned to face her, but like the turning of a page the night disappeared and she was standing in front of Kingsfield, her hand raised to shield her eyes from the dazzling sun. The light, the house, the grass, the trees, it all swirled around her in a kaleidoscope of colour and sensation. For a moment she thought she was going to be sick, or faint. Her legs trembled and she barely made it to the bottom step where she sat down and put her head in her hands.

A few deep breaths and the dizziness and nausea faded. When she was sure she could lift her head without any ill effects, she looked around at the empty grounds. It took her a moment to think why she had left the house then she remembered hearing a child crying and coming to see if the mother needed help. Since there was no one there, what she heard must have been part of the hallucination, because what she thought she had seen could not possibly have happened. For a start it was daylight and secondly, perhaps more importantly she had felt as if she were actually there, taking part in some sort of magic rite. Jo shook her head.

When she came back to live with Nan, when she was so unhappy and confused, there were times, when in spite of herself and her misgivings, she had slipped up to Kingsfield, where Ann had been waiting. There may even have been a game they played at the Stones. A stupid ritual to conjure up a sweetheart, or keep a lover close, but Sophia had not been there, or had she? Jo's hands dropped between her knees, her shoulders slumped. Was this another memory beginning to surface? One so deeply hidden that she had not yet been able to face it.

What hold did this place have over her? Jo glanced up at the house. The mellow stone glowed in the evening light, the windows shone, the half open door threw a shadow across the marble hall. Jo blinked and looked again. There was something wrong. When Richard had shown her around, the door had been locked, securely fastened with a padlock.

Her first thought was that it was beginning again, that she was slipping back into some past over which she had no control. Turning her head, however, she could see the streets of Weston Ridge and beyond them the line of factories along the Severn. She was still in her present. Nothing had changed.

If the door to Kingsfield was open then someone had broken into the house. Jo reached in the back pocket of her jeans for her phone. It wasn't there. In her rush to find the crying child, she had left it on the kitchen counter. She'd have to go back to The Granary and ring Richard. Or she could leave it until he came. She glanced at her watch. It wouldn't be long, then he could come and check or even call the police if he thought anything had been stolen or damaged.

She was about to leave, when a flicker of movement caught her attention.

"Oh no you don't. If you're in there then I'll lock the door, so you won't be able to get out until the police arrive." Jo stormed up the steps. Hand on the doorknob she was about to pull it to, when it occurred to her that it would be stupid not to look inside. If the intruders were kids, or even teenagers sneaking in for a quick grope, then calling the cops would be overreacting. She would, however, do no more than look. It would be stupid to risk anything else, especially now when she had her child to protect.

Her hand on her stomach, she took a deep breath. Then she gave the door a little push. The hall was full of shadows. The air still and veiled with dust. She glanced around quickly, there was no one there. Reluctant to search any further she moved away and was about to shut the door behind her, when the crying came again. There was a child here, a child that needed her. Jo hesitated and in that moment a shaft of sun lit up the staircase and she saw standing at the top, a woman in a red dress. Her hair was wild, her eyes blazing,

"You robbed me of my child," Sophia hissed. "My baby was left weeping alone in this cruel house with no one to care for her. You and that girl, that evil twisted whore, you sent me into the darkness."

"No." Jo flinched, her hands flying to her mouth. "I couldn't have. I didn't mean to. I didn't know. I didn't know what Ann was doing."

"You gave her the strength to banish me. Without you she was nothing. But now I have you and what is most precious to you within my grasp."

Jo backed away. The stone threshold slid beneath her feet, the air thickened. A heavy cloying scent pressed down into her lungs, holding her powerless as Sophia lifted her arm. Jo saw the flash of the knife. With a desperate effort she turned to run down the steps but her legs would not obey her. *Come on,* she willed herself and was almost out in the sunlight, when the pain slashed through her and she fell.

"Jo are you all right?" She looked up. She was sitting on the steps of Kingsfield, Richard's hand on her shoulder. "Darling I was worried. When I arrived the front door was wide open and I couldn't find you anywhere."

"I thought I heard something, someone. I came to see. I must have forgotten to lock the door. I know I left my phone behind. Oh." Jo leaned against him and bit back a sob as pain gripped her.

"What is it?"

"Nothing," she lied, but as he helped her to her feet she swayed with dizziness. Richard slipped his arm around her waist, then the sun disappeared, there was a terrible pounding in her head, her body slumped and something broke inside her.

Lying on the sofa in The Granary Jo kept as still as she could, but already she could feel the hot trickle of blood between her thighs.

"I'm sorry," she said stretching out her hand for his.

"I only want you to be well," he said, his voice distant but controlled. She let her hand fall back and closing her eyes against her tears turned her face away.

CHAPTER SIXTEEN

Next morning, Richard made her an appointment with the consultant, then insisted she came back to the apartment where she would be closer to medical help.

"I don't want anything to happen to you Jo," he said as he helped her out of the car.

"I'm all right," she said stiffly. "I've had an early miscarriage that's all. It happens to a lot of women." She walked to the lift, pressed the button and stood staring at the arrow showing its descent to the ground floor.

"You're all that matters to me," Richard said as they stood in the steel box, side by side but not touching. "After that last time I thought we'd agreed to wait."

"You agreed. I was in intensive care. I was doped up to the eyeballs, hardly in a position to give informed consent."

"I'm only thinking of your health. Once you're better, we can try again."

"When will that be?" She whirled round at him. "How long am I going to have to wait? It's all right for you, you've got children already, but I," she broke off.

"Jo. It's not that I don't want us to have a child, but this was not the right time."

"It happened," she flared back. "That night you came to The Granary. Or have you forgotten. It's not that long ago and you were keen enough at the time." She glared at him; he stared back then their eyes dropped, each of them remembering that violent, savage coming together. "Anyway it's over." Jo shook the memory from her head. "It's all gone." The word echoed with loss. She folded her arms, pressing them against her breast, but Richard made no move to comfort her.

"I want you to stay here. You can't go back to Kingsfield on your own," he said. "There's nothing to do. I've sorted it all. I put your cat into the cattery and they can keep him for as long as you need."

"But you're not even going to be here. You're going away," Jo interrupted.

"I'm going to New York for a week. It's not long. You could come with me," he added, in that neutral tone that suggested he didn't really mean it. "Or I could cancel, or send someone else in my place."

"No one can take your place," she said. He looked at her with the fleeting hope in his eyes that she was talking about their relationship. Unable to bear his look, Jo turned her head. "You go. I'll be OK."

"Promise," he tried to speak lightly but there was a world of meaning in that word.

"Promise," she repeated without looking at him.

"You're quite sure?" he persisted

"Yes," she said quickly. His fussing was meant to show he cared. But how much did he really care, when he would not talk about what she so desperately wanted and needed? Richard had made up his mind and there was nothing she could do to make him change it.

She could hardly wait for him to leave. Every move he made, everything he said irritated her almost beyond bearing. To avoid a row, she spent her time either resting or sitting out on the balcony sketching. The drawings she produced disgusted her. They were airy-fairy little offerings with no depth or meaning. The sort of pretty Bristol scenes she could sell as postcards in St. Nicholas's Market. As long as Richard was with her she could not begin to explore the darkness that haunted her.

When he had gone she'd go back to Kingsfield, shut herself up in her studio and take out her paints. Her hands itched for her brushes and colours, for pristine untouched canvases.

The morning he left, he kissed the top of her head, touching her for the first time since he'd helped her out of the car.

"Take care and text me," he said.

"And you me," she replied automatically. Then the door shut behind him and she was free.

Jo was in the bedroom packing when the intercom announced a visitor.

"It's Caro," came the rich husky voice. "Let me in will you Jo."

"Caroline." Jo suppressed a sigh. Richard's second wife, the mother of his daughter, was the last person in the world she wanted to see, now or ever, but what excuse could she give?

"Just a moment." She found the remote, pressed the button for the entrance and winced. There was still a dull dragging pain at the base of her spine, but already it was fading and in a day or two there would be no trace of her pregnancy. It would be as if she had never conceived that child. Jo clenched her teeth. However wretched she was feeling, Caroline must not know.

Richard's ex-wife was already at the door of the apartment. A short, fat woman in a scarlet salwar kameez. A magenta silk scarf held back her thick black curls. Her tiny hands were laden with rings, her wrists with bracelets and an ornate necklace perched on her huge breasts.

"Jo." Caroline lunged towards her, lips puckered in a kiss. "It's been a long time. Too long," she added as Jo managed to avoid her embrace. "I've been so very, very busy."

"Me too." Jo bared her teeth in what might be mistaken for a smile. "So busy in fact that I need to get back to work. I have an exhibition coming up. I'm afraid I can't spare you much time." She looked pointedly at the door. A hint Caroline ignored, walking past Jo into the living room and plumping herself down on a sofa.

"Very minimalist your apartment," she said. "Not my style of course, but it works in this faux loft setting." Jo said nothing and her visitor swept on. "Personally I prefer something more colourful, more ethnic. I have to say, I find all this rather cold. But then we are very different people, aren't we. I have my business, my passion for the East. It's what fires me, what gives me my reason for being. There is nothing more fulfilling than discovering some unknown craftsmen in a little mountain village and bringing his work to the notice of the world. It's my karma. I know it is. Somewhere in a previous life I was a great artist. I had talent, but I committed some terrible sin and the only way I can redeem myself is by seeking out others and giving them success." She paused waiting for Jo to comment. Jo said nothing. All she wanted was for her visitor to leave. Caroline's mouth tightened. "Talking of business that's why I'm here. I've got to make a quick trip to India and I need somewhere to leave Strif."

You want me to have your daughter to stay? Now? Think again.

"Why would she want to come here?" Jo said carefully not wanting to risk a long and explosive row. "She's never wanted to before."

"Oh that's when she was little," Caroline waved a hand dismissively. "She's fifteen now. And there's no one else to have her, while I'm away. I'm going. My flight's booked. I'll tell her it's all right shall I? No doubt she'll turn up when she wants, but that's Strif for you. Does what she likes, when she likes. A free spirit my daughter. Rather like me." She heaved herself to her feet and padded swiftly to the door.

"Wait," Jo said, but she wasn't fast enough. Caroline had gone. Jo scrolled down her phone searching for her number.

You bitch, she thought as it came up unrecognised. *You're going to make sure we can't get hold of you. Cow. If you think I'm waiting around for that brattish daughter of yours, you've got me completely wrong. I'm going back to Kingsfield. Strif's got her dad's number. He's got mine. If she actually bothers to turn up, we'll deal with her. If not, then tough.*

Storming back into the bedroom, she finished packing, sent Richard a brief text telling him where she was going and hurried out of the apartment. The Mercedes was in its parking space, Richard had had it brought back for her, and she drove away with an increasing sense of freedom. She stopped only to pick up Diablo from the cattery. The kitten miaowed pitifully all the way until they turned into the drive at Kingsfield.

The Granary drowsed in the late afternoon sun. Jo opened the car door and leaning inside let the kitten out of his travelling cage. Tail erect he stalked around the courtyard, sniffing and growling softly, inspecting the boundaries. Not until he had decided that all was safe did he follow her inside.

Jo did not stop to unpack. She had told Caroline she needed to work and that was what she was determined to do. Once in the studio, however, the ideas that had seemed so vibrant and exciting in the apartment now seemed flat and stale. It had all been done before by people with a greater talent than hers.

She glanced out of the window and let her gaze roam over the rich greens of the surrounding trees. At the tail end of summer there were so many shades and subtle permutations. The shapes of the trees too were distinct, ranging from tall thrusting conifers to the dainty silver birch at the edge of the lawn. Each tree had its own personality and its own mythology.

She thought of her vision of Damien as the Green Man and reached for pencil and paper. Then her hand dropped again as she wondered whether it was the picture of Helene and Cecile as mother and daughter she wanted to work on. Unable to make up her mind she hesitated, half closed her eyes. Employing a technique she had used before, she would let her subconscious decide. Without looking at what she was doing, she drew the first line. Cecile who was fluid, watery, Piscean would embrace Helene, who was more solid, earthy and yet who had a wisdom, which was not totally of this world. Perhaps to represent them as people was not the way. There was something more abstract she wanted to say. She would start with some fundamental shapes.

The work came easily, flowing effortlessly onto the paper. An oval for a face, a straight line for the backbone of the figure, a curve for the folds of the skirts. At this point, Jo glanced down and frowned, both women had worn trousers and while she was not seeking a realistic representation, neither did she want to turn them into a sentimentalised picture of the bond between mother and child.

The face that stared up at her was neither gentle nor kind. Sophia's hair writhed about her face like the Gorgon's snakes, her eyes were cold, her face contorted with hatred, the knife in her hand poised to strike.

Seizing the paper, Jo ripped it in two. As the pieces fluttered to the ground, she forced herself to begin again. If Cecile was water then Helene was a tree. Catching her lower lip beneath her teeth, she leaned over the paper and drew one long line, which curved and shaped itself into the figure of a woman in a scarlet dress, gazing with desperate longing at the blank windows of Kingsfield House.

"You robbed me of my child." Dear God could she really have done this? Was she in some way responsible for such sorrow? It was not possible. She had never meant Sophia any harm, all she had done was to do what Ann had wanted. She reached for her phone. Fingers slippery with fear, she found Cecile's number. When there was no response from her mobile, she tried the shop and let the phone ring and ring until at last it was cut off. Wherever the two women were they were beyond her reach.

She was alone; caught in a process she could neither halt, nor control. It was like the time she had gone into premature labour. Once it had started there was nothing anyone could do until the miscarriage had reached its natural end.

When Jo had left Weston Ridge, Ann had promised she would wait for her. Now Jo had returned, was it her body she wanted, or her soul? In the past they had been two little girls playing together, sharing each other's secrets. Jo had managed to convince herself that nothing strange had happened on those silent afternoons, when the sounds of the estate had disappeared and the air smelled clean and new.

After Melinda died she refused to remember, but as soon as she had seen the portraits in the museum, she had known.

The people she had seen and spoken to had lived over two centuries ago. They were long dead, so either she had slipped back into their time, or they had come forward into hers. Was she their ghost, or were they hers?

Richard had sensed them too that day in the house, when the air was restless and full of whispers. However much he would deny it, she knew he had felt something.

Cecile and Helene as soon as they realised where she was living had shown their concern. Even Damien had mentioned local legends. Apparently it was well known that Kingsfield House was haunted. But what was happening to her was more than that. Seeing a ghost might terrify you, might leave you unable to sleep without the light on, or look in dark corners. It did not, however, play on other emotions, or affect what you did. Jo shuddered remembering the strange overwhelming passion that she and Richard had shared.

She had been powerless to prevent it. Somehow Sophia's spirit had taken her body and fuelled it with her own frustrated passion. That time it had not lasted, but what if Sophia was not willing to let her go? What would happen to that part of her that made her what she was? The part that some people call the soul. Would it be condemned to wander the earth for all eternity, unable to die because her body belonged to someone else; unable to live because she was no longer herself?

The fear of forever being on the outside, of existing without love or joy, threatened to suck her down into the depths. She would not, she could not, contemplate such a fate. She had to prove to herself that it was all crazy nonsense. When she was little she kept drawing Ann's face. It was a childhood habit nothing more. All she needed to do was to concentrate on what she was doing.

Jo took a new pencil and a fresh sheet of paper. She drew the outline of the window then started to sketch a squirrel sitting on the branch of a tree. A fluffed up tail, bright eyes, paws held up to its chest. She breathed out, loosened her grip on her pencil, leaned back and looked critically at her drawing. It wasn't bad; she had caught the creature's expression of cheeky expectancy. In fact it was better than she expected from a quick sketch. Then the pencil fell from her fingers, an icy chill coiled up her spine, the breath caught in her throat and for a split second the world went dark.

Beyond the squirrel, on a patch of scrubby lawn, stood a small figure in a wide skirted dress. At the bottom of the drawing, in a thin spiky script were the words *Beware, my beloved sister.*

Fear washed over her in waves, her body juddered and shook. She flushed with heat and shuddered with cold. What could she do? Cecile and Helene had disappeared, Richard was in New York. Her first instinct was to escape. She could get in the car and drive back into the city, but if she did, she would never be free of Sophia or her past.

CHAPTER SEVENTEEN

A sharp nip on her ankle followed by a firm head butt on her calf, broke through Jo's terror. She bent down, picked up the kitten and held him close. Diablo wriggled and twisted in her arms. She pressed her face against his soft fur and murmured in his ear, but the kitten lashed out with his paws. Surprised, she dropped him. Tail erect he marched to the door and miaowed.

"Little devil, just when I need you you're off," Jo muttered as she watched him scamper into the bushes. "It's not the first time. You tried to hitch a lift with Damien."

What had he said before he left? "Phone any time. I'm always on call." The tattered envelope was still where she'd left it on the unit, the number of Our Lady of Sorrows' presbytery scrawled on the back.

"Hullo," his voice was warm and welcoming.

"Hi, it's Jo."

"Jo, are you all right?"

"Yes." Her voice was as steady as she could make it. "I mean no. Something's happened."

"Do you want me to come over?"

"Oh yes. Please." *Bring bell book and candle. Holy water and a crucifix.*

"I can be up there in five minutes, so hang on in there."

He didn't ask what the emergency was. He just said he was on his way. Jo felt her legs crumple. She clung onto the work surface, using it for support as she inched her way round to the nearest chair. Her skin was filmed with sweat. Her T-shirt hung cold and clammy on her back. She wanted to curl up on the sofa, to hide her head under the pillows like a child in a thunderstorm, but she did not dare move.

Outside the sun was shining in a blue sky fluffed with white. The luxuriant summer leaves were bright against the conifers. A robin stood on the feeder chasing away all other

- 133 -

birds. Somewhere in the undergrowth, Diablo stalked shrews. Down the hill in Weston Ridge people ate and shopped and gossiped; children went to school and mothers took their babies to the clinic, while up here in Kingfield she was fighting for her soul. Damien was there in less than five minutes. Leaping out of the car, he stood on the threshold with a small black kitten at his side. Jo's hand shook as she held it out to him.

"I came as quickly as I could."

"Like an avenging angel." Her voice quavered, her eyes filled, but she managed a smile.

"Hot, sweet tea first. You look as if you've had a shock."

"Won't a Florentine do? I've only got Earl Grey and that tastes awful with sugar," her voice was stronger now.

"Joanna Docherty how typical. Only Earl Grey indeed. Did you learn nothing from all your years in Weston Ridge?"

"Tea makes the world go round. Sure, I was brought up on it. Strong enough to stand a spoon in and vital in a crisis. Nan thought every problem could be solved by brewing up. Personally I prefer coffee, with a dash of milk but I'll have the tea if you insist."

She sat down and he busied himself with the ritual, which she thought must be so familiar from his visits to old ladies, so necessary and comforting and almost sacramental in its sharing and soothing.

"Drink," he said, heaping in two large spoonfuls of sugar.

"Sticky brown mud." She looked up at him from under a fall of hair, sipped, made a face then sipped again. He was right. Something hot and sweet was what she needed. She could feel the strength flowing back into her. He waited until her mug was half empty, then said,

"How can I help?"

Jo put down her tea and pushed her hair back behind her ears. What could she say? How could she explain what was happening to her without making it sound as if she was going mad? After a long moment in which she searched for the right words and could not find them, she said quite simply, "I'm being haunted."

He glanced behind him. Then to her relief he said gently, "Tell me about it."

Jo twisted her hands in her lap. Biting her lip she said, "I think I'm being taken over."

"You mean possessed by a spirit?"

"Yes. And I don't know what to do."

"Neither do I," he said. Her heart lurched. She shut her eyes briefly. "But I know a man who does. Father King, he's the diocesan exorcist. The Church, you see, is one institution that will take you seriously. We do believe in ghosts, or rather in troubled spirits." Jo smiled tremulously and Damien asked, "Can you start at the beginning, so I can understand exactly where you are with this?"

It was too much. The images were crowding in on her. The voices echoing in her head.

Her hands flew to her ears. Pain flashed across her temples. Blood beat in her head, but she took a deep breath and began, "I was ten years old and I was in trouble with Granddad…"

Jo told the whole story from the first meeting with Ann in the summerhouse to the drawings she had made that afternoon. As she talked and Damien listened without interrupting, her fear receded and a furious anger rose in its place.

"I won't have her being me." Jo banged her fist on the table. "She can't do this to me. I won't let her."

"In that case she won't succeed. You're strong now, not like when you were a little girl. Back then, when it began, you were lonely and vulnerable."

Jo shivered. "Is that why it happened? Why I began to see them?"

"Possibly," Damien said cautiously.

"At the beginning, it all seemed quite normal. Even promising not to tell was something little girls did with their best friends. Then when I realised what she was, I liked the idea that I had something no one else had. Besides, she seemed to understand what I was going through. Whenever anything bad happened she was always there for me."

"Until your mother died."

Jo bent her head.

"I always thought that was my fault," she said at last.

"If Ann caused the accident, it can't be."

"If it wasn't for me, she wouldn't have been there."

"Not even a ghost can put ice on the road."

"But I kept going up there. If I hadn't gone on seeing her, she wouldn't have had that hold over me. Whenever I went to see Nan I would sneak up to Kingsfield."

"I don't think that had anything to do with what happened. The ice was there that night. Nothing you could have done would have changed it."

It was as if a weight had been taken from her shoulders, the burden of guilt lifted from her soul. "Maybe it is time I stopped blaming myself and accepted what happened. The strange thing is that whatever Ann did, I don't feel that she is evil."

"She may not mean you any harm. My guess is that she needed you to help her survive."

"She was fighting for her life, or at least her love. Nicholas meant everything to her. Without him I think she would have died. No, it's not Ann, it is Sophia who frightens me. There's such anger and hatred there." Jo shuddered at the memory of the figure she had drawn. The face contorted with fury, the raised knife. "She made me lose my baby," she whispered.

"I'm so sorry Jo." For a moment Damien's hand rested on hers and it took all her strength to hold back her tears.

"It's all right. At least it's not, but..." Jo shrugged. Damien's grip tightened on her fingers then he withdrew his hand and poured more tea.

"Better?" he asked as she took a sip. Jo nodded.

"A little. I'm still scared. I think Sophia is out for revenge."

"I agree. But you are not necessarily her only target. On reflection everything that happens at Kingsfield seems to involve children or babies."

"What do you mean?" Jo felt as if pieces of a puzzle were about to fall into place.

"What you've got to remember Jo is that a lot of what people say about this place is only stories and we have no way of knowing how true they might be. All I can do is tell you what I know. The more lurid tales you can read up in local histories or old newspapers. OK?" She nodded. "Two years ago a little girl called Jodie Clarke went missing. She was three years old and her mother swore that she had left her playing in the back garden for a minute, while she went indoors to see to the baby. When she got back, the child was gone. The garden of their house in Arnold Grove backed onto the Kingsfield estate. The woods were searched, and the house and the outbuildings, but the child was never found." Jo let out her breath. "Is this OK? Are you sure you want more?"

"If I'm going to fight, then I've got to know what I'm up against."

"Sure?"

"Yes. Please don't try to protect me. It won't help me or the situation I'm in."

"OK, if that's what you want." She nodded and he continued, "When we were kids Kingsfield was a mother and baby home run by the nuns as a place for unmarried girls to come and have their babies. During that time, two of the girls killed themselves. One not long after she had her baby, the other some weeks after she had left. She came back and hung herself in an outhouse. There was another case too. One of the girls killed her child; suffocated him with her pillow when the nun in charge of the nursery brought him to be fed. "

Was this the baby I heard crying? Please God no, Jo thought.

"There's more." He was looking at her with concern.

"I'm fine," she said defiantly. "Stop treating me as if I'm made of china and might break at any minute. I'm tougher than that. I thought we'd already established that."

"OK. But you looked a bit grim when I arrived."

Jo shrugged. "I'd had a shock," she looked at him and smiled bleakly. "You were right. I needed a jolt of sugar. Now I'm fine. So you can tell me the rest."

"Before Weston Ridge was built, a little girl called June Pilling was murdered up here. She went to play with her dog in the woods and was found later by the Satan Stones. Her throat had been cut. She was ten years old and no one was ever convicted of the crime. Her sister, who still lives in one of the old cottages on the main road, told me that all the children had been warned against going into the grounds, but she was sure that June used to go and play up there, with another little girl."

"Could that have been Ann?"

"Again, that's a possibility. Or it could have been a friend, another child who was too afraid to talk to the police. It could even have been an imaginary friend."

Jo bridled. "You don't think that's what I've been doing, imagining it all?"

"No I don't. If I did I wouldn't be sitting here feeding your imagination, I'd be telling you to see your doctor, or a psychiatrist."

Like Richard, who thinks that this is all in my mind; that I'm suffering from some sort of post miscarriage syndrome.

"There is something here Jo and if it involves you I will do everything I can to help. I don't know enough about these things. I'll have to find out what has to be done. OK?"

The tension drained out of her and her stomach rumbled loudly. They looked at each other and laughed.

"Supper?" Damien said.

Jo glanced out of the window, where the shadows lay long on the grass. "I had no idea it was so late. I've got some cheese and pasta. I could throw something together, or we could stuff ourselves with the Florentines."

He grinned. "I wasn't inviting myself to supper. A pub meal and a drink was what I had in mind."

Jo hesitated. "Can you? I mean are you allowed?" she said.

"Priests do eat, you know. If we choose a very discreet

pub, where no one will see us, it won't cause too much scandal and gossip. You'll be quite safe," he grinned. "The old ladies of the parish won't be talking about you. On a more serious note, we are old friends Jo and you do need to get out of here, if only for the evening. How about it?"

An evening with someone who takes me seriously. Who is good company and who knows the people I used to know.

"You're on. Give me a minute." She fed the kitten, ran upstairs, pulled off her T-shirt and put on a silk blouse. She hung her silver cross around her neck and put silver studs in her ears. Then she was ready.

As the door of The Granary shut behind them, the mobile she had left in the kitchen began to ring, but the windows were double glazed, the walls thick stone and no one heard.

CHAPTER EIGHTEEN

The crying sliced through her dreams. A loud demanding wail that faded into a miserable, sobbing whimper. Half asleep, Jo fought free of the bedclothes and fumbled for the light. Her feet were on the floor by the time she found the switch.

"I'm coming, don't cry." Her voice echoed into the emptiness. "God what am I doing? There's no baby here."

Fully awake she slid back into bed and sitting up against the wall, pulled the duvet up to her chin. The night was very dark, the un-curtained window made a black arc against the white wall and she was alone. She wrapped her arms around her knees and tried to stem her fears. The house was full of shadows but she was facing whatever might enter her room.

Her heart thudded in her throat; she pressed her hand over her mouth to stifle a moan and forced herself to take a calming breath. Filling and emptying her lungs relaxed her shoulders and she leaned back against the pillows and tentatively stretched out her legs. In a minute or two, she would get up and walk over to the half open door. She would reach round for the hall switch and the whole house would light up and she would walk down the stairs to the living room, where Diablo must be curled up on the sofa. She would heat milk, some for him and some for hot chocolate for her, then with the kitten tucked under her arm she would go back to bed.

The cry came as she was about to move. A faint, plaintive whimper, followed by a stronger wail, a desperate and lonely sound. Jo pressed her hands against her ears. The crying grew louder. She dug her nails into her palms and watched as red half-moons developed on her skin. She was awake. This was no dream. Somewhere in this house a baby was crying. It lay in its crib, hands balled into fists, face screwed up, red and furious and screamed and screamed and screamed.

Sweat slid between her breasts. Her feet pressing hard against the mattress rooted her to the bed.

A bundle of black fur hurtled through the door. Tail bristling, ears erect, eyes wild, Diablo dived under the covers. She felt him trembling, stretched out her hand to stroke him and was met by a low growl from the back of his throat.

"It's all right. It's only me." As she spoke, the crying stopped. The kitten cuddled close and the house was filled with silence.

Diablo slept; Jo did not. As the first streaks of dawn lit the sky, she got up, slipped a long cashmere cardigan over her nightdress and went down the stairs. Opening the back door for the kitten, she breathed in the green smell of damp earth. In the trees around The Granary, the birds were stirring, the air was fresh and clean. It was so still that she could hear the early morning bus going down the hill into the estate.

The little cat scampered back across the yard and as she began to close the door behind them, her fingers sought automatically for the sign carved deep into the wood. The surface was smooth. The sign that she had felt to be a blessing had gone. A finger of sunlight slid into the kitchen, but what had once been so safe and ordinary was no longer what it seemed. Nothing was stable, nothing fixed. It was as if time and reality were fragmenting.

Jo felt very weary. She sat down at the table and rested her head on her hands. Her breasts strained against her nightdress and somewhere a child stirred and snuffled in its sleep.

"Stop it," she said. "Leave me alone."

The knock on the door startled her. She pulled her cardigan around her and went to open it.

"Damien! How did you know?"

"Know what?"

"That I needed you."

He smiled a little sadly. "I was thinking about our conversation yesterday. I needed…" he hesitated. "I wanted to see if you were all right." He stepped past her and into the kitchen. "You look as if you've had a bad night."

"You mean I look terrible."

"You look frightened," he said gently.

She nodded quickly. "Things are getting worse."

"Do you want to talk about it?"

Jo glanced around, uncertain who or what might hear. "I think so. I don't know what else to do." She gnawed her bottom lip.

"Jo what exactly has happened?"

"There's something in The Granary. They've got in. Before, they were only in the grounds or in Kingsfield itself. Except once but that wasn't ..." she stopped. Catching her lip with her teeth, she looked away. The colour flared in her cheeks. She could not tell him about Nicholas and Sophia in the barn and what had happened afterwards with Richard. But he was waiting. She had to say something.

"And now," he prompted.

"It was last night, or in the early hours of the morning," she said, her voice trembling. "I heard a baby crying. Here in this house. It was as if it was in the next room. It screamed and screamed and then it sobbed and whimpered and finally stopped. I got out of bed to go to it. I was going to feed it, when I realised, it couldn't be here. It could not be real." Not wanting him to see her pain, she bent her head, letting her hair cover her face. "Every time I get pregnant I lose my baby," she whispered. Damien said nothing. "Go on," she flared. "Tell me it's my lost babies that I hear crying. That's what everyone else would say."

Damien considered. "Have you heard them anywhere else?"

"No." She shook her head quickly. "I've dreamed about babies, my babies, other people's babies. I've had to stop myself from snatching them out of prams and running away with them. Especially when I think their mothers don't care, or aren't looking after them properly. Anything I see, or hear, or read about babies makes me weep, but before coming to Kingsfield I'd never heard one cry. Not as if it was really happening."

"It's this place then. If it was your grief that made you hear the crying, it would happen wherever you were."

Jo let out a long breath. She was almost dizzy with relief. Impulsively she reached out and took his hand. He held it for a minute before letting it go. "Thank you."

"What for? I haven't done anything"

"Yes, you have. You're treating all this craziness as if it's true."

"That's because it is," Damien said seriously. "What we've got to do is to find links between what happened in the past and what has happened since."

"Sophia." Jo shivered. "She's the link.

"What do we know about her?"

"That she's cruel, malicious, evil. That she and Ann were bound up in some sort of magic or ritual." Jo stopped and ran her fingers through her hair. "This is crazy. These things don't happen."

"Except that they do and we don't, or won't, acknowledge them. Every day of my life I perform a ritual which transforms the divine into the ordinary, or if you like the other way around."

"The bread and the wine," Jo said.

"Let it become for us the Body and Blood of Jesus Christ, Your only Son, our Lord," Damien quoted the words of the Mass. "Whatever you do or don't believe Jo, there are powers, energies and forces out there we do not understand."

"Some of which are good," Jo said slowly. "And some evil." She ran her hands along her forearms, holding herself tight.

"Or people learn to use them for good or evil," Damien said.

"Which is why you think we need to know more about Sophia. Then I can deal with whatever she wants and after that I can get on with the rest of my life."

"You are not going to deal with her on your own Jo. You must never do these things alone. It is potentially too dangerous."

"I know that. I've seen and felt what she can do and believe me I want all the help I can get. Where do we start?

She must have come from somewhere, there must be family, or some background to her, but when I was in the museum no one seemed to know who she was. Her portrait was labelled as being that of an unknown woman."

"Researching Sophia should be easy enough. We can Google, or even better still we can go back to our primary sources and look in the parish records. All births, deaths and marriages will be recorded there."

"Which parish?"

"We'll start with the nearest."

"Our Lady of Sorrows?" Jo managed a smile.

"Hardly." He grinned back. "Too Catholic, too new. The church was built when they put up the estate. No. St. Michael's is our best bet. That has been there since the Middle Ages, so the chances are it's the one the lords and ladies of Kingsfield would have used for their christenings, weddings and funerals. There are definitely some eighteenth century graves in the church yard."

"You'll come with me?"

"Of course. I told you, you mustn't do this on your own."

"You're going to be my spiritual health and safety back up."

"Anything you need Ma'am. The white knight at your service." He gave her a mock salute.

Jo grinned and pushed back her chair and as she did so her nightdress twisted in the rail. She pulled at the skirt then grinned ruefully as she realised what she was wearing. "I'm not even dressed."

"It was probably too early to call." Damien glanced at his watch, frowned then leapt to his feet. "Sorry, I've got to go. I promised Sister Rosemary I'd spare her some time this morning and if I don't she'll give me one of those *it was so much better when Father Egan was in charge,* looks of hers."

He checked that Jo knew how to get to St. Michael's, arranged a time and was gone. Jo showered and washed her hair. It was like getting ready for a date, she thought as she sprayed perfume between her breasts. Smiling wryly at the mirror, she slicked shadow over her lids and curled mascara onto her lashes. A trace of lipstick added a little colour to her face, but still she looked too pale and gaunt. She slid black jeans and T-Shirt over black underwear, tightening the belt to keep the trousers in place. She put on silver earrings and a large silver ring that hung loosely on her middle finger. At the last minute, she fastened a matching necklace around her neck, glanced in the mirror and took it off again.

You're being stupid, she told herself. *All you are going to do is look at some parish records. There's no need to make a special effort.* But somehow, after letting Damien see her, dishevelled and unwashed, dressed in a cardigan for comfort like an old woman, there was.

CHAPTER NINETEEN

Jo drove through the bright afternoon. Cows grazed in fields of rich green grass and the hedgerows were full of late summer growth. The road that ran along the top of Weston Ridge led past a row of detached houses and into what had once been the small hamlet that nestled round St. Michael's. A narrow lane lined with old cottages led up to the church and it was here Jo parked the Mercedes. She got out of the car and looked around but there was no sign of Damien.

Tired after her disturbed night, she stretched, yawned and lifted her face to the sun. At this time of day shadows had been banished and she was safe. *Once I've freed myself of Sophia* Jo thought, *then the fear that waits with the twilight will be gone forever. I'll be my own person again. I'll be able to get on with the rest of my life. But what will that life be? Will it be with Richard? Or is the rift between us too deep?*

I know he only wants to protect me. Trouble is I'm not the fragile creature he thinks I am. Or wants me to be. I'm strong, strong enough to face this and to face anything else that life might throw in my direction. If only he'd listen, then he'd know what I really wanted. But he can't. He wants to wrap me up in cotton wool all the time, while I need to be left to make my own mistakes. To find my own way through this mess. Jo caught her bottom lip in her teeth.

"I don't want to hurt you. I really don't, but if you can't see it from my point of view, then..." she said aloud, squeezing her eyes tight to keep back the tears. "I don't want us to split up. But..."

The sound of Damien's old Ford drawing up interrupted her and there was something oddly comforting and reassuring about him as he got out of the car and came towards her. Like her he was smartly dressed, the worn jeans replaced by new ones, a roll neck shirt under his jacket, shoes instead of trainers, his ponytail tied neatly at the back of his neck. He looked good, handsome even. It seemed natural to stretch out her hand and for him to take it and hold it for perhaps a moment longer than he should; his grip was firm, his skin warm against hers.

"You look better," he said. Jo laughed.

"I should hope so. I was a total wreck this morning. I'm hoping this is where we'll find the answers."

"It should be," he said confidently. "As I told you, the parish records should have all we need to know about Sophia, Ann and Nicholas. I rang Amy Gordon the vicar, when I got back this morning and she says Mrs. Armitage at Honeysuckle Cottage will let us see them. She's the church warden and lives next door to St. Michael's."

Set sideways to the road, Honeysuckle Cottage was long and low. Its thatched roof hung over deep set leaded windows giving it an air of secrecy. Damien pushed open the wrought iron gate and led the way up the narrow path twisting through two large flowerbeds to the door at the side of the house. Looking beyond it, Jo saw a sweep of lawn, fringed by ancient apple trees. A rope bell pull hung in the latticed porch and when Damien tugged it, its chimes echoed through the house and set off a frantic barking.

"Down Geordie," were the first words Mrs. Armitage uttered as she opened the door. A dog with long ears and a brown face hidden by dreadlocks appeared at her side. "She's very friendly, too friendly I sometimes think, but better that way than the other."

"She's lovely. Aren't you girl," Damien hunkered down and stretched out his hand. The water spaniel, her bare tail wagging furiously, bounded past her mistress and gave herself up to being fussed.

It's like a walking hearth rug, Jo thought, *but the face is beautiful, soft as velvet and those eyes under that fringe of ringlets are like chocolate.* The dog gave her a sideways glance; her owner gestured her back and Damien stood up.

"I'm Father O'Connor and this is Mrs..." He hesitated for a moment.

"Avery," Jo said quickly, as she realised that she had never told him her married name.

"Amy Gordon said we were to come here for the keys to the church."

"Of course. I was expecting you. If you would like to step inside for a moment, I'll get them. Don't worry about Geordie; she'll have a run in the garden."

Inside, the cottage smelled of dog. A row of leads hung on a peg beside the door and the walls were covered with pictures and photographs of water spaniels. Some were old prints, others recent photographs with rosettes attached.

Mrs. Armitage a sensible looking, middle aged woman in fawn coloured trousers and sweat shirt with a water spaniel logo on the breast, handed them a pair of heavy iron keys, plus a bunch of smaller ones.

"The big ones are for the church, the slightly smaller one for the vestry and everything else. The registers are in a cupboard with a padlock. Do you want me to come with you, or can you manage? I normally go with visitors, but you Father, being a man of the cloth, I know I won't have to worry about any unseemly behaviour. People don't seem to understand, you see, that the church is a sacred building. Even if they don't believe, I think they should still treat it with respect. They talk at the tops of their voices, they laugh and make jokes and I've even found cigarette ends in the vestry before now, so you see why I have to be careful."

"I quite understand," Damien said gravely.

Jo nodded, hiding her smile at the thought that she obviously looked like some sort of hooligan, or was it her lack of enthusiasm for Geordie that made Mrs. Armitage direct all her remarks to her companion?

In contrast to the brightness outside, the church was dim and cool. Solid pillars soared to a vaulted roof and their feet echoed on the stone flags. A brass eagle formed the lectern, a gold crucifix and candlesticks shone on the altar, above which was a stained glass window showing Christ in his glory, the Archangel Michael brandishing a fiery sword on one side, St.

George complete with dragon on the other. Jo breathed in a smell of polish and candle wax and the sweet scent of flocks.

Damien crossed in front of the altar, stopping and bowing his head to show his respect and Jo found herself copying the gesture. The vestry was lit by a narrow plain glass window. Along one side hung a row of cassocks and other vestments, opposite these there was a large table and two wooden cupboards, one of which was padlocked. Damien fitted the key into the lock and opening the door lifted out a heavy leather bound book.

"This looks like the oldest," he said, laying it on the table.

"It can't be." Jo traced the date with her finger. Engraved in faded gold letters, on the spine was 1832.

"What's the problem?" Damien looked over her shoulder.

"It's too late. Ann's picture was painted in about 1760, by this time she'd be in her eighties, if she was still alive. Sophia's even older, so she's very unlikely to be here. Though we could look I suppose," her voice faltered. "There must be something else. There must." Sinking down on her knees, she began taking out the rest of the books, handing them up to Damien one at a time, until the cupboard was empty except for a faint trail of dust.

"I'm sorry Jo. It seems my idea isn't going to work."

Jo sat back on her heels and rubbed her arm across her face. She had been so sure they would find what they were looking for the disappointment was almost too much to bear. Beneath it lurked the fear that they would not be able to stop what was happening with Sophia and it would destroy her. She shivered and Damien moved towards her.

"Are you all right?" His voice was warm and concerned and she wanted to throw herself into his arms, to hide her head in his chest and whisper her fear, but she knew she must not. He was a priest and she was married to Richard. She swept her hair from her face and got to her feet.

"I'm OK," she lied. "It just got to me for a moment, but I suppose it was too much to hope that it could be this simple."

"Logically it should have been. Ann and Nicholas were

local gentry. Their names and those of their household should be here in the records."

"They weren't though, were they?"

"No. But that doesn't necessarily mean we've come to the end of the line. If Sophia had a child, then if that child had children, or grandchildren they might show up in a later volume. Look, here, the dates would fit." Damien opened the oldest book and began to read down the long columns. Unable to stand the wait, convinced that he would find nothing, Jo walked back into the church.

As soon as she stepped out of the vestry, she sensed the change. In what had been an empty building, the pews were full. A murmur of voices rose like surf breaking on the shore, but however hard she tried, all she could see were the vague outlines of shadowy shapes. Then the temperature dropped and not even the sudden shaft of sunlight that lanced through the stained glass could warm the icy air.

The bride and groom stood at the altar. Ann in blue silk, flowers in her hair and in her arms, a wisp of lace at her throat, her face turned upward in adoration of the man at her side. Dressed in black and silver, Nicholas looked down at her. His height and the breadth of his shoulders made his bride seem very young and childlike.

Jo could not move. As the skin prickled at the back of her neck, she saw Nicholas raise Ann's hand to his lips, saw her cheeks flush and her body sway towards him in utter submission.

"He is mine." The voice hissed through her brain. Jo swung round. She caught a brief glimpse of a woman in a red dress standing at the back of the church.

There was a muffled thunk as if someone had dropped a solid object, then the sound of a door shutting and Damien was standing beside her.

"Did you see them?" Jo whispered. Without speaking, he made the sign of the cross. "You did?"

Damien shook his head. "I felt something." He suppressed a shiver. "I saw nothing."

"They were here. In the church. It was her wedding day." Jo tried to stop her voice from trembling.

"So we know where they were married."

"You didn't find anything?"

He sighed. "Nothing. No mention of D'Aubeneys at all."

"There must be other records." Jo clenched her fists in frustration.

"They could have been destroyed, or taken somewhere else. It happens. One thing is fairly certain. If they were married here, then the chances are they were buried here and if she was a member of the family, as she appeared to be, then Sophia should be here too. In fact the graveyard might be our best bet."

"Or the church." Jo looked round at the memorial tablets set into the walls. "You take one side; I'll take the other." Slowly, reading carefully as she went, she made her way down the west wall. Some were simple brass plaques, like the one mourning the death of a young lieutenant killed at Balaclava. Others were ornate pieces of sculpture, surrounded by flowers and weeping cherubs, such as the tablet celebrating the virtues of a beloved wife of a long dead rector. There were none for the D'Aubeney family. When she reached the door, Damien was already waiting for her.

"Nothing my side," he said. Jo shook her head sadly.

"They were all so young."

He nodded briefly. He seemed very remote and withdrawn. Without thinking she tucked her arm through his, leaned her body towards him, drinking in his warmth. She had only to turn her face…

"I need to lock up." Abruptly he pulled away from her and Jo stumbled back into the shadow of the porch. Hot with embarrassment and arousal she fought to slow her breathing at the same time trying to keep her eyes from Damien's body as he slid the key into the lock.

She did not wait to see him put it back into his pocket and turn to her. Going out into the sunlight, she made her way along the lines of ancient headstones. Most had been eroded by wind and rain, others were covered in moss and lichen. A few however had worn better than the others. Jo read lists of names where a whole family had been buried in the same spot, often the children dying first to be joined later by their mother and finally by their father. Some stones had the outline of angels carved on them, others Death's head. One, the final resting place of an African slave who had converted to Christianity and been freed by his master, was headed by a crude portrait of the dead man.

"We're getting close. The D'Aubeneys were slavers, so was Ann's family," she told Damien who had caught up with her. He stood, hands in his pockets, looking at the headstone.

"No. I don't think so. The lords and masters wouldn't have been buried so close to their servants. I've got a better idea where we might find what we're looking for." Without waiting for her, he walked off round the side of the church, where there was a large square tomb surmounted by an urn. He read the inscription, frowned and shook his head. "It reminded me of the urns on the roof of Kingsfield, but I was wrong. I'm sorry Jo. It looks as if we've come to a dead end."

He turned to go and she was about to follow when she felt a tug at her sleeve.

"Damien wait. Ann's here. I know she is. But where?" This time the pull was sharper, drawing her downwards. Jo sank to her knees beside a simple slab. "I've found it." She leaned forward and touched the weathered lettering, reading softly, "To the memory of Ann D'Aubeney, born 1747 died 1764. May she rest for ever in Peace."

Kneeling beside Ann's grave, Jo bowed her head and let the images flow through her memory. A dirty child in a torn silk gown. A girl racing down the stairs to throw herself into her cousin's arms. A radiant bride with an armful of flowers.

"Amen."

Lost in her memories, Damien's voice startled her. She looked up, blinking away her tears.

"She was only seventeen when she died. My God, that's only two years older than my stepdaughter. Nowadays she'd just be starting her life; she'd have everything to live for."

"Life was short in those day, especially for women." His voice was hoarse and full of pain.

Jo glanced at him quickly but he was looking away from her and she said, "I think she might have died in childbirth, but if she did then what happened to the child? There's no mention of it on the gravestone. Could it have lived, if the mother died?"

"It's unlikely, but not impossible."

"If the child did die then it must be here somewhere."

"Do you want to look?"

Jo brushed the dirt from her knees. "Yes. But if her baby didn't die, we will be looking for an adult not a child."

"In that case he or she may not be here. In fact if Ann's baby was a girl, I would think it highly unlikely that she is buried here."

"You're right. The chances are she would have married and moved away and a son could have died abroad, or in London, or anywhere. What is strange is that, apart from Ann, there is no mention of the family anywhere. Isn't it usual for the local squire and his family to be buried in the same churchyard for generations? But as far as the D'Aubeneys are concerned, it's as if they never existed."

"It is odd," he said. She glanced at him. His face was set and he did not meet her eyes.

This is hurting him she thought. *Why should he be so upset at the death of a girl who lived two centuries ago?*

"If you like we can go. I can always come back on my own."

"You need to find what you came for." He turned and walked away from her. His shoulders hunched, his hands thrust into his pockets, he radiated an aura of grief and despair.

Jo cast a quick glance around the headstones surrounding Ann's simple grave. Nothing.

"Damien." He was standing at the gate and did not look at her when she called. She hurried up the path towards him.

"You were right. Wherever they are, they're not here. Any of them."

"Shall we go?"

"Are you all right?"

"I shouldn't have come."

"What is it?"

He shrugged. "I had no idea it would get to me."

"Because she was so young?"

"My wife," he turned to hide the pain in his eyes.

"Oh God, I didn't know you were married."

"Before I was a priest, obviously." His mouth twisted into a parody of a smile. "She died. She had a brain tumour. She was twenty three."

"I'm so sorry." Jo reached out to touch his sleeve and she was in his arms and he was holding her hard and she was holding him. They clung to each other. She raised her face to his. She kissed him, softly at first, gently, then harder, thrusting her tongue between his lips. She felt him respond, his arms tightening around her, pulling her closer, moulding his body into hers. She wanted him, she needed him, but even as she whispered the words, he pushed her away.

They stood staring at each other in horror.

"Jo, I'm sorry," he said at last. "I shouldn't have done that. This shouldn't have happened."

"No it shouldn't," Jo's eyes filled with tears. How could she have done anything so stupid? Damien was a friend, he was in pain, what he needed from her was comfort and understanding, not a display of full blown lust. What was wrong with her?

She rubbed the back of her hand across her lips, rubbing away the taste of his kiss.

"It wasn't me," she stammered.

"God no. It was my fault."

"No," she stretched out her hand then dropped it before she could touch him. "It's like before. It's like that time with Richard. She takes me over. She's here. It's Sophia that wants to fuck you in a graveyard, not me. I care too much about you

- 154 -

and myself to do this. Don't you see, she wants to ruin everything I've got? Come on, we've got to get out of here."

Hurrying down the lane towards Honeysuckle Cottage, they were greeted by a bundle of brown curls. The water spaniel danced around them bare tail flicking wildly, then as if she understood their distress she stopped her cavorting and gently pressed a wet nose into the palm of Jo's hand. Repeating the action with Damien, she sat and waited until her owner caught up with her.

"Did you find what you were looking for?" Mrs Armitage asked. Jo shook her head.

"There were no registers for the years we needed."

"Oh my goodness, I should have told you. I do hope you haven't had a wasted journey, but the earlier ones were destroyed. There was a fire in the vestry some time in the eighteenth century, I think it was. It was a great scandal at the time. Some people said it was deliberate, others that it was the work of the devil. Luckily whatever caused it didn't cause much damage."

Jo had a sudden vision of Sophia's face as she stood at the back of the church. She had gazed with such venom at the bride and groom.

She did it. I don't know why. I don't know if it makes things better or worse, or why she'd want to destroy the record of Ann's marriage. Still if she did want to wipe it out of history, she didn't succeed. I know Ann married Nicholas. Apart from that what else did I learn? Only that Damien is full of pain and unhappiness and thanks to Sophia I nearly ruined everything we had. He's a friend and I want to keep him that way and even if I wanted something more I'm not going to get it.

"I have to be free of her. I have to get her out of my life," she told Damien as they walked back to the cars.

"You will. You are strong enough."

Jo pulled a face. "How can you can say that after what nearly happened back there?"

"Because it didn't. With two different people it might have

done. You can fight her Jo and I'll do everything I can to help."

CHAPTER TWENTY

In the fading light the driveway gaped between crumbling gateposts. There was no sign, no nameplate, no certainty that this was the right place. On the other hand there was nowhere else it could be. The girl looked back, but the car was already disappearing down the hill. She raised two fingers and swore loudly. Her voice echoed eerily in the empty road and with a shiver she heaved her bag over her shoulder. It was chilly and she had the feeling that it was getting colder. There was something about this place that was really creepy, but the house could not be far and she was starving and desperately needed the toilet.

Around the first curve the darkness closed in on her. The stone under her feet was damp and slippery, the trees arched overhead cutting off any light from above. It was like walking in a tunnel, or stepping into a tomb. She gritted her teeth. There was no turning back. She had nowhere else to go. She only wished it wasn't so dark and the air wasn't so hard to breathe. It was getting harder and harder to walk, but if she stopped she would be lost forever in the dark. Her heart was banging in her chest. She was sweating; her hands and hair were damp, a chill running up and down her back.

She had to get out; she had to get back to the road. She would hitch a lift with the first car that stopped. She would go anywhere, so long as it was not here. She turned and faced impenetrable blackness. Its menace loomed over her, hedging her in and forcing her on towards Kingsfield House.

*

The garden was dark, the house flooded with light. Standing in the kitchen Jo was about to feed the kitten when her phone rang. It was Damien.

"Jo. How are you?"

"I'm OK." She forced a smile into her voice.

"Really?"

"Really." She paused, then added, "And you?"

"I'm fine. I'm ringing, apart from making sure you're OK, to tell you that I am going to see Father King tomorrow. He's the diocesan exorcist. The official guy who gets rid of ghosts and spirits and he's our next step in dealing with Sophia. Are you alright with that?" There was a pause. The very mention of Sophia's name made Jo shudder.

"Jo?" Damien prompted.

Pulling herself together she said, "Yes, definitely."

"Good then I'll say goodnight and God Bless."

Jo shut her eyes. Bowing her head she tried to absorb his blessing, using it to make her strong against the force of Sophia's hatred. She experienced a fleeting moment of peace then it was gone.

Picking up a tin of cat food, she waved the opener in front of Diablo's nose. Instead of butting against her arm to remind her to hurry, as he usually did, he retreated, his fur bristled, his tail rose and he began to growl.

"Flavour not suit you?" Jo said, the breath tight in her chest. Trying to ignore the animal's obvious nervousness, she spooned a little of the meat into the dish marked CAT. Diablo twined around her legs and looked pointedly at the door. Jo put the dish on the floor. Somewhere in the distance, a car stopped. Its door slammed then it drove away. Jo found she was holding her breath. The house vibrated with silence.

"Come on, it's good stuff." Her voice sounded shrill and artificially bright. She moved the cat food around with a fork. The kitten gave a brief mew. His fur subsided and after a preliminary sniff, he began to eat. There was a knock at the door.

Jo's heart lurched. It couldn't be Damien, she'd only finished speaking to him a moment ago and he'd have told her if he was coming to see her. Richard was in New York. The only other people who knew she was here were Cecile and Helene and they appeared to have abandoned her. She reached into her bag for her phone. Holding it like a weapon, she moved towards the door.

"Well are you going to let me in?" The girl standing on the threshold was small and thin. She could have been pretty. Her features were delicate, her eyes huge, but her hair hung in greasy strands over her shoulders, her skin was waxy, her nose pitted with black heads and pierced by a silver stud and her eyes were heavily lined in black. There were loops of silver in her ears and bands of tarnished silver and plaited wool around her wrists. She wore a large jumper and tight trousers that stopped just below the knee revealing thin white calves above scuffed pumps.

"Strif, what are you doing here?" Jo stared at her stepdaughter.

"Are you going to move out of the fucking way?" Strif picked up her duffle bag, deliberately swinging it in front of her so that Jo had to step aside to avoid being hit. Then she strode into the house, the curve of her jumper revealing quite plainly that she was near the end of her pregnancy.

She can't be. It's not possible. This can't be happening, Jo thought. Her head spun at the craziness of it all and she had to dig her nails into her palms to stop herself from screaming out something she would later regret.

"I need the loo."

"Help yourself. It's over there." Jo gestured towards the cloakroom door. She stepped back to give Strif room, moving slowly and deliberately as she tried to hold back the pain that flared in the middle of her chest, crawled up into her throat, her eyes, the back of her neck and down each limb, so that her hands shook and her legs ached with the effort of staying upright and not curling into a screaming, howling ball.

There was a sound of running water; the door opened and Strif came out pulling her jumper over her bulge. "I needed that. I thought I was going to pee myself in the car."

"You came by car?" Jo felt a sudden surge of energy. If someone had brought the wretched girl to Kingsfield, then they could bloody well take her back. Strif gave her a look of utter contempt.

"I hitched," she said.

"From town?"

"No, from Mars."

"You shouldn't have done that. It's not safe." *You stupid, stupid girl. Anything could have happened. To you and to the baby.* "Weren't there any buses? Couldn't you have taken a taxi?"

"Yeah well. Anyway, I got here didn't I?"

Jo bit her lip. She knew that Richard gave his daughter a monthly allowance, which would more than pay for a taxi. So why hadn't she used it? And what was she doing turning up at Kingsfield without warning? Surely in her condition she should be at home, or at the very least with friends who cared about her?

"Does your Mum know where you are?"

Strif shrugged. Thin shoulders moving beneath a dirty jumper. The gesture which was at once defiant and vulnerable, brought everything into focus and Jo realised that as far as Caro was concerned Strif was with her and Richard. No doubt she'd sent her to Wharfside, only for Strif to find no one there. When she'd left the apartment she should have texted or phoned her stepdaughter as well as her husband to say where she was going. That would have been the sensible thing to do. Deep down Jo knew the reason why she had not done so. She had hoped that Strif would find somewhere else to stay while her mother was away at least until Richard came back from New York.

"Her?" Strif blew down her nose. "I don't think so. I haven't seen her for months."

"What!" Jo exclaimed. How could any mother not know where her teenage daughter had gone? "OK," she continued carefully, not wanting to cause a row. "Didn't she send you a message to tell you when she was going to be away? In case you needed her."

"No. Why should she? I told you. We don't speak."

So your mother had no idea where you were, or what you were doing, which probably means that we were meant to find you as well as look after you. Or, typical Caro, was she going

*to blame us for your disappearance? Setting herself up to play
the distraught mother when she got back from her trip.*

"We don't get on. She's out of her head. You know what
she's like." Strif's voice was hard and she rubbed one grubby
hand across her nose. Jo nodded.

"Where have you been staying?" she said more gently.

"Around," Strif snarled.

*Fifteen years old and no one knew where you were, or
what you were doing. What is worse, no one cared enough to
find out.*

"You should have come to your Dad's."

"No I couldn't," Strif scowled. "I was with someone.
Besides, you were there."

Ignoring the provocation Jo said, "Does Caro know about
this?" She glanced at the girl's stomach unable to bring herself
to say more.

"No she fucking doesn't." Strif's eyes slid to the fridge.
"Got anything to eat. I'm starving." Without waiting for Jo's
response, she opened the door and pulled out a block of butter
and a lump of cheese. "Is this it?"

"I can make you an omelette or some scrambled eggs."
Laced with strychnine, or arsenic.

Strif screwed up her face. "I need proper food. For the
baby," she said with deliberate cruelty. She cupped her hands
under her bulge. "Can't you send out for a pizza, or
something?"

Jo felt very, very tired.

"No. I can't," she said. "It's late and I'm not taking you out
either, even if there was anywhere half decent open. You'll
have to make do with what I've got. And before you say
anything milk, eggs and cheese are all very good for," she
forced out the word, "the baby." She moved past Strif, leaned
into the fridge, took out a box of eggs and cracked them
viciously into a bowl. "If you want salad there's plenty in the
crisper. That's good for you too."

"You sound like my mother," Strif sneered.

Jo slammed two pieces of bread under the grill, threw a

lump of butter into the pan, turned up the gas and heated it until it sizzled. Strif straddled a chair; resting her chin on the back, she watched as Jo hacked at the cheese, beat water into the eggs and threw the mixture into the pan, jabbing at it with a fork until it began to set. Then she flung in the cheese.

"You can get the lettuce and tomatoes out," she told Strif.

"Can't."

"Why not?" Jo whirled round furiously and saw that Diablo had settled himself on Strif's knee. Eyes shut, he was purring happily as she tickled him under the chin.

Traitor. I thought you were on my side. You warned me she was coming. So how come you're doing the sweet little kitten bit? If you had any loyalty at all, you would be hissing and spitting and scratching her eyes out.

A spurt of fat leapt out of the pan. Jo flipped the omelette onto a plate and thrust it at Strif.

"I need a knife and fork. Or do you want me to eat with my fingers?"

Jo yanked open the cutlery drawer. Her hands trembled as she picked up the knife. It was too blunt to do any real damage, but a fork shoved in somewhere soft and yielding might be much more effective. *Dear God what am I thinking of? She's a kid and she's in trouble. I've got to stop this before I do something to her. She can't stay her. She's got to go.* Jo threw the utensil down on the table.

The girl ate as if she were starving, shovelling the food into her mouth and chewing loudly. *She is doing it to wind me up.* Jo thought. *But why? Why is she here? Why didn't she stay where she was?*

"How did you know where I was?" she said. Strif pushed away her plate and opened her mouth. Jo clenched her teeth. *If she belches, I'll slap her. I won't be able to stop myself.*

"That was easy. Dad had left some stuff in his study."

"You went to the flat?"

Strif bristled. "I've got a key. Anyway you weren't there. Seb was with some girl."

"Seb?" Jo's voice rose. What was Richard's son doing at

Wharfside?

"Yeah. Dad said he could stay for a few days, seeing as you weren't there."

"Couldn't he have looked after you?" Jo asked foolishly. "I mean until your dad came home?" Strif threw her a withering glance.

"I told you. He was there with some girl and in case you've forgotten there's only one bedroom and only one bed in your fucking flat."

"He shouldn't have let you go off like that. He should have rung me. You should have rung me."

Strif shrugged. Her face looked pinched. "I promised him I would and I tried. But then I didn't have any credit left on my phone."

Don't let me feel sorry for her, Jo prayed. *She's a nasty, vicious piece of work. She's come down here to make trouble. She hates me, she always has. This is just another phase of her unremitting war against me, but this time she holds all the cards.* Instinctively, she wrapped her arms around her waist, feeling the hard outline of her ribs above the slight hollow of her stomach. She swallowed. "You know your Dad's away at the moment," she said as neutrally as she could.

"Yeah. Well." Strif's head bent over the kitten. He lay stretched out over her legs and she stroked him with long smooth strokes. He purred and trembled with pleasure.

"It's a bit like camping here just now. I'm not organised. I haven't even got a spare bed."

"You going to put me out in the street then?"

"Of course not. I'm just telling you the house isn't finished. You need somewhere…" *Somewhere where you can be looked after. Where people care about you. Where your mother doesn't disappear off abroad whenever she fancies it. Where she bothers to find out where you've gone. Somewhere where they will help you get ready for the baby. Somewhere, where your stepmother doesn't want to kill you.*

"You can have my bed for tonight." Strif screwed up her face, but Jo ignored her. "I'll sleep on the sofa and tomorrow we will sort something out."

The girl sniffed loudly and rubbed her hand over her nose. "Whatever," she said. She turned her attention to the kitten then looked up suddenly. "I don't know if I want to stay anyway." *Thank God. The sooner you go the better.*" I don't see what you see in this place. Stuck up here on the hill like it was in the middle of nowhere. That drive's as black as shit and you can't breathe. The air's like tar."

"Oh?" Jo tried to sound noncommittal, but the familiar chill slid up her spine. Something had happened to Strif out there in the drive and she needed to know exactly what she had seen and heard. On the other hand, she did not want to put any ideas into the girl's head, so she would have to be careful about how she reacted. "Perhaps you're tired and that's why it seemed hard."

"Oh yeah." Strif gave her a scathing look. She yawned and stretched her arms above her head. Her bracelets jangled and she gave out a smell of stale sweat and old deodorant. "I want a bath."

"There's plenty of hot water," Jo said carefully.

"You got any baby oil? For the stretch marks."

Ignoring the barb Jo said, "You can use my body lotion for tonight." Strif wrinkled up her nose. "It's that or stretch marks," Jo said.

Strif disentangled herself from the chair. Dragging her bag behind her, she trailed after Jo up the stairs. Jo ran the hot water, poured in generous amounts of bath oil and brought a pile of new towels from the airing cupboard. Strif dawdled about, turning taps on and off, rummaging in her bag, demanding shampoo and conditioner and toothpaste.

Watching her, Jo thought that Strif was behaving as if she did not want to be left alone. But there was nothing to hurt her, not up here. Unless…

"Dear God," Jo breathed, pressing her hands against her stomach. Then shaking her head briskly to chase away the fear she told herself that Strif's pregnancy was too advanced for her to miscarry. At the very worst all that would happen would be that her baby would come a week or so early.

"God, my back hurts." Strif sat on the toilet and began pulling off her trousers.

"If you need any help, I'll be downstairs," Jo found herself saying.

"I can take a bath on my own," was the instant reply.

Jo ignored her. "If you need anything and I mean anything just shout."

Only please don't call me. I don't want to see the curve of your body, where your child conceived so easily, carried so effortlessly, lies curled up in the safety of your womb. I don't want to see your breasts, already swollen with the glands that will make the milk to feed your baby.

Jo shut the bathroom door and went down the stairs. Every step was like wading through sand. Her thighs hurt, her arms hung heavy by her side. Her jaw ached from the effort of holding back her anger and pain. In the kitchen, she rang Richard.

"Jo?" He sounded surprised, but was he pleased? To her fury she felt the tears spill over into her voice. "What is it? What's happened?"

"When are you back?"

"Tomorrow. Had you forgotten? Dear God, Jo tell me what's wrong."

"I'm OK. It's Strif."

"Stephanie!"

"She's here. At Kingsfield. I can't explain, all I know is that she's pregnant and I can't deal with it." She was weeping openly now, the hot tears rolling down her face, soaking into the top of her jumper.

"She's what? She can't be. She's fifteen years old for God's sake."

"I know," Jo gulped.

"What the hell's she doing there? God when I get hold of whoever's responsible, I'll kill him. I'll be with you as soon as I'm back. Hold on in there. It will be OK. I promise. Love you."

"Mm," Jo grunted. It was easy for him to say, all those thousands of miles away, while she was left dealing with this horrendous situation. Seized by an irrational surge of anger, she dropped the phone on the table and only some deeply buried instinct for survival stopped her from sweeping it to the floor and trampling it to pieces. Richard knew how much Strif's pregnancy must hurt Jo, but he didn't even ask how she was. He was ignoring her pain, as he always did, hoping that it would go away, that she'd end up seeing things from his point of view, that if they couldn't have a child they could be happy together without one.

"Oh yeah!" Unconsciously she mimicked Strif. As if the words had conjured her up, there she was. Her newly washed hair hung soft and wispy around her heart shaped face. Her skin glowed from the heat of the bath. Her eyes devoid of make-up were wide and lost. In one of Jo's long white nightdresses, she looked like a little girl on a Victorian Christmas card.

I remember the first time I met you. An expensively dressed little girl, cool and self-possessed, sitting and eating sushi with her soon to be stepmother. You were polite and well behaved and you made it very obvious that you didn't like me and you'd do everything you could to get me out of Richard's life.

Me? I was so naïve. I thought it would be like it was with Melinda. That as you grew up we could be like sisters, united by our love for your father. I did whatever I thought you wanted. I gave you whatever you asked for. And however hard I tried, I always got it wrong and was left feeling stupid and inadequate. In the end, you didn't even bother to come and stay anymore.

"I'm going to bed."

God bless, goodnight and don't let the bedbugs bite. You see you almost caught me there. You can just stop looking so innocent and so vulnerable. Under that sweet exterior, you're as hard as nails. It comes from having Caroline as a mother. She never gave a damn about you and you don't care about

- 166 -

anyone else.

"The kitten can sleep with me. I'm not used to sleeping on my own."

"Fine," Jo said. Knowing that Strif wanted her to, she was determined not to ask who it was she had been sleeping with.

Diablo scampered up the stairs and disappeared behind Strif's skirt. She bent down and picked him up. He put his paws on her shoulders, she turned and smirked at Jo, then carried him tenderly into the bedroom.

Oh for goodness sake stop playing games. Go to sleep and leave me alone.

A door shut. There was a whimper, or was it a mew? The sound floated down the stairs and hung in the air like gossamer.

CHAPTER TWENTY-ONE

Jo heard the sirens wailing as she went to fetch her bedding. She stopped half way to the airing cupboard, but the upstairs windows were too high to see out and the view from the ground floor would be obscured by the trees that surrounded the house. The high-pitched sounds grew louder and louder and as they penetrated the double glazing and ricocheted around the walls she realised that the accident must have happened close by.

She went downstairs and put her sheet and duvet on the sofa, then stood wondering what she should do. She had no training in first aid, nor any morbid desire to watch mangled remains being removed from the wreck of some car, but there were few other houses along that stretch of road and once on an icy January night someone had stopped at an accident and saved her life. Maybe there was something she could do to help, even if it was only to make hot drinks for the rescue crew.

She went into the hallway and took her jacket from its hook. The torch was in her car so she slipped both sets of keys into her pocket. It was darker outside than she had expected. The narrow slits of windows at the front of the house threw little light onto the cobbles and she had forgotten to switch on the outside light, so approaching the car was like being wrapped in a black blanket. She moved cautiously, stretching out her hands to feel her way, until her eyes became accustomed to the gloom and her fingers felt the smooth metallic flank of the Mercedes.

Raising the lid of the boot, she took out the torch. She pressed the button. Nothing. The security lights had not come on either, making it almost impossible to find her way down the drive to the road. Jo shrugged, there was nothing more she could do, but as she turned back towards the house, the security lights sprang into life. At the same time her finger pressed down and a broad beam of torchlight splayed out across the courtyard.

As she turned into the drive, she listened for sounds of voices, cutting equipment, vehicles coming or going, all the expected noises of a road accident. It was very still. The light she held fanned out in front of her; it caught the ragged shapes of the bushes that bordered the drive, the dark square of the house and the wavering outline of the white figure that stood in her way.

"I knew you would come." Ann moved towards her, holding out her arms, her skirts flowing over the curve of her stomach. "I often think of you. Tonight when I slipped out of the house I knew you were near. I hope you come to bring me good fortune." She slid her hand into Jo's. "I shall need it when my time comes." Her hand trembled and Jo tightened her grip on the thin fingers. "They say it will not be many days now. I should stay in my room and rest, but I needed some air. I was a little sick and dizzy."

And far too thin, Jo thought. *Your head looks too heavy for your neck, your arms are like sticks and with that belly you look like a famine victim. Is the child sucking all the nourishment out of you? Or are you ill?* She blinked away the image of the plain stone slab in St. Michael's churchyard. There was nothing she could say or do. Whatever lay ahead for Ann and her child had already happened. The girl beside her breathed sharply.

"It grows cold. We should go in." She staggered a little, falling against Jo, who braced to hold her upright. The stars shone sharp in an autumn sky. The lights from the house spilled into pools of candlelight on the flagstones. The long windows glowed gold behind their shutters. The light from the torch grew thin and weak. Jo pressed the button and the beam died.

Ann was leaning heavily against her arm. Her feet dragged, her skirts trailed and she seemed to have difficulty catching her breath.

"Don't leave me," she whispered. "I fear I have walked too

far. If I can rest for a while I will soon recover."

Jo saw the sheen of sweat on the hollow planes of her face. "You'll catch cold if we stand out here. It's not much further. Can you make it to the house?"

"If you help me, I can."

Jo looked around. "Is there a side door we can use?"

Ann shook her head. "The front entrance is the nearest."

I don't want to do this, Jo thought. *I don't want to go into that house. I can feel myself growing thinner and fainter, more and more insubstantial as if she is leaching the very life out of me.*

Ann gave a little cry and pressed her hand against the small of her back.

Jo wanted to go back down the drive, where the emergency light of the ambulance flashed and the police measured the length of the skid on the road, then home around the corner to the converted barn where Strif slept curled in her bed with Diablo at her side, but Ann's hand was still on her arm and they were climbing the sweep of steps that led to the double doors, where footmen in livery and powdered wigs bowed to the lady of the house and stared straight through her companion.

She threw no shadow on the stairs; her feet made no sound on the wooden floorboards. By the time they reached Ann's room, Jo could not feel the touch of her hand on her arm. It was as if she did not exist.

"I must go." Was it her own voice or the echo of some other sound in her brain?

A fire burned in the grate, candles stood on a chest of drawers and on a low table beside a sofa. The air was warm, perfumed with lavender and sweet apple wood. Ann sank down on the sofa. Her eyes closed; long pale lashes swept her cheeks, her chest rose and fell, breasts round and full against the tight bodice. Thinking she was asleep, Jo started towards the door.

"Don't leave me. Please," Ann's voice was very faint. "Stay with me for a little longer." Her eyes opened and with a great effort, she turned her head towards Jo. "Now that you are here, I know that everything will be well." She struggled to sit up. "I have been so afraid. They all tell me there is nothing to fear, that I am young and strong, but..." she bit her lip. "Sometimes I cannot breathe, my head feels so light, but my ankles swell and the child, it drags me down. My Nicholas is gone away on business to the city and I was all alone until you came." Jo took one of Ann's pale limp hands and held it. Ann's fingers closed round hers, her eyelids flickered and for a moment it seemed as if she slept.

The door opened. A footman entered, carrying a tray. On it stood a bowl, a glass and a bottle of wine. Ann glanced at the tray and screwed up her face. "Take it away. I don't want it," she whimpered.

Jo looked at the thin arms and the hollow face. "You must eat," she said briskly. "Come on, let me help you." She took the bowl and dipped the spoon into the thick gruel. "Just a little," she coaxed. Ann made pushing movements with her hands.

"It makes me ill. I cannot bear the smell. I cannot bear the taste. The very thought revolts me."

"Your baby needs food and so do you. You will need all your strength." Ann shook her head wearily.

"I cannot," she whispered. "If I eat too much I shall grow huge. Oh why is Mercy my nurse not here? She would help me. When I was a little girl, before I came to Kingsfield, she would give me medicine when I was sick. Then I got well, but now there is no one."

"You have Nicholas," Jo said softly, hoping this was true.

"Ah yes," Ann sighed and for a moment her hand rested on her belly. Thinking she was a little calmer Jo began to move away, but as she did so Ann clutched at her hand.

"Please don't leave me I beg you. You must stay with me. You promised, you are my sister in blood. We are bound together for all time," her voice faded and her eyelids fluttered and when she opened them again, they were bright with fever.

"It's all right, I'm here. Hush now," Jo soothed. She

slipped her arm under Ann's shoulders and lifted her up. Holding her close, she coaxed her to take a little wine to help her sleep. The girl's head was heavy on her breast, her bones sharp and thin.

"Promise me it will not make me dream," she whispered, her eyes large and frightened. "I dream of such horrors. Of death and monsters. Always monsters with their staring eyes."

"Shh," Jo soothed, lifting the glass to Ann's lips.

Ann took a sip and a faint flush rose in her cheeks. "It warms the blood, I thank you," she murmured. Her eyes closed. Jo settled her back against the cushions. Ann turned herself awkwardly onto her side and put her thumb in her mouth.

Candle flames flickered then died. The fire shrivelled into a pile of ash and charred wood. The room grew cold, the air musty. Jo's hand closed around her torch; her fingers pressed down on the switch and the pale beam shone in an empty room. She edged her way towards the door and bare boards creaked beneath her feet.

The marble staircase curved down into the black well of the entrance hall. Where moments ago there had been light and warmth, now there was nothing but a deep, cold darkness. She felt her way, one step at a time. Her right hand she pressed against the sweep of the banister rail, even though it was too wide to hold, too slippery to cling on to if she lost her footing. Her left hand was clamped around the torch, focusing its light downwards. She ignored the wild leap of her shadow behind her, the sound of her footsteps in the empty building and the prickling at the base of her spine, where at any moment she feared she would feel the malevolent thrust of a hand propelling her down onto the stone floor at the foot of the stairs.

Her thigh muscles ached, her shoulders were tense with the effort, but at last, she was on level ground. Only a few more yards and she would be at the entrance. Unwilling to let go of something solid, she trailed her hand along the wall. Her fingers tangled in cobwebs, something scurried across her feet, but it was the laugh, low and wild, that sent her racing towards the door. The torchlight wavered and dimmed. Her hands clutched at the doorknob pulling, turning, tugging frantically as nothing moved. The torch died. She felt herself falling into nothingness. She stretched out her arms to save herself and her hands touched solid wood. One push and the door swung open and let her out into the night.

Below her she could see the orange glow of the streetlights of Weston Ridge, hear the whisper of traffic on the main road, see the shapes of the factories beside the river. She wished she could run down the hill, through the woods and into the warmth and safety of Nan's kitchen, but Arnold Grove was no longer home. Other people lived there now; other children played in the long back garden and crawled through the fence to run wild in the wood.

She rubbed her hands down the legs of her jeans. Her skin felt grimy, her mouth was dry and her legs trembled as she walked down the steps. She did not want to go through that tunnel of trees. It gaped before her, thick and sinister, but it was the only way back to the light and safety of The Granary. Totally enclosed, she could see nothing, hear nothing, but her own breathing. Trying to orientate herself, she shuffled forward, one step and then another, only a few more and her feet would touch the rounded shapes of the cobbles and she would be home.

Surely she should have reached The Granary by now? She had been walking for long enough. She could not have missed the turning. If only she could see she would know where she was. Should she turn back, or should she go on? If she continued down the drive, she would eventually reach the road. There were lights there and people, while here there was nothing but darkness.

She tried to hurry, but something held her. It pressed in on her, holding her back, an evil presence that wished her nothing but harm. She raised her arms to her face, pushing away the thing she sensed but could not see. There were hands around her throat, a pillow over her mouth. She was suffocating, gasping for breath. Lights spun through the darkness; her legs would not hold her; she was falling, falling.

Her bones jolted against the ground. Stone grated against her palms as she raised herself to her knees. Down here the air was thinner. It slid easily into her lungs giving her the strength to pull herself forward.

"Like the worm that slithers through the grave, I will step on you. I will crush you. I will destroy you," Sophia's voice sounded in her brain.

"No!" Everything she was fought against the evil that threatened her. She curled her fingers around a gap in the stones. Her nails sank into the ground and she smelled the damp, living smell of the earth. Lifting her head, her eyes strained into nothingness, but she knew what she must do. Bracing her arms and feet, she began to push herself upwards. Sweat ran from her face, her chest, soaking through her clothes as she battled to stand upright.

"I am not afraid. You cannot hurt me." The hand she lifted to cross herself was heavy as death. The prayers she murmured futile as guilt, but the air seemed to shift. It grew a little lighter, less dense. Instead of holding her immobile, it caught at her legs like an undertow. She threw herself against it and arms outstretched, legs braced against the current, she waded into the blackness.

Was she heading in the right direction? Was she going backwards or forwards? Would she find herself in the road, or at the front of the house where she would have to go through all this again? She felt the scream rise in her throat, heard the voice in her head.

"You are alone. No one will hear you. No one will ever hear you in the eternal silence. Can't you feel it closing you off? Shutting you away from everyone forever."

"Nan!" She was six years old, alone and screaming in the dark.

Nan came running, her hair in pink plastic curlers, her dressing gown tied with a cord around her waist. "It's all right, I'm here. It's only a dream you had," she soothed.

I'm dreaming. This is not real. In a minute I will wake up in my own bed. I will. Jo clenched her teeth and clung to the image of Nan sitting at the side of her bed, smoothing her hair from her forehead. She forced herself onward, her breath coming in short gasps, her feet dragging. She would not stop. She would go on. She would not give in.

Something lifted around the edge of the darkness. What had been impenetrable began to lose substance and it was possible to make out the beginnings of shapes. The terrible heaviness was gone. She could move faster; she could run. It was like being washed onto the shore after struggling through a heavy sea. Bent half double, she stumbled over the cobbles as before her she saw the outline of The Granary with its narrow line of lighted windows. The security lights came on, blindingly white as she burst out of the shadows.

Jo sprinted to the house. Her hand fumbled for the key and she was inside, leaning against the wall, taking deep jagged breaths. She was clammy with sweat, covered in mud, but she was safe. For the time being.

"Thank you, thank you God." Why was she praying? What was she doing? Gratitude could come later, if at all. The first thing she had to do was to make sure that everything was all right. Fear swept through her like fire. A horror of what she might find drove her up the stairs two at a time.

The door to her bedroom was ajar. Strif slept on her side, her hair fanned out on the pillow, her face slightly flushed, breathing softly. The room smelled of Eternity and warm cat.

Jo checked the bolts and the locks on every door again and again. Lights blazed throughout the house, but still the shadows lurked, half glimpsed from the corner of an eye, as she waited, hands clenched, in what might be a prayer, for the first sign of daybreak.

CHAPTER TWENTY-TWO

Jo was standing at the side of the room. The floor sloped slightly, the floorboards were pitted and dark with age, the plaster stained and cracked. If she looked up, she could see the oak beams that ran the length of the ceiling and seared into the centre of one was a date, 1532. In her dream, she knew that she was in one of the old timber framed houses that filled the narrow, twisting streets around the docks.

The room was simple but clean. Most of the space was taken up by the four-poster bed. Its canopy and hangings were embroidered with birds and flowers and the coverlet was drawn back to reveal fresh white linen and a pile of pillows. Beside the bed was an old sea chest, on which stood a pair of candlesticks and a pewter brazier. There was a carved wooden chair, a stool and a low table on which stood a basin and a ewer.

A fire burned in the grate, but one of the windows had been left open and beyond the latticed pane, the last hectic flush of pink hung above the tangle of masts and sails, as the sun setting behind the hills at Dundry bled ribbons of red into the river. The colour, swirling and dissolving into the water, mimicked the blood stained plug of mucus that lay at the bottom of the chamber pot.

There were two women in the room. The elder of the two was black. With a fine boned face and slender neck, she carried herself like a queen. Her hair was cropped close to her head, her wiry curls touched with silver and her skin glowed with a blue sheen in the soft evening light. The other woman was Sophia, her hair lay loose on her shoulders and she wore a white shift over her distended body. The older woman glanced in the pot.

"It has begun," she said.

Sophia's hands rested on her belly. She smiled a slow cat like smile.

"Will it be long now?"

Aphra shook her head. "Do as I say and she soon come." She moved across the room to close the window. Then lighting a taper from the fire, she set it to the pile of leaves on the brazier. The herbs caught and crackled and wisps of aromatic smoke rose into the air. "Do you feel it?" Her voice was low and hypnotic. "She start her journey into this world. Your baby she come. Here." She reached up and pulled at the laces of Sophia's shift. The material ripped and fell to the floor, leaving her naked. Her bare skin was the colour of coffee; her nipples brown as chocolate. "No hurt."

The older woman reached into her mouth and taking out a wad of half chewed leaves, passed it to Sophia, who put it into her own mouth and gave a short sigh of pleasure. The skin, stretched tight over her belly, rippled. With her hands on the small of her back, she flung back her head, thrusting out her hips as if in the act of love and gave another little moan.

"Mother," her voice was lazy and warm.

"Daughter, you do good."

The air grew hazy with smoke. Sophia breathed in deeply and Aphra began to chant. She moved backwards and forwards and the words strange, yet familiar hung like incense in the air, as her daughter started to dance.

In the firelight, Sophia's body gleamed with moisture. She moved lightly, her feet pounding out the rhythm. Sweat stood on her brow, but there was no sense of pain, rather a moving in concert with her body, as in grindingcorn, or chopping yams, she was at one with her task.

The light faded. Aphra lit the candles and set them on the floor. Her daughter slowed, her movements were heavy and languorous. The smile on her face was rapt. Her eyes narrowed in concentration. She gave a cry and crouched down to squat. Her hands closed around the posts of the bed; her whole body strained, her breathing quickened. The woman took the stool and placed it behind her. Sophia rested her buttocks on it; her legs splayed open and the dark triangle between her thighs began to part. The whole of her body bore downwards and Sophia gave a triumphant shout. Her mother knelt before her and she delivered her child into Aphra's hands.

The baby gave a loud and lusty yell. She was a girl, a well formed child with a head of tight black curls.

"His daughter," Sophia cried and taking the baby, she held her to her breast.

"He will own her," Aphra said. It was a statement not a question.

"She is mine. I am his. He has no choice in the matter." Sophia looked up from her child and into Jo's eyes. Her face, so tender and gentle when she nursed her baby, became cruel and knowing.

There was so much hatred in her glance that Jo shrank back against the wall, shaking her head against its rough surface as if to rub away the sense of menace. Her eyes smarted from the smouldering herbs, the thick, sweet smoke slid into her lungs. She coughed and woke.

The laugh mocking and challenging rang around the dusky room. It drifted up the stairs to the bedroom, where Strif whimpered and cried out in her sleep.

It was a dream, Jo thought. *An evil dream, that's all. She can't do anything to hurt us. She does not exist. She is dead, long since dead.*

The room was icy. A feeling of dread hung in the air. In the bedroom above her head the kitten growled. Jo struggled to sit up. She wrapped the duvet around her and stumbled towards the light switch. Beyond the bare windows, the night coiled around the house and the feeling of danger grew stronger.

Get out of here. Get out of my head, she thought, then her fingers found the switch and the room leapt into view. The deep coloured rugs, the cushions lying where she had thrown them on the floor, the sofa with her tangled sheet.

Get out. I've got nothing you want. So leave us alone.

She saw again the child's mouth pulling at her mother's breast, the whole of Sophia's body given up to the pleasure of feeding. Her own pain ripped through her and with it the beginning of understanding. Sophia had given birth to Nicholas's child. Ann afraid of the power that might give Sophia over her husband had persuaded Jo to take part in whatever dark magic had sent Sophia through the Satan Stones. Torn from her baby, the child neglected, left uncared for in some distant corner of Kingsfield, Sophia had sworn her revenge on the two girls. Jo pressed her hands against her stomach. Sophia had caused her to miscarry, Ann would die in childbirth. Any mother and child who came within the reach of this vengeful spirit was in terrible danger.

Tonight, alone in this house, she was responsible for Strif and her unborn child. She glanced at her phone. Four o'clock. Richard would be on his way, somewhere high above the Atlantic. She scrolled down, until she found Damian's number. There was no answer. She tried again but the phone rang out. She would have to wait until he called her in the morning. For the time being all she could do was keep watch and hope.

Oh God, Damien, she thought. *Where are you? Why is there no one here for me? Please God let it be all right.*

CHAPTER TWENTY-THREE

"Christ I'm starving." They stood together on the bottom step, the girl in the long, white nightdress, the small black cat at her side.

Jo struggled out from under her duvet. Her back ached, her limbs were stiff, her eyes dry and sore. The pale light of dawn had given way to bright sunshine, so at some point she must have slept. The fear and panic of the night had gone. She felt nothing, but a profound weariness. "Strif don't swear," she said.

"Why the fucking hell not?"

"Because I don't want you to."

"Caro doesn't mind."

"Caro might not, but this is my house and I do."

"Why?"

Because you're doing it to wind me up and make me angry. You need me on your side. I'm almost too tired to think and I have to try and figure out what has to be done. The trouble is there are too many emotions flying around this place and I think that's how they get to us. Ann and Sophia use my anger and pain as a way in. But I don't expect you to believe me. I don't expect anyone to, except Damien.

"I don't like it," she said.

"You're going to throw me out?"

Jo sighed. "Not this morning."

"You're gonna wait 'til later."

"No. I told you No one's throwing you out. When your Dad gets here, we'll decide what we're all going to do."

"You've told him?" There was a note of anxiety in Strif's voice and Jo could not help a slight twinge of satisfaction. From their first encounter Strif, then a demanding four year old, had made her position clear. Richard's daughter and Jo, her hated her soon to be stepmother, were locked into an eternal battle. Strif was Daddy's little girl, he loved her best

- 180 -

and no one was going to take her place in his affections. Ever.

"I rang him last night. He's on his way."

"Sh…" Strif began then stopped. "Is there any toast?"

"When you're dressed, I'll make some."

They sat at the table. Jo sipped scalding black coffee. Strif devoured a plateful of scrambled eggs on toast, with only a passing reference to the lack of tomato ketchup. Diablo, having been fed first, lazed on the windowsill. When she had finished, Strif got up and without being asked took her dishes to the sink and began to wash up.

Because of her size, she had to stand some way from the basin. Wearing black leggings and a creamy, washed out cotton jumper that clung to her bump, her arms and legs seemed thin and spindly. She was bare foot and the narrowness of her ankles made her look very young and vulnerable. As she leaned forward to rinse her plate, the sun caught glints of gold in her hair.

With the image came another memory, of another time, another girl. Glints of gold in candlelight, pale hair caught by the light of the fire. Ann asleep on her couch, very white, very thin and getting close to her time.

"Leave it," Jo said abruptly.

"I've nearly finished." Strif swirled clean water around in the scrambled egg pan and placed it on the draining board.

Jo pushed back her chair. "We're going shopping," she announced. Strif looked at her as if she were some kind of slimy creature that had crawled into the room.

"I don't do shopping," she said.

Neither do I, Jo thought, *not any more, not since Melinda died. But I have to get you out of here. You can't stay, not even for a few hours. It's not safe. When Richard comes he can sort out his son and girlfriend and take you back to Wharfside. Damien will help me do whatever I must here and then we'll see. You mustn't be here. I don't know why, I just know that if you stay something terrible will happen.*

"You do now," she told Strif.

The girl looked at her, then, as if she sensed something in

Jo's tone, gave way. "If you say so," she muttered.

Don't let her pick up my fear, Jo thought. *Let her think whatever she likes about me, but please let her hurry up.* She wanted to scream at her stepdaughter to get out, to grab her by the arm, pull her out of the house and drive her away as far as she could, but knowing that Strif would always do the opposite of anything she suggested, she forced herself to smile. "I'm sure there are things you need."

Strif glanced down at her stomach then looked away. "Suppose," she said.

"So, let's go."

"OK. I'll just do my eyes."

Must you? Jo thought. *Of course you must. You know how much I hate the way you look. Those great black lines around your eyes, your lashes clotted with mascara the cheap jewellery and dirty clothes you wear to make yourself look as scruffy and common as you can. You do it on purpose, but you're not going to get a rise out of me. Not today.*

Strif moved slowly and heavily up the stairs. Half way up, she stopped and rubbed the bottom of her back. Jo wanted to ask her if she was all right, but the kitten miaowed urgently and she had to hurry to let him out of the front door.

Sunlight filtered thinly through the trees as Diablo scampered off into the bushes. Jo watched his little black body disappear into the undergrowth, waited for a moment then called his name. The kitten did not come back. Reluctant to leave him, but desperate to get Strif and go, Jo stepped back into the hall. There was no sound from the bedroom.

What are you doing up there? She thought impatiently. *Even if you were covering the whole of your body with make-up you should have finished by now. Don't you understand, we've got to get you out of here?*

Jo gritted her teeth. If she called she knew from past experience that her stepdaughter was perfectly capable of taking off all her make-up and whatever she was wearing and beginning the whole process again to ensure that they would be late. Perhaps if she started the car Strif would hurry. As she reached into the pocket of her jacket for keys and phone, it occurred to her that once she had Strif in the Mercedes she could take her straight to the apartment. She could ask Seb and his friend to find somewhere else to stay, or pay for them to go to a hotel. But what if Strif refused? Could she force her? Could she make her stay in the safety of the flat, or would she have to watch her every move until Richard got home? Whatever she wanted Strif to do she was sure to do the opposite just to spite her.

"Why do you always have to be so difficult?" Jo groaned. "Not you," she hastened to say as Diablo, tail held like a pennant, picked his way delicately over the cobbles. "Look after the house for me. Keep her out," she murmured, bending over to stroke his fur. The phone rang. *Damien,* Jo thought. *Thank God.*

"Jo, darling, we've landed. We're taxiing in now. A few more hours all being well and I'll be with you. Whatever happens, I'll be at Kingsfield this evening. So hang on in there with her, OK."

"But I was…"

"Got to go. Love you."

"Well what are we waiting for? I thought we were going shopping." Strif appeared at the top of the stairs. "You can take me to Mothercare."She walked past Jo, her body taking up the whole space and opened the front door. Immediately, the kitten shot out into the sunlight.

Great, Jo thought. *I wanted you inside, where you'll be safe.* "Get in the car," she said sharply. "Let's get out of here." Strif pulled a face and made a great fuss of heaving herself into the passenger seat. Jo swung the Mercedes out of the drive, into the main road and accelerated faster than was wise under the iron bridge and down the hill towards the safety of the city.

CHAPTER TWENTY-FOUR

The afternoon was heavy and close. The clouds hung low over the hills, turning the sky grey; the air metallic. When they got back from their shopping, there was nothing Jo felt she could do. She needed to work towards her exhibition, but that would mean ignoring Strif and ignoring Strif would inevitably lead the girl to do something stupid, so instead she sat and stared at the television on the kitchen counter. She had switched it on to keep the silence at bay. She and Strif only spoke when necessary. For the rest of the time the air was dense with emotion.

Anticipating this situation, Jo had turned the set around so that it could be seen from the living area and rearranged the furniture to accommodate it.

On the screen, a husband and wife screamed at each other. He suspected her of sleeping with his brother, she knew he was having an affair with his secretary. Jo surfed through the channels, until she found a long haired girl in dungarees explaining how to make a container garden in a shaded back yard. She concentrated on learning how to protect hostas from the depredations of slugs, so that she could shut out the storm clouds beyond the window and the sound of Strif coming down the stairs. The girl moved heavily but with energy, her bare feet slapping the wooden floor as she crossed the living area and positioned herself between Jo and the television.

"Isn't there anything better on?"

"Find it." Jo handed her the remote control.

Strif took it, then put it down and wandered away. She pulled open a kitchen drawer and rearranged the contents; she straightened the cushions on the sofa. She came back to the kitchen and wiped around the sink.

For God's sake can't you keep still? Jo's skin crawled with irritation, but she focused her attention on the girl in the dungarees, who was now heaving flagstones into her yard ready to lay them on a bed of sand.

Strif took a cloth and started to polish the taps. Jo clenched her fists, as she fought back the impulse to scream at her stepdaughter. What was it she had said to Damien about how Ann, then Sophia had used her emotions? When she had first met Ann she had been lonely and miserable. She thought her grandparents did not love her, that no one did. No wonder she had been so open to Ann's demands for attention and affection. Then Sophia had recognised her need of Richard and had used all the long suppressed feelings Jo had for her husband to make sure she would conceive the child that she would miscarry. As for the time in the graveyard. If she and Damien became lovers that would have destroyed her marriage and his vocation.

Whatever happened she must not lose her temper. If she did, who knew what evil she might unleash? When Richard came, she would insist they leave. Even if they went to a hotel for the night, it would be safer than staying in The Granary.

Rain spattered against the window. There was the sound of a car in the cobbled yard. Strif's head jerked round. She bit down on her lower lip as Jo pushed back her chair and smoothing back her hair, walked slowly and deliberately to the door. She must not throw herself into his arms. She must not scream and cry and demand that he remove Strif immediately. She had to stay calm and rational and in control if she wanted to convince him to agree to her plan.

"Richard." Jo lifted her face to be kissed, but his lips skimmed hers briefly, his eyes on his daughter, who was standing by the sink, her face pale and drawn, a film of sweat on the white skin shining like grease.

"Dad." Strif, as if fully aware of the effect she was having, kept her eyes down as she moved slowly towards him.

Richard stood awkwardly, uncertain whether or not to put his arms around his daughter, then kissed her quickly on the top of her head and moved away before she could react.

He's angry, Jo thought suppressing a small glow of pleasure. *He's finally seen his darling daughter for what she is and he's furious.*

"I'm glad you came," she said. "We need to sort things out. Tonight." *Keep it cool. If you don't, he'll just think you're hysterical.*

"You mean me," Strif flashed.

"Who else?" Richard said coldly.

"You can't do anything to me now. She, Caro, would have made me get rid of it, but now," Strif grinned triumphantly. "It's too late."

"It certainly is. Just for once your mother might have been right. Look what you've done with your life."

"Richard, don't," Jo's voice was sharp with anxiety. Richard glanced at her. She shook her head, but Strif was already on the attack.

"Oh yeah! And what do you know about it?"

"I know you're going to have to take responsibility for what you've done."

"And you don't think I can. It just goes to show you don't know anything. You don't know anything about me."

"I know that you are fifteen years old and fifteen year old girls are not supposed to be mothers."

"Oh no. Well, I bet I'll look after this baby better than you looked after me."

"How do you intend to do that?"

Strif shrugged her shoulders.

"Or is the father of this child going to take some responsibility?"

Strif glared at her father.

"Well is he?"

Strif pulled a face.

"Richard I'm sure we can work something out," Jo tried to intervene.

"You don't know who he is, do you?" Richard sneered. There was a crash and a splintering of glass, as Cecile's mirror fell from the wall. The light wavered and a sliver of cold air snaked around Jo's shoulders.

"Richard please stop. This isn't going to get us anywhere.

- 186 -

We need to think."

"There's nothing to think about. It's all too obvious."

"I'm going to have a baby, a baby, a baby." Strif was dancing defiance at them.

"Strif!" Richard and Jo spoke together.

The air in the room coalesced. It grew dark and thick. Strif's whole body shuddered. She wrapped her arms around her stomach and staggered back against the table.

"Stop it. Stop it now." Jo went to the girl and put her arm firmly around her shoulders. For a brief moment Strif leaned against her, then she pushed her away and ran out of the room. Richard lunged after her.

"Leave her." Jo put her hand on his arm. "Please," she added softly, trying to diffuse his anger.

He shook her off. "Don't interfere, Jo. I'll deal with it. She's my daughter." It was as if he had slapped her.

Where were you when she needed you? What were you doing when Strif was little? When she needed the stabilizing influence of her dad. You were busy working, making your mark, becoming one of the leading architects in the world, while your daughter, your vulnerable little girl was left to the tender mercies of that bitch of an ex-wife of yours. No wonder Strif has turned out the way she has. The words trembled on her lips, but she bit them back. They must not fight. There was enough anger and pain here. They must keep calm, for Strif's sake.

"I think we should all go."

He swung round to face her. "What the hell are you talking about?"

"We need to leave here. At least for tonight. "

"Jo have you gone completely crazy? First you refuse to stay at home, now you want us all to go to the flat."

"Which we can't do because according to Strif your son by your first wife and his girlfriend are there."

"With my permission," Richard said stiffly. "Seb texted me and since you'd decided, against all advice, not to be there I saw no reason for saying no. They'll be gone tomorrow, so what's the hurry?"

"It's this place. There's something here. You felt it yourself, that time we went round Kingsfield. It's evil and it wants to destroy us. Can't you see what's happening?"

"Oh for goodness sake. Strif gets herself pregnant and all you want to talk about is some spooky feeling you have about the house."

"That's not fair. It's Strif I'm worried about. She's in danger and if we don't get her out of here, I don't know what's going to happen."

"Nothing is going to happen to her. She's going to have a baby; that's all. It will ruin any chance she ever had of a decent life and a good career, but that's as far as it goes. I know this is hard for you and I'm sorry you've had to face it like this, but that's it Jo. Anything else is fantasy."

"She can't stay here."

"You mean you don't want her here."

"No, I don't. I never did. But that's not the point. Please Richard, take her away. Take her to a hotel. Take her anywhere. Just get her out of here."

"You're obsessed. There is nothing wrong with Kingsfield. Whatever you think is going on, it's all in your mind."

In the corners of the room, the shadows thickened; the air became charged.

It's starting again, Jo thought. *She knows she's winning. She knows we're not going to leave.* She lowered her eyes, her lashes swept her cheeks, as if to brush away the tears, then she looked up.

"Please Richard, do this for me," she murmured.

"No," he said abruptly. "I'm tired, jet lagged. There's absolutely no reason on earth either to throw Seb out, or take a pregnant girl to a hotel at this time of night. If you still want us to go, then we'll go tomorrow. Perhaps by then you will both have calmed down and I will be able to get some sense out of Strif. Tonight she can sleep on the sofa."

Jo turned away from him; she saw her face reflected in the window. It looked like a white mask floating in the darkness.

Around it shadows of trees swayed in the rising wind. She felt the room grow colder as she waited for Richard to speak. The silence rose like a wall between them. She had begged him and he had refused her. Was this the end? Had Strif finally defeated them? With all their past histories, had their marriage ever stood a chance?

Their relationship had begun with a death. Had it been doomed from the start, like all the others? All the important people in her life had died, her father from an overdose, her mother in the accident, Ray's suicide. Even Ann's friendship had always had a sinister undertone. *Best friends, blood sisters,* the words echoed down the years. Was Ann still reaching out for her; making sure that she would always be hers?

Jo put her hand up to her face to wipe away her tears and something in her gesture must have touched him.

"Jo," he said and coming up behind her, he slid his arms around her waist. There was a moment's hesitation, a suppressed sob and she leaned back against him and he buried his face in her hair.

"It will be all right," he whispered. In the black glass of the window, their bodies merged. The room was warm, the air still.

"She's gone," Jo murmured.

"Strif?" he said puzzled.

"No. I don't know," Jo realised she had spoken her thoughts out loud.

Richard sighed.

"I didn't handle it very well, did I," he said ruefully. "Should I go and say something?"

"Mmm," Jo nodded, rubbing her head against his chest, enjoying the feel of him.

"I can't bear to think of it. Some lout with my child. Getting her drunk, or stoned then..." he shuddered. "God I could kill him. And Caro. Leaving her, all on her own, to cope with this. Dear God what good is her mother going to be?"

"None at all. That's why Strif needs you," Jo swallowed

back the flood of resentment that surged through her veins.

He let go of her reluctantly. "You're right," he said. "We're all she's got. You and me Jo, we're in this together. Aren't we?"

"Of course we are," she said firmly unable to bear the hurt on his face. "You know," she took a deep breath and looked him straight in the eyes. "I do love you."

"Thank God, I thought…"

"Don't," she put her finger on his lips. "We've had some tough times that's all. Go on, I'll make us some coffee. You go upstairs and get Strif.

Jo's hands trembled as she filled the kettle. It was true what she had said, she did love her husband that was something she could no longer deny. It wasn't necessarily going to solve the problems between them, but it was something to hold on to.

She heard Richard go to the foot of the stairs and call, then the sound of his footsteps as he went up, followed some minutes later by the echo of leather on bare wood as he came running down.

"She's gone."

"Oh God." Jo's hand flew to her mouth. She thought of the dark tunnel of trees that led from Kingsfield to the road and the indefinable feeling of menace that lurked there. Strif's brittle air of defiance would stand no chance against the evil that lay in wait for her and her child.

"She left this." Richard handed Jo a note.

"You don't want me, so I'm going. Send the stuff on later. Strif."

She's done it to make us feel bad, Jo thought. *She feels unwanted and so she's lashing out at us.*

"She can't have gone far. I'll get the car. You stay here and phone if she comes back," Richard said heading for the door. Jo locked and bolted it behind him. Then, although she knew that it was impossible for him to have missed his daughter, she searched the house. She went into the downstairs cloakroom, then the cupboard in the hallway. In both cases, she left the doors propped open as if there were someone in the house who might come in after her and lock her in the dark. She looked in the laundry and the kitchen. The living area was empty, the glass from the broken mirror spread over the floor.

Upstairs the bed had been made. The basin and bath cleaned; towels neatly lined up on the rail. In one of the empty rooms, stood the Moses basket piled high with the baby clothes she and Strif had bought that morning. A stack of nappies stood beside it. Everywhere was eerily tidy.

Jo placed her phone in the middle of the kitchen table. She brushed up the glass and emptied it into the bin, glancing constantly at the mobile, as if she could force it to ring. She wiped the surfaces, leaned against the sink and peered out of the window as if she could see beyond the circle of light that surrounded The Granary. The wind was gathering force, the rain beating against the windowpanes. She looked at her watch. Richard had been gone for half an hour.

If anything had happened to Strif in the drive, he would have found her by now, in which case, she must have reached the road. Then what had she done? Where had she gone? If she had hitched a lift, she could be anywhere.

Jo could not keep still. She paced from kitchen to living area and back again. As time passed and the phone remained silent, her anxiety grew.

Please God she was somewhere safe. Surely no one would hurt a pregnant girl. The floor lurched, sending Jo's stomach into her throat, turning her legs to water. What if Strif hadn't made the road? What if in the dark she'd taken the wrong turning and instead of going down the driveway had found herself at the front of Kingsfield House?

Jo clenched her fists and tried to still the wild beating of her heart. Then picking up the phone, she took her jacket and stepped out into the night.

CHAPTER TWENTY-FIVE

Rain sliced through Jo's clothes; it beat down on the cobbles and hazed the beams of the security lights, blurring the transition between the artificial brightness of the courtyard and the primeval darkness of the drive.

Driven by the storm, Jo fought to keep her footing on the rain slicked stone. Nothing was what it seemed. Lights slid behind the windows of the house, candles wavered and flickered, merging and dissolving into darkness. The wind tore at the trees, branches flailed and creaked. Voices muttered and rose beneath the tumult, then died away as the wind slackened. The rain was chill, yet sweat flowed from her body. The roar of the elements drummed against her head, her heart pounded in her chest, heat and cold merged into one. She was trapped in a nightmare, where her legs would not move and the weight of her body dragged her down, yet at the same time, she was running towards Kingsfield, leaping up the steps and shouldering her way through the door. After the battering of wind and rain, the house was silent, watchful and waiting.

She's here, Jo thought, *I know she is. They are all here.* She could sense them; smell them. The reek of hot wax, the acrid smell of coal burning fires, the heavy scent of flowers and musk overlying the rank perfume of unwashed flesh. They were there at the edge of her vision, beyond the corner of her eye. She spun round to catch them and saw nothing but shadows. Above her head, she could hear footsteps, the rustle of skirts, the opening and shutting of doors.

Where are you? She clenched her fists. *Where? Damn you.*

As if they were mocking her, the noises ceased. All she could hear was the pounding of the rain against the windows and the wail of the wind in empty chimneys.

She must be here, she must. But where? Where would she go and hide? Jo flung open doors to empty rooms, where shafts of darkness lay like ladders across the floor and the air was stale and still. She stepped into the corridor that led to the kitchen quarters; breathed in must and grease; called Strif's name and heard her own voice falter and die.

Then at last it came, a strangled, gasping sound that sent her racing up the stairs, the light around her mellowing and warming. The bedroom door was ajar, shadows looming over the bed where Ann lay. She was very pale, her eyes were closed, her legs spread wide, her body heaving.

"No!" Jo screamed. This was not what she had come to find. The room dissolved. Strif sat spread-eagled on a dirty floor. Her chest heaved.

"I can't breathe," she gasped. Jo knelt beside her. "Mum," Strif whimpered. Her body shuddered and she clutched desperately at Jo's hand. "The baby's coming and it hurts."

"I know." To Jo's relief once the contraction had passed, the girl's breathing returned to normal. "Listen Strif we need help. I'm going to phone for an ambulance."

"Don't go."

"I won't. I promise." *There's no way I'm going to leave you here,* she thought. *Not in this room, not where Ann died trying to have her baby. Not where Sophia is still waiting for another death.* She took the phone from her pocket and keyed in the emergency number.

"Where are you?" the dispatcher said.

"Kingsfield House," Jo gave directions. "It's empty, but the doors are open. She's upstairs, first bedroom at the top. And please, hurry."

"We'll be with you as soon as we can."

Strif racked by another pain cried, "I didn't know it was going to be like this."

Nor did I, Jo thought. *We're in the middle of something I don't understand. All I know is I have to keep you safe until help arrives. Where's your father when we need him?* She tried Richard's number. To her relief he picked up straightaway.

"Jo where are you? What's happening?"

- 193 -

"I've found her. She's here. She's in the main house. Richard, hurry."

"I'm on my way." Even as he spoke the phone was wrenched from Jo's hand and sent flying across the room.

Sophia was here, but there was no time to react. Strif's breathing had changed. She was giving short sharp pants, her feet were braced down against the floor and in the dimness of the room Jo could see the top of the baby's head. As the contractions reached their climax and the desire to push became overwhelming, Strif screamed. The sound echoed in the empty room, tearing through the curtain of time so that her screams joined the low animal like moans that came from the girl on the bed, as she too struggled to deliver her child. Jo could see them both, Ann moving her head feebly on the pillows and Strif panting and grunting, pushing and crying out loud for her mother.

A sudden, overwhelming hatred seized Jo, raging through her like a fever. She crouched down, muscles tense, hands trembling, avid with desire. Her body shook as Strif clutched at her arm, nails digging into her flesh, each stab of pain, an almost sensual pleasure, as it fed her rapidly growing rage, her mounting need to kill, to snuff out the emerging life. The girl gasped and cried out.

"The floor's too dirty."

Jo's mouth twisted into a smile.

Nothing's too dirty for you. Filth, that's what you deserve. A miserable snivelling child, flat chested and plain, coming here, stealing my man, taking him from my bed. Giving him my child.

"Please Jo. It's coming."

The voice inside her head subsided. Another side of her reached out and found a clean T-shirt in Strif's bag and stretched it out on the floor under the girl's straining thighs. Strif gave a cry and the child slid out into Jo's waiting hands.

*

It was his child. The boy that should have been hers. The child that would be acknowledged. The son that would inherit, not the daughter that must be hidden, never mentioned, only seen on secret visits. He would have not only Kingsfield, but the Great House, set among the cane fields where her mother's people had toiled and died. All that would be his when he came to manhood. If he came to manhood.

She wrapped him in the cloth, she held him close, his damp head against her arm, his puckered face looking up at hers, his mouth nuzzling, sensing the milk welling in her breasts. She pulled the cloth tighter. She swaddled the sleeping baby, drawing the linen tightly over his head, letting it fall over his face, her fingers lingering over the tiny button of a nose.

Ann had robbed her of her child, so she would take hers. Nicholas' son and heir, the boy he had scorned her daughter for. Her child was cast away, his would inherit everything. If he lived which was unlikely. His mother was already past help. She was bleeding heavily, gouts of blood sliding down her legs, her life seeping away. Now for the child. All it needed was a little pressure. It was as simple as dealing with an unwanted cat. She could not do it herself, trapped in this layer of time to which they had sent her, but the girl could. That pale whey faced creature that was almost hers. She knew only too well the pain of seeing other women with their babies when hers were gone. Lost to her for ever.

*

"Jo," Richard cried. His voice sliced through Sophia's bringing her back to the present where she found she was standing at the top of the marble staircase. There was a baby in her arms wrapped in an old T-shirt. There were, however, still voices in her head, images too. A girl, white and drained, lying on a bed, the sheets soaked with blood, her eyelids fluttering, her breath faint.

"Jo," he called again, racing up the stairs towards her.

It was like drowning in darkness, sinking down into unfathomable depths then surfacing into a terrible fear. She could not look. Remembering what she had heard, Jo dared not think what she had done. Instinctively her arms tightened around the child as her legs weakened and she fell against her husband.

"What's happened? Where's Strif?" Richard's voice was harsh with fear. The baby cried, a strong healthy cry.

"It's OK," Jo cried in relief. "It's all right. Oh thank God, it's all right."

She thrust the child at him and ran back into the room. Already she could hear the sound of the siren as the ambulance turned into the drive, could see the flash of light through the open door.

The smell of blood was strong, hot and metallic. Strif lay crumpled against the wall, her eyes shut. Jo knelt beside her and took her hand. Her skin felt cold, her hand limp unmoving, then fingers closed around hers.

Time switched and swirled.

"Oh my love, forgive me." She heard Nicholas say. His eyes were full of pain as he raised Ann's pale hand to his lips. Somewhere a baby cried. "Ann," his voice broke.

"It's all right love, we're here. You can let go of her hand." There was light and noise. Nicholas, Ann and their child had gone. In their place electric torches, bags full of equipment and people in yellow coats moving swiftly, competently. A small figure was loaded onto a stretcher and carried down the stairs and into the waiting ambulance. At her side, Richard holding his daughter's hand, whispering her name in a desperate attempt to keep her from slipping away.

CHAPTER TWENTY-SIX

Jo stood on the steps of Kingsfield House holding the baby. Richard's grandson. Strif's child. Not Ann's. She held him awkwardly, not wanting to be seduced by the warm, sweet smell of him, the softness of his skin, the round firmness of his limbs. The delicate fineness of his bones, the fragility of the skin stretched over the soft spot on his skull. He wriggled and snuffled against her and she was struck once more by the horror of what she might have done. Jo closed her eyes against the thought, bit down on the cry that rose to her lips.

"Strif!" Richard's voice was hoarse. He glanced up before getting into the ambulance. His face was ashen, lines etched deep around his mouth and eyes. Jo ran her tongue over dry lips.

"She's going to be all right," she said. He looked at her briefly. She braced herself, but there was no disgust or repulsion in his eyes, only his terrible fear for his daughter. Whatever had been her intention, when she stood at the top of that staircase with the new born baby in her arms, he must have arrived in time to stop her.

"Strif will be OK," she said firmly, making herself believe it. "She's young, she's strong."

Richard's mouth trembled. She wanted to reach out and touch him, but her arms were full. The baby whimpered. Jo made soothing noises and stroked his cheek with her finger. How could she have come so close to hurting him? He was so little, so vulnerable. Every instinct she had was to protect and keep him safe; she would never have harmed the baby.

"I'll take him, love," the paramedic held out his arms. "Paediatrics will need to take a look at him. It's just routine, the birth being unusual and all. You can come with us." He saw Jo glance into the lighted interior of the ambulance. "Or you can follow on if you'd rather."

"I'll do that. Thanks," Jo said. Reluctantly she handed over the baby. Somehow it did not seem right for her to go with Richard and his family.

The ambulance doors slammed shut. As it sped down the drive, Jo kept her eyes on the taillights, forcing her attention away from the brooding presence of the house.

Don't look back, she told herself as she ran back to The Granary. *Get in the car and drive.* Moments later, fumbling for her keys, muttering half-forgotten prayers under her breath, she unlocked the Mercedes and slid into the driving seat. Hands clutching the wheel, shoulders hunched, she turned into the tunnel of trees. Branches swayed in the wind. The powerful headlights threw grotesque shadows in her path. On either side the darkness closed in around her. Her chest was tight, her throat dry. Leaves skittered against the windscreen, the trees reached out towards her. Stifling her panic, Jo inched towards the pinpoint of orange light that marked the end of the drive.

*

Richard was in the waiting area. Unable to keep still, he was walking up and down.

"How is she?" Jo asked.

"They haven't said. She's in surgery."

"Dear God," she pressed her hands against her mouth. Her skin smelled stale. There were traces of blood on her palms. She sank down onto a plastic chair and shut her eyes against the harsh florescent light.

"You don't have to stay. You can go home," Richard's voice broke through her exhaustion.

Home where's that? The thought of Kingsfield made her shudder, but Seb was at Wharfside and there was nowhere else to go.

"Of course I'll stay, I've only just come."

"It could be hours yet."

You think I don't care, but I do, Jo thought wearily. *I might not like your daughter, but I never seriously wished her any harm. I tried to warn you about getting her away, but you didn't listen.*

"I can't leave her," Jo said. *I did my best. I stayed with her. I didn't let her die alone in that room. Sophia was there, just as she was when any baby was born at Kingsfield.*

"The baby's all right." Richard stopped mid pace and looked at her. "The doctor said you did a good job there."

"What?"

"You cut and tied the cord."

"I did?"

"There was no one else."

"I know but…" Jo shook her head. How had she known what to do? What had she used? She had brought nothing with her. In spite of the heat of the hospital she felt very cold.

"Are you all right?" For the first time since he had burst into the house, he was focusing on her.

"Yes. Why?"

"I was thinking of you, in that empty house, standing there holding the baby in your arms."

Jo's stomach plummeted. Dear God, perhaps she was wrong. Had he seen her hand hovering over that tiny face? Did he know how close she had been to pressing the life out of that small body?

"You saved them Jo. If you hadn't thought to look in the house, God knows what would have happened." He turned back to his pacing and Jo shut her eyes in relief. He did not know. He would never know. As soon as this was over, they would start again all three, no all four, of them.

"Mr. and Mrs. Avery," the doctor stood at the door. He looked young and exhausted. Jo forced herself to her feet. Richard's hand reached out for hers. "Your daughter has lost a lot of blood, but she's young and healthy. We've stopped the bleeding and she's going to be OK. They're taking her back to the ward now and you can go and see her."

*

They sat with her until she woke. Richard held Strif's hand. Jo watched the small body stretched out beneath the sheet, eyes closed, lashes long and dark against the white cheeks and thought of that other girl on her blood soaked bed. The girl who had teased her and played with her and shared with her the secret of her great love. The love that had destroyed her. Tears flooded her eyes and spilled down her cheeks.

"Don't cry," Richard said, his voice husky with his own unshed tears.

"Sorry. Must be reaction. Give me a minute and I'll be back." Jo headed for the ladies, where she locked herself into a cubicle and wept and wept. For Ann, for herself and for all the girls who had borne and lost their children in Kingsfield House.

Strif was awake when Jo returned. She was so pale, she was almost an outline against her pillow. *White on white, no colour, just form and texture. It was like the work I did with Kit, before he died,* Jo thought. Richard sat on a chair at one side of the bed, the baby lay in his crib on the other. Strif's eyelids fluttered.

"Nicholas," she whispered.

"Sweetheart," Richard leaned towards her protectively.

"It's his name."

"Nicholas," Richard said out loud. He smiled and pressed his daughter's hand. "It has a strong sound. I like it."

Standing at the foot of the bed, Jo felt her knees buckle. She gripped onto the rail to keep herself upright. *You can't,* she thought. *Choose any name but that. It's tempting fate. It's letting him into your life. It's too dangerous. We have to break free of them.* Fighting to keep her voice steady, Jo looked at Richard. "It's not a family name or anything is it?"

"No. Why?"

She lowered her gaze. "I was wondering why you chose it Strif."

A frown, faint as a ripple on the surface of a pool, passed over Strif's face. "I heard it. When he was being born. I dreamed, I saw…"

"Sweetheart don't talk. You're too tired. Now is not the time to be thinking of names. It can wait until later." Richard looked reproachfully at Jo.

"But it's important. I know it is…" Strif's voice trailed into sleep.

The fear Jo had been holding at bay coiled through her veins. Nicholas had been there with them. Strif had seen and heard him. One birth had mirrored the other. Each girl had struggled and screamed and bled; each girl had been without anyone who cared for her, and yet that was not quite true. Jo, by calling the ambulance, had saved Strif's life and in the end Nicholas had been there for Ann as she bled to death. Jo had a sudden memory of her racing down the staircase at Kingsfield and throwing herself into her guardian's arms and his pleasure at seeing her. Whatever his passion for Sophia, there had been some feeling for his young wife and genuine grief at her death.

"You don't like the name," Richard broke through her thoughts. Jo fought down a feeling of helplessness and forced herself to appear indifferent.

"Strif will do what she likes," she said, as nonchalantly as she could manage.

The baby gurgled; one tiny hand shot up above the rim of the crib.

"He's a lovely lad."

Flinching against the pride in Richard's voice, Jo nodded. Richard stretched out his hand and the baby's fingers closed around his. Jo could bear it no longer. She clutched at the strap of her bag, pulling it hard across her shoulder. "There are things Strif will need. I'll go back to The Granary and get them."

Richard spared her a glance. "Drive carefully," he said.

She walked out of the ward and past the nursery, where she could see the rows of cribs. One image gave way to another and she saw in her mind's eye fleshy coils of entrails, slippery with blood, and a heart, still beating, twisted around the Moses basket that waited in the spare bedroom. The pattern twined through the strands of willow, then dissolved and reformed itself into the shape of a blood stained child. Horrified, she pressed her palms against her eyes. The image faded. Bile rose in her throat and she swallowed acid.

Only a few hours ago, she had stood at the top of a stone staircase with Strif's baby in her arms and a voice in her head urging her to cover his face, to stretch the cloth over his mouth and nose and hold it down, until he could no longer breathe. Only Richard's arrival had saved him. If her husband had not come in time, what might she have done? Jo pressed her fists against her forehead.

"It wasn't me," she whispered. That need to destroy had come from Sophia. Her spirit had possessed her that night. It was the only explanation for what had happened. And yet she was not entirely blameless.

Jo moved her head from side to side, but there was no escape from the fear that it was her desperate need for a child and her resentment of Strif, that volatile mixture of dislike and pity that characterised her feelings for her stepdaughter, that had given Sophia her way in.

She used me, Jo thought. *She could do it again. And I don't know how to stop her.*

CHAPTER TWENTY-SEVEN

In the hospital car park, Jo fumbled in her bag for her phone. Her hand shook as she found Damien's number. He had to be there. Regardless of what had happened or not happened between them, he had to listen to her. He was the only person who would understand. He had sensed Sophia, Ann and Nicholas in the church. He knew what they were and would know what to do. He would help her fight. That was his job; he was a priest, for God's sake. With Damien's help she could unpick what was Sophia and what was her own part in what had happened. Once she had done that, then she could break free.

The phone rang and rang. Where was he? How could he leave her to face this on her own? Whatever was going on at Kingsfield was evil. It fed on grief and anger and showed itself in the deaths of children. The phone rang out.

Forcing herself to stay calm, she drove slowly back to The Granary. As she approached the pair of stone pillars that marked the entrance, her eyes were drawn to the road into town. If she took that route she could book into a hotel and there would be no ominous silences, or voices from the past. Once in her sterile, anonymous room, she would ring Richard and tell him where she was. But how would she explain her actions? If she told him the truth, he would think that the shock of Strif's baby had finally sent her over the edge into the breakdown he had feared since her last miscarriage.

There was no other way; she would have to go back to The Granary. She slowed, indicated and turned into the drive. The storm from the night before had subsided but rain drummed on the roof of the car, the windscreen wipers worked furiously. She would run into the house, grab what was needed and get out. That was the sensible thing to do. It would prove that she was still rational and concerned for Strif and the baby.

It was so dark under the overhanging trees, that her arrival triggered the security lights. She jumped out of the car and head down, raced for the door. The kitten was waiting on the doorstep. Wet, bedraggled and hungry he wound himself around her legs, mewing and butting her calves. Jo was flooded with guilt. In her desire to escape she had completely forgotten Diablo. She couldn't take him with her, either to a hotel, or to Wharfside. Temporarily he could go back into the cattery but long term she would have to re-home him. She looked down at the small furry body pressing against hers and knew that she would never part with him. Diablo was her cat, her guardian, he had to stay and he came with The Granary. Did this mean she had to stay too?

Jo found a tin of cat food and spooned some into his dish. Diablo threw himself on the meat, as if he were starving. Tail quivering he fed with utter concentration, while Jo drummed her fingers impatiently on the work surface. When the kitten had finished, he stalked into the living room and settling himself on the sofa began to clean his whiskers.

"Don't make yourself too comfortable. I'm going out again in a minute," she warned. The cat looked at her, then lifting up his back leg began to lick his private parts. "Balls to you too," Jo cried. Giggles rose in her throat; laughter fuelled by panic exploded into the room. It ricocheted from the walls. It swelled and grew until her stomach ached and tears poured down her face. She sobbed and gasped, then as a wave of grief and envy overwhelmed her, she howled and screamed.

Startled the cat scampered up the stairs. Jo yelled and swore. She cursed God and the universe for the unfairness of life. She paced and kicked at the furniture until finally, all emotion gone, she was completely drained of feelings. Her body relaxed, her mind was blank. She walked easily from bedroom to bathroom collecting disposable nappies for the baby, deodorant, shower gel and a big T-shirt for Strif.

"I've been stupid," she told Diablo, who had curled up on the bed. "You and I both know that I can't run away from here. I, God help me, helped to bring Sophia here, so I'll have to get rid of her. Then we can all make up our minds about what we're going to do. And that," she added bravely "Has got to include Strif and the baby. We can't leave her to Caro. That's the plan. OK cat?" Diablo looked at her with his big eyes and Jo bent down and tickled him behind the ears. "Good, now that's settled, let's check that bag and get going."

The bag was packed, she was ready to leave. She glanced at her watch and saw that it was almost the end of visiting hours.

"Be good," she told the kitten. He opened one eye. She scratched him under the chin and he stretched luxuriously, making it plain that he wanted more fuss. "That's your limit," Jo said. "I'll be back soon."

She went downstairs with every intention of leaving, but with every minute that passed it became increasingly difficult to leave the house. First she had to check the taps for drips and electric sockets in case they had been left switched on. When she finally got to the front door, she discovered she had left her car keys upstairs. Back in the bedroom, she stood in front of the mirror, tied back her hair then let it fall loose again. She petted the cat, which reminded her that she must wash his dish and finally when there was nothing more she could do to delay the moment, she went out into the gloom of early evening.

It was a short dash from the door to the car. Jo threw the bags on the back seat, shook the raindrops from her hair and put the key in the ignition. As she pulled out of the courtyard, a whirl of mist rose from the drive. Jo switched the wipers to full and the screen cleared, but the mist thickened; it blotted out the surface and began to solidify. Slowly, inexorably, it took on the shape of a woman.

Jo braked. She leaned forward, her hands gripping the wheel and peered through the glass. Ann stood in front of the car. One hand was raised, her wet hair fell in strands over her shoulders, her dress clung to her body and the rain ran down her face like tears.

"You're dead," Jo said. Her foot touched the accelerator.

"You can't be here. You died over two hundred years ago."
Ann did not move. The car crept forward. Jo closed her eyes,
the wheel beneath her fingers was slippery with sweat.

My sister, my best friend. The voice from so long ago filled
her mind. She killed the engine and sank down in her seat.
Help me. The girl stood solidly before her. Jo got out. She
went round to the boot and took out the torch. Then she swung
round and trained the beam straight at Ann, who flinching
against its brilliance covered her eyes with her arms.

Jo lowered the torch. The hem of Ann's skirt was crusted
with mud, her slippers were sodden, her ankles streaked with
dirt. The wind lifted her hair and blew her dress between her
legs. Water dripped from the lace around her wrists and ran
down her fingers. It trailed down the already sodden skirts just
as it ran down Jo's neck and soaked into the shoulders of her
jacket. This was no apparition. Whatever Ann was, she was
real. Jo drew in her breath.

"You must come," Ann held out her hand.

"I can't. I have to go out. There are things I must bring for
the baby. They can't wait. He needs them tonight." Ann gave
a cry. She grasped Jo's hands. Her skin was cold and wet, her
fingers little more than bone.

"They all die," Ann said.

Strif's baby too. Terror swept over Jo; she tried to pull free,
but the thin hands held her. "Let me go," she cried.

"I cannot. We must do this. I have to help you. As long as
she stays no one is safe." Ann bent her head and Jo saw the
fullness of her breasts, the curve of her stomach. She smelled
the milk in her and the acid note in the breath of a girl, who
had been starving herself. She thought how young she was
and how sad and her fingers curled around Ann's and Ann
tugged at her hand and they began to walk towards the house.
Remembering, how in other times, the stars had shone bright
and candles burned in the windows, Jo switched off the torch.
Instantly, Ann's grip tightened. "No, leave the light. We will
need it."

The ground was broken and uneven, flagstones jutting at

odd angles, puddles glinting darkly. The walls of Kingsfield were blank, stained with damp and patches of lichen. At the front of the house, the orange glow of the estate lit up the sky. From the end of the terrace it was possible to see the tall lamps of the motorway interchange, the endless stream of headlights and the dark shapes of the factories crouched along the side of the river.

Clinging to each other, they hurried across the lawn. The wind drove the rain into their eyes. Patches of long grass whipped against their legs. Shoes caked with mud, weighed down by their clothes, water running down their backs and into their mouths, they struggled towards the trees.

Under the oaks, the wind was still, the rain softer. Pinpoints of colour refracted in the darkness, as Jo shone her torch down the avenue. A narrow corridor of light opened up between the trees, edged by the stumps of ancient rock, squat and brooding, lining the way to the Satan Stones.

Ann's pace quickened, so that they were almost running. When they reached the Stones, Jo held the torch steady, focusing it on the upright thrust of the monolith, the worn circle of the round stone, its centre a dark hole. The slight rise on which they stood was running with water. Ann's thin-soled slippers slithered in the mud. She stretched out her hands to save herself and slid to her knees. She tried to get to her feet, but could find no purchase. Unable to stand, she crawled towards the Queen Stone.

A small puddle had formed at its base. Ann scooped it up and let the water fall through her fingers. Leaning forward, she stroked the earth and when she looked up, Jo saw that she was weeping. "Help me," she cried.

Jo shone the torch into the depression. "What do you want me to do?" Ann's hand shot up and fastened on her wrist. The expression on her face changed, became fierce and feral. Her nails dug into Jo's skin and as she pulled her off balance, the torch beam flared over the Stones and Jo crumpled down beside her. Ann crouched over the hole and began to dig. Hands black with mud, she scrabbled like an animal and all the time she wept. Jo put out her arm to comfort her and she flinched, as if she had been struck.

"Help me," Ann cried again. Her face was streaked with black, her body shook and her eyes were wild. Jo thrust her hands into the earth. The soil was cold, heavy clay. She grubbed up a handful, then another and another as she was seized by the need to dig. The rain beat relentlessly on her head and shoulders. The hole grew bigger; the water rose and as she hacked a gap in the mud, it spilled down the slope revealing a slab of stone.

Ann cried out. Clutching herself, she rocked back on her heels and screamed. Jo slid her fingers under the edge of the stone. Working her way underneath, the rough surface tore at her skin. Soil clogged her nails, the weight pressed down on her wrists. The muscles in her back jarred; her thighs burned. She breathed in, pushed up and one corner was free.

Jo tugged and pulled, cursing in frustration. On hands and knees, she crawled around the stone brushing away every trace of dirt, clawing at the rim of mud that held it in place. At last, shaking her hair from her eyes she knelt up and with her hands under the loose end, her feet sinking into the ground, she gave another push. The stone began to move. She had her arms under it now, then her shoulder. Balanced against her, it stood upright, before falling with a thud onto the slope of the hill.

Embedded in mud, a delicate tracery of bones curled around a tiny skull. Spine rounded, knees tucked beneath the chin, the child lay as if in the womb.

"She died. I let her die," Ann whispered.

"Sophia's child?" Jo asked. There was no reply, only the faint pressure of a shoulder pressed against her side. Jo reached out to pull her close, but Ann was gone.

CHAPTER TWENTY-EIGHT

The stand of trees behind the Satan Stones blocked the wind and blotted out the sky. In the light of the torch the child's bones lay curled as if in sleep. Sobs rose in Jo's throat. She thought of Ann desperate for Nicholas's love and the pain he had caused her by his passion for Sophia. Whatever she did, she could not prise the lovers apart, until at last, convinced that Sophia was going to poison her, she had persuaded Jo to help send her spirit into some other time. Had they killed her? Was that what Ann had intended? Or was Sophia already dead when they performed the ritual? Jo screwed up her eyes and pressed her lips together. Whatever they had done, they had not only unleashed Sophia's venom and hatred they had also robbed her baby of her mother. It was this child, abandoned and unloved that was heard over the centuries crying in the empty house. That child had died and Ann had had her buried beneath the Stones.

Was this reparation? Did she hope that Sophia's spirit would come back and claim her baby? Once she was pregnant did she realise the full horror of what she had done? Jo thought of Ann as she had seen her in the last stages of her pregnancy, the emaciated body, the distended belly, her fear of pain and death, then the birth itself, the hot smell of blood and her terrified cries. She had been little more than a child, when she died.

Kneeling on the rain soaked mud, Jo made the sign of the cross and taking her jacket spread it over the makeshift grave.

"You poor little thing, with no one to care for or love you, you didn't have a chance. We didn't mean for this to happen. We didn't know. But it's all right now. I'm here," Jo murmured. She folded back the material that covered the little head and tucked it tenderly around the space that held the bones. Then she sat back and rested against the upright stone.

The beam of the torch formed a circle of warmth and light.

She would sit and keep vigil with the baby for a little longer. It was what Ann wanted. In the end, after her own death she wanted to free them all from Sophia's curse.

"You see, it will be all right. It will." Jo leaned forward and pulled back the coverlet. She was not surprised when she saw, not the pitiful little skeleton she had found, but a baby's face, her round cheeks, the tremble of her top lip as she breathed quietly and peacefully. The baby stirred and put her thumb in her mouth. Jo lifted her jacket and gathered her close. It was time to take her home.

She could not manage the child and the torch, but at the end of the avenue the sky shone orange, lighting her way. The rain was cold; the wind wild, bending the tops of the trees. Her shoes squelched in the mud. She quickened her pace, eager to get back to The Granary.

The house was warm and full of light. Carefully she set down her burden, her jacket wrapped tenderly around the tiny bones. Then she sat down at the table and waited for Richard to come home.

*

Jo heard his car pull up; heard the front door open and shut, but she did not move. What happened next would be the test of their relationship. Either he would decide that she was in the middle of a breakdown and would want to look after her, dismissing what had happened at the Stones as a hallucination, or and this was what she hoped for, he would listen to her suspending his own beliefs and prejudices to take what she had to say seriously.

"Jo?" Richard spoke softly, his hand resting gently on her shoulder.

She blinked and saw the anxiety on his face. "It's OK. I'm all right. I've done what she wanted. It's all over now."

"What is?" He struggled to keep his voice steady.

"The haunting. Sophia, Ann. This is Sophia's baby. It's all right. I'm not mad. Honestly." Jo willed herself to go on. Richard had to listen, he must. Looking up into his face she knew without any doubt that she could not bear to lose him.

Through all the horror of the past few hours, he had been the one that had kept her safe from Sophia's power. There was a bond between them that not even her malevolence could break. Richard might be over protective; she might be spiky always wanting to break free, to be herself, but deep down there was love. If, however, he did not believe her where could they go from there? Her unexpressed grief over the loss of her babies, his fear of losing her had almost driven them apart. They had not listened to each other and if there were to stay together this must change. If not, however much she loved him, could she bear to stay?

Ignoring what lay on the table, Richard said, "Tell me."

"It's all bound up with the house. When you asked me if I'd ever sneaked up there as a child and I said I didn't remember. Well I didn't. I couldn't. I must have blanked it all from my mind, but since I've been here and …" she hesitated, swallowing back the pain, "lost the baby, that seemed to unlock memories and…" again she paused, uncertain how he would respond.

"Go on," he prompted and listened carefully as she told him everything she had done. When she was almost finished Jo took a breath then said,

"Sophia was there the night Strif had her baby. I saw…" she faltered. "I don't know how to describe it. All I can say is that I felt Sophia's anger and I knew that she was the one that was responsible for all the terrible things that have happened at Kingsfield over the years."

"And now you've found her baby?"

"Yes. Buried under the Stones. Ann led me there. I think she was trying to make up for what we had done. She wants to free me, to give me the chance she never had. If the child is no longer at Kingsfield, if we can find where Sophia is buried and reunite them, maybe that will put an end to it all."

Richard took her hand. For the first time, they looked at the tiny skeleton, nestled in the folds of Jo's jacket. Taking a deep breath Jo finished her confession.

"When I carried her here, it felt as if she was alive."

Richard tightened his grip on her hand. "It's all right. I know she wasn't. I think it might have been Ann's way of making sure I would bring her home rather than leaving her where she was. What happens now?"

"Leave it to me." Richard stood up. "I'm afraid we're going to have to ring the police. It's the only way, if we want to get her buried with her mother. Don't worry, we'll think of a good story for them. "

*

The police came later that evening. A young constable and a slightly older WPC, who quickly took charge. Richard and Jo sat on the sofa; he had his arm around her shoulders and she rested against him. She was very tired, but quite calm. Looking directly at the policewoman, she said,

"I went for a walk."

"In this rain?" There was a note of disbelief in the WPC's voice. Richard pulled her closer and she began the story they had prepared.

"I was going to the hospital with the things my stepdaughter needed for her baby. I'd got in the car and had started down the drive, when suddenly it hit me," Jo's voice shook. The policewoman looked up from her notebook, her pen poised. "I'm all right. It was just that we'd been trying for a baby for so long and I couldn't, I can't. I...." She stopped; shook her head and continued. "Anyway I couldn't go and see Strif feeling the way I did. I had to clear my mind, so I got out and started walking. I know it was a stupid thing to do, but I was in no state to think clearly. I took the torch and started towards the house. I didn't mean to go far, but the more I walked the better I felt, so I kept going. When I got to the Stones, I could see that something had scrabbled in the earth. I looked down and that was when I saw it."

She paused. So far everything she had said sounded plausible. She turned her mind from the image of the tiny skeleton lying in the mud and the even more vivid picture of the baby snuffling in her sleep.

"I'm sorry. I know I shouldn't have disturbed anything, but

it looked so little and so lonely." She closed her eyes. Richard's arm slid from her shoulders and he got to his feet.

"As I told you on the phone, my wife has not been well. She needs to rest."

The policewoman put away her notebook.

"That's all right, Sir. We've got the statement. We'll need to go up to the site, but there's no need for Mrs. Avery to come. So if you could show us the way."

*

"It's going to be OK," Richard said when he returned. "The policewoman was very understanding. She says they'll have to run forensic tests and look up their old files on missing children, but there was a scrap of lace in the hole which will probably date the child and if it does, then it's out of their hands."

"And the baby?"

"We'll find some way of proving she's Sophia's child."

"Thank you," Jo took his hand and lifted it to her lips.

*

They lay together in bed. Her head on his chest, his arm around her shoulders, cuddled close in the musky dark. They had slept long and woken late. Uncurling against each other, they kissed and came together again.

"I don't want to get up." Jo snuggled under the duvet. "I could stay here for ever."

Richard nuzzled at her shoulder.

"So could I, but there are things to do."

Jo rolled away from him. "Strif's things. I never got them to her," she said, throwing back the covers.

"She said to thank you."

"She did!" Jo stopped on her way to the shower. "Really? Strif?"

He nodded. "Really. She knows what you did. You saved her life, Jo and she is grateful. She might not seem it, but believe me, she is."

Struck by a sudden image of a spiky Madonna balancing a baby on thin knees, Jo ran downstairs for pencil and paper.

"Hey where are you going?" Richard called after her.

"Studio."

"What about breakfast. I'm starving."

"Don't worry. We'll have some before we go to the hospital."

"You mean you've got some food in the house?" he teased.

"Pig!" she threw back at him.

She perked coffee first. Then she sketched. Mother and child sitting; mother with child on her hip; mother lifting her baby up in the air, fat legs flying. Upstairs the shower ran, the electric razor buzzed, but she remained absorbed, until she heard Richard on the stairs. Then she pushed the drawings away, took croissants from the freezer, butter from the fridge and marmalade from the cupboard.

She filled a jug with milk, pouring some into Diablo's bowl. The black cat drank delicately and when he was full, settled in his spot on the windowsill. Jo set the table with blue and white china, arranging each piece as carefully as a still life. The kitchen was full of sunlight. Richard's favourite burnt orange marmalade glowed like amber, the coffee tasted smooth and rich with an underlying hint of bitterness. The croissants were buttery and crumbly. Flakes of pastry fell into their laps as they ate and Jo put out her tongue to lick the sweetness from her lips. She smiled and Richard leaned towards her.

"Later," she said. "I've got nappies to deliver."

"In that case you'd better get dressed." He cupped a hand around her breast, she blew him a kiss and stood up. Richard switched on the radio. Kingsfield House was headline news, on the local station.

"Police say they are keeping an open mind about the discovery of a child's body in the grounds, a police spokesman said this morning."

"God," Richard groaned. "Not the best publicity for our development."

"I don't know. It might not be that bad," Jo said carefully. "When they find out the truth, it might give the place a certain frisson. Some people like a tragic past. But if it does put off buyers you could sell that piece of land. It's far enough from the house not to make too much difference."

"You could be right. In fact it could be a selling point. It adds to the mystery of the Stones."

He's listening to me again, Jo thought. *We're going to be all right.* She smiled at him. It was a long time since she had drawn his face and it had changed, grown more solid, yet less fleshy, as if the bone was coming to the surface. Had she changed in the same way? She wanted to see them side-by-side in the mirror. A study in light and dark, she could call it. She rested her hand on his shoulder. He caught her fingers and kissed them.

"If you're not thinking of going," he said.

"We must."

"If you're sure." He slid her finger into his mouth.

She dropped a kiss on the top of his head and pulled away. "Not now." She felt very calm and a little detached. It was as if she had come to the end of a long illness, or rather a fast by which she had been strengthened and purified. Everything seemed new and vivid. Colours were brighter, objects more solid and tangible. Perhaps finding Sophia's baby was enabling her to come to terms with her own loss.

*

They went together to the hospital. Strif was sitting up, her drips and monitors had been removed and there was a hint of colour in her face.

"You can pick him up," she told Jo.

Although she knew it was the greatest compliment a new mother could pay, the symbol of her trust and the start of their new relationship, Jo approached the crib nervously, afraid of how she might feel. The baby looked up, his face creased and pudgy. A fat, little hand reached out and grabbed at her finger. She made soft, gurgly noises at him and he seemed to smile. Reassured, she picked him up. He was warm and firm. A nice cuddly, baby, nothing more.

CHAPTER TWENTY-NINE

"Strif can come back here. It will be all right," Jo said. She looked up from the sketch of mother and child that lay on her worktable and smiled at Richard.

"To The Granary?"

"Where else? She's due out of hospital in a couple of days and there's no room for them both at Wharfside. We only have the one bedroom and I don't see you giving up your king-size-plus for Strif and the baby. That apartment was never meant for a family." Even as she said it, Jo realised how true that was. Was that why she had been drawn to The Granary, to the house with room for a nursery and a large garden where children could play? If that was so it was the worst place she could have chosen. Not only had Sophia caused her miscarriage, her vengeful spirit would be a danger to any baby that lived at Kingsfield.

Jo shook her head ruefully at the irony. Richard drew her close and kissed the back of her neck. She let herself lean into him, drawing from his strength and solidity.

"If you think it's a good idea then we'll have to go shopping. We'll need a bed for Strif and some things for the baby," she said. Richard groaned.

"How much more can such a small baby possibly need? Neither of the other two had half of what he already possesses and now you tell me there is more."

"That's the way it is these days." Jo turned in his embrace so that she could reach up and kiss him. "Especially when you've got rich and doting grandparents."

"I wouldn't call Caro either rich, or doting," Richard said.

"Well maybe she will be when she sees him."

"When will that be? So far no one's been able to reach her. She's been known to go away for months on one of her sourcing expeditions. If that is what it is. My guess is she's holed up in some ashram doped up to her eyeballs."

"Do people still do things like that?" Jo disentangled herself gently. "Still even if they do it doesn't make any difference. She's not here. We are and we have to do what's best. At the moment there's nowhere else for Strif and the baby to go. When her mother comes back we'll see. Though I still think both of them will be better off with us."

"You're sure you're OK with this?"

"Quite sure," Jo said firmly. She was not going to give in to pain that lurked somewhere inside her at the thought of preparing a nursery at The Granary for Strif's baby and not one of her own.

"And the ghosts?"

"We found Sophia's grave and her baby will be buried with her. I've even designed the headstone. I would say that's enough. They're gone. It's been quiet here. It's been good."

"For me too," Richard said softly. "Even though the nights are drawing in I could get used to this rural living."

"Well don't spoil it with your expensive development," Jo replied. "Or at least make sure The Granary is well and truly hidden behind the trees and then we could all live here happily ever after."

"You and Strif!"

"Well…" Jo drawled. "I can try." She was determined to welcome Strif and Nicholas and to find some way that they could all be together.

*

Mid-afternoon and the sky was grey as slate. Rain dripped from the eaves, streaked down the windows and splashed into the sodden ground. Upstairs, the baby slept in his basket, while Strif lay on the sofa in front of the television, one hand dipping into a jumbo size packet of crisps, the other randomly pressing buttons on the remote control.

Jo straddling a kitchen chair, her sketchpad balanced on the back, bit her lip. The angle of the head was wrong. It should lie below the top of the sofa, so that the girl appeared cradled by the furniture. She wanted to capture contrasts. The sharp angularity of face and limbs, the soft roundness of the cushions.

Strif yawned and wriggled her shoulders. The crisp bag fell to the floor.

"What do you think of Blane?"

"Sorry, who?" Jo abandoned one sketch and began another.

"As a name." Strif's hair stood up at the back of her head. Her eyebrows were raised, her mouth puckered. "I thought you'd like it better than Nicholas anyway." She stretched her arms over her head. Milk leeched in star shaped patterns from her breasts. "I don't know why I chose it really. It was probably something to do with losing all that blood." She swivelled round to look at Jo. "Was there lots?"

"Of blood?"

"What else?"

"Don't be so ghoulish, Strif. You had a haemorrhage. You survived."

"I nearly didn't," she said proudly. The face on the paper took on a malevolent aspect.

"It's all over and you're OK," Jo said tersely.

There was a pause then Strif said almost too casually. "When it happened to you, did you see things?"

The sketchpad slid from Jo's fingers, the pencil followed, rolling away under the sofa. "What sort of things?" Jo said, carefully.

"People; a different room. I don't know. When I was having him, there was stuff I saw. Or maybe I didn't. I don't know." Strif's eyes skittered around the room. "There were voices."

"Can you remember what they said?"

Strif lifted her shoulders. "He said he was sorry. He held my hand."

"Who Strif? Who was he?"

"Nicholas," she whispered. "That's why I have to call the baby that. It's his name."

There was an inhuman yowl, followed by a hiss and a thud, as something fell to the floor. Strif swung herself off the sofa and pushing past Jo, tore up the stairs. When Jo arrived the duvet had been flung from the crib and Strif was standing by the window her face vengeful, the baby held against her shoulder, flushed and rosy with sleep.

"Your fucking cat. It could have killed my baby. He could have been suffocated, or got some disease or something and it's all your fault."

"Mine?" Jo shut her eyes against the onslaught.

"He's your cat. He must have got in somehow. You must have left the door open. Or something." Strif was sobbing; her body shuddering, her shoulders jerking. "Get it out of here."

The kitten cowered under the chest of drawers. Jo knelt to coax him out and he shrank further against the wall, his eyes yellow with fear. She slid her hand towards him and he bared his teeth and hissed.

He hadn't been trying to hurt the baby, Diablo had been trying to protect him. Right from the start he had attached himself to Strif. It was as if he had known that one day she would need him.

"It's all right," she murmured.

"No it's not," Strif howled. She was crying loudly, rocking herself backwards and forwards, clutching Nicholas like a doll. "Get rid of it. Now. I won't have it in here."

Jo clapped her hands and growled. Crawling on his belly the cat slithered out of the room. She shooed him down the stairs and cornering him in the kitchen, carried him to the door.

"It's only for a little while," she said, as she set him down in the rain. Diablo gave a little mew of protest and tried to dodge back through her legs. Then he cried out in disbelief as she shut the door.

"Is he gone?" Strif sat on the bed and put the baby to her breast. Two small hands closed round alabaster flesh, red lips sucked vigorously. The girl's face was drowsy with pleasure.

Averting her eyes, Jo examined the bedroom door. The handle was new and it took some effort to depress. No kitten could have done it. She pulled the door shut, then leaned against it, gently at first, then with more pressure and still it remained firm.

"Tomorrow we'll get a bolt for the outside of the door. To make absolutely sure this can never happen again," she said.

"Well it wasn't my fault. I closed it," Strif said defiantly.

So did I, Jo thought. *I was so careful. And if I didn't let the kitten in who did?*

*

In Westbury village Mr. Nowell's windows were filled with pots and pans, gardening tools, brushes, mops and haphazard piles of crockery. The whole collection blocked the light so that inside the shop everything was seen through a sepia haze. Winding her way past display cabinets filled with saucepans, casserole dishes, hammers, thick china cups and plates and plastic ware, Jo waited to be served. Behind the counter, wooden drawers, each one labelled in faded gold print, rose half way to the ceiling. Above them were shelves stacked with cardboard boxes.

Mr. Nowell's elderly assistant carefully wrapped three screws in a twist of brown paper, fastened it with tape then wrote out a bill. He handed the purchase to his customer and turned to Jo. "What can I do for you today, Madam?"

"I need a bolt for the outside of a bedroom door."

"To keep something out, or something in?"

"Does it make a difference?"

The man's head wobbled on his neck. "It might well, Madam." Climbing shakily onto a pair of steps, he pulled out a drawer marked "Tacks" and drew out a silver bolt. "I trust this will serve the purpose Madam."

I hope so too, Jo thought. *But I am not sure that it will.*

A gust of rain caught her as she walked out of the shop, then the clouds rolled away and a watery sun appeared in an eggshell sky. Drops of water sparkled on the windscreen; the pavements dried; the light grew stronger; sunshine hazed through the branches of the trees and when she walked into the house a sudden shaft of sun fell onto the sofa, where Strif lay. Her head was back against the armrest, her mouth slightly open, one arm lay at her side, the other dangling over the edge, while the baby sprawled precariously on her stomach. Strif murmured and shifted in her sleep. The baby gave a startled little cry and began to roll towards the wooden floor. Jo skidded towards them. Sliding onto her knees, elbows scraping the ground, she cushioned his fall. As her arms closed around him, Strif woke.

"Where is he?" she sat up, eyes blurred with sleep. "Why have you got him?"

"He fell." Jo's heart was beating wildly against the baby's body.

"He can't have. I was holding him. He was asleep beside me. I was between him and the edge. I was… " Strif's voice rose.

"It's OK," Jo soothed. "These things happen."

"He can't have fallen. He can't move yet. He's too small." Glaring at Jo, Strif snatched the baby from her arms. Nicholas began to scream. In his fury he arched his body away from his mother and her grip on him tightened. "See what you've done. You've gone and upset him."

"I haven't done anything."

"I know what you're thinking. You're thinking I can't look after him, 'cos I'm too young to have a baby."

"I did not say that."

"No. But that's what you meant."

"Don't put words in my mouth."

"Why not? That's what you're always doing to me."

Jo felt her temper slip its leash. "That's not true. It's never been true. I've always treated you with respect. I've never tried to interfere in your life. But since you asked. Yes, I do think you are too young."

"See, I told you." They glared at each other. Then Strif's bottom lip trembled and she buried her face in the baby's hair.

"Anyone's too young to have a baby at fifteen, but that does not mean to say that you can't be a good mother," Jo said gently.

The baby's sobs hiccupped to a standstill.

"Then why were you looking at me like that?" Strif muttered.

"Shock, surprise. If Nicholas had fallen on the floor, he could have been badly hurt."

"There you go again, blaming me." The front door opened.

"Don't let that fucking cat in here," Strif yelled.

Richard looked from his daughter to his wife. Strif scowled, Jo smiled warily. He kissed her lightly. "Anything I can do?" he murmured.

"I can cope," Jo said.

Strif sank back onto the sofa, lifted her jumper and began to feed the baby. Jo went into the kitchen and started chopping onions for a pasta sauce. Outside the window the edges of the day fuzzed into evening. A small black shadow sat on the windowsill and miaowed reproachfully.

Richard came down, hair still wet from his shower. Jo sneaked a wet cat in through the window and shut him up in the cloakroom. They ate in silence. Strif nursed the baby throughout the meal, ostentatiously moving him from one breast to the other, while shovelling pasta into her mouth. Jo moved her food around her plate. Richard ate quickly and drank most of the bottle of wine he had opened. Their faces were pale and flat under the central light and when Jo flicked it off and switched on the lamps, their figures blurred into shadowy shapes, hunched over the table.

Richard read "The Evening Post", spreading it out, so that its pages trailed over his dirty plate. Strif lifted the baby onto her shoulder, rubbing his back and rocking backwards and forwards in her chair, until his face wrinkled, he opened his mouth and burped. Milky crud lay thick on her jumper. In the cloakroom Diablo began to scratch at the door. The smell of dirty nappy seeped into the room. Richard looked up from the paper.

"Isn't it time you took Nicholas upstairs?" he said.

Jo scraped some of her meat into the cat's dish. She did not look at Richard. Strif pushed back her chair.

"If you're up to it, in a day or two we ought to get him

registered." Richard was determined to ignore his daughter's bad temper.

"Whatever," Strif snarled. Richard drew in his breath. "I think having a baby is cool," Strif looked pointedly at Jo. "Come on baby, let's go and give you a bath."

"Do you want any help?" Jo asked.

"I can manage, thank you."

Expected though it was, the rejection hurt, but what hurt even more was the sight of Strif's thin little figure going up the stairs. There was a brave hopelessness about her. A pathetic defiance.

"You having a hard time?" Richard slipped his arms around her.

"Motherhood hasn't sweetened her," Jo leaned back against his warmth. "She's just a kid. She should be at school worrying about GCSEs not getting up in the night to feed her baby."

Richard sighed. "I've been a lousy father."

"You did your best," Jo said.

"It would have been different with ours."

Would have, already past tense, strange that it did not hurt so much anymore.

CHAPTER THIRTY

Night gathered around the house, the fire burned low in the stove and shadows stretched out on the walls. Jo and Richard sat on the sofa, the cat between them purring gently. Richard played with her hair and Jo leaned back and relaxed. Growing sleepy in the warmth, Richard went to lock up, Jo to let Diablo out. The night was cold, the wind fierce, the rain slanting down from a turbulent sky. The kitten scampered off into the bushes and was back in minutes, his fur laced with raindrops. Ignoring his supper, he sat at the bottom of the stairs looking at them expectantly.

"Can we take him with us? He's got used to sleeping with me," Jo said.

"So long as he doesn't get any ideas about crawling in between us," Richard said.

They went up to bed together, holding hands like children, she leaning slightly against him. The sheets were cool, the bed deep and soft. Jo stretched out beside her husband. He put his arms around her and held her close. She reached up and kissed him. He stroked her hair and she snuggled closer. They held each other carefully, tenderly, not willing yet to ask anything more than to sleep in each other's arms.

Richard's breathing slowed, became more regular. The cat purred at Jo's feet. The darkness in the room was so thick, that even with her eyes open she could see nothing. The duvet was feather light, Richard's body warm, Diablo a hot, heavy shape against her legs. Drifting into unconsciousness, she was suddenly aware of silence. She sat up, fumbling for the light switch. Beside her, Richard struggled out of sleep.

"The cat," Jo cried. "I can't see the cat."

"He's there, at the end of the bed."

"I couldn't hear him. I thought he'd gone."

"If he's going to cause this much trouble, I'll take him downstairs and shut him in the cloakroom."

"No. "

"Then leave him alone and let's go back to sleep," Richard reached out for her, but she shrugged off his arm and slipped out of bed. "I thought you wanted him to stay."

"I do. I'm just making sure the door's shut."

"Of course it is," Richard yawned. "I shut it behind us." Jo pressed down the handle and let it go again. "I told you, I shut it," he said impatiently.

"I know, but he got into the baby's room this morning. He could have suffocated him. I've got a bolt to put on the door tomorrow, but tonight…"

"Tonight I want to sleep." He held out his arms and she went into them. For a long time, she could feel his heart beat against her chest then she began to dream.

Ann stood by the Stones a small bundle in her arms. At the foot of the incline a man servant dug a hole, then she knelt and slipped the little body into the grave. The moon was red as blood. A white owl cried a plaintive, mourning call and as she rose to her feet a tiny hand reached up and…

The crying woke her, jolting her out of the nightmare. Heart pounding she lay stiffly under the covers, telling herself that it was not Sophia's child that cried but Strif's. That little one had died from one of the many illnesses that plagued babies in the eighteenth century. Perhaps the neglect and lack of love she had suffered had made it more likely, on the other hand infant mortality was so high in those days that even if her mother had been there she might not have been able to save her. Whatever else Sophia might blame them for she and Ann could not be held responsible for the death of her child. It had happened long ago, there was nothing Jo could have done to prevent it and she had done what she could to re-unite Sophia with her daughter.

In the room next door Strif got up and the crying stopped. The wind moaned in the chimney, the trees lashed out at the sky. It was a wild night, full of tortured dreams. The kitten whimpered in his sleep. Jo leaned down and stroked him and gradually her thoughts calmed and she lay back against the pillows. Beside her Richard breathed evenly. Her eyes closed. She dreamed.

*

In a bedroom in Kingsfield, Nicholas and Sophia faced each other. His face was set and cold, hers wild with fury.

"How dare you bring her here to Kingsfield? You have gone mad Sophia. Do you really think I would ask my new wife to accommodate a bastard child?"

"She is your bastard, your daughter," Sophia hissed. "You were eager enough to take part in her making." She held up the child. "How can you deny the product of your love?"

"I do not deny her. I will make provision for her and for you."

"Make provision. What kind of words are those? I am Sophia, your love. We have loved each other since we were children. This is our child, our beloved daughter, see how beautiful she is." Sophia thrust the baby at Nicholas. Shuddering he recoiled.

"She is black as the ace of spades."

"No. See. Her skin is pale, as white as mine," Sophia ripped away the child's dress. The skin beneath the white linen gleamed like copper.

"You are the daughter of a slave. I will have a legitimate son to inherit my house and fortune."

"The fortune that whining miserable child you married, brought you."

"The fortune I am making to support my family. The children Ann and I will have and of course your child."

"My child. You cannot say that. She is ours, ours, ours," Sophia's voice echoed as the door closed behind him. "Ours," she cried again, beating at the wall with her fist.

*

Something was banging. A dull persistent thud of unutterable loss and misery. Jo tried to focus. Was it in her dream? She sat up slowly and listened. She could still hear it. Was it a door? Or something outside the house that had loosened in the wind? Carefully, trying not to disturb Richard, she slid her legs out of bed, but before she could get up a hand grabbed at her.

"Where are you going now?"

"To see what's making that noise."

Richard pulled the switch. Light flooded the room. Diablo yawned showing sharp white teeth. Richard frowned.

"Sounds like a window."

"I'll check." She was at the bedroom door.

"I'll come with you."

Richard turned towards the stairs to check the ground floor, but Jo stopped him. She had no doubt where the sound was coming from. As she pushed open Strif's door the air was icy. The wind blew the clouds from the moon, splashing puddles of silver light onto the floor.

Strif lay on the bed her baby in her arms. Their faces drowned in moonlight, hair glistening, clothes clinging to their bodies. The duvet lay on the floor, the sheets were wet, the pillow soaked. Richard slammed the window shut. Jo knelt beside Strif. Her skin was cold, the baby's lips blue. Jo rubbed the girl's hands and called her name. At first there was no response, then Strif's eyes fluttered open. She looked up and smiled.

Richard brought towels. He stripped Nicholas and wrapped him tight. Jo pulled Strif's T-shirt over her head. She was limp as a doll, eyes blank, lips still smiling as if lost in some mindless dream. Jo forced her to her feet and walked her into the bathroom. She turned on the taps and hot water steamed into the room. Strif blinked against the light and began to shiver. Her whole body trembled. Nicholas whimpered.

"I'll put the heating on," Richard said.

"And bring some hot drinks, tea, coffee, anything," Jo said.

She helped Strif into the water and handed her the naked baby.

"I'm cold," Strif murmured, her voice faint, as if it were hard for her to speak.

Jo scooped water over Strif's back. Nicholas lay on his mother's stomach. His arms and legs moved, as if he were trying to swim.

"What happened?" Jo said. Strif leaned back; she lifted her baby, so that his head was on her shoulder as she sank deeper into the water.

"It's cold in the ground," she said.

"Strif!" Jo cried, her voice sharp with fear.

"What?" The snarl was back. "There's no bath oil in this water. If I don't have some, my stretch marks will show." Jo almost wept with relief.

Later, Richard stoked up the log burner and they sat wrapped in duvets, Strif wedged between them on the sofa as if by staying either side of her they could keep her safe. She slurped the tea that Richard had brewed, but her belligerence had faded and after a while she snuggled down against the cushions and began to yawn. Richard brought down the Moses basket and Jo made up a bed on the sofa. They sat at the table in the kitchen watching Strif and her baby sleep.

"There was nothing wrong with the window latch. I checked it," Richard said.

"I know. There was nothing wrong with the door handle and still the cat got into the bedroom."

"That suggests it was no accident," Richard said reluctantly.

"It's crazy, but I think you're right. There is no other logical answer and it's the third thing that's happened today. First the cat, then Strif apparently letting the baby roll off the sofa and now this." Jo let the coffee, black and bitter, slide down her throat. "I think something wants to…" she put down her mug. "Oh God Richard I don't even want to think this, but it isn't all over. They're still in danger."

Richard looked across at his daughter and her son. The lights in the kitchen had been turned down low, in the stove the wood glowed red above a bank of ash.

"Sophia hasn't finished with us. Is that what you're saying?" he asked. Jo hung her head and nodded.

"I wish Strif had never come to Kingsfield," she said. "If only she'd stayed in Bristol, if only you'd been at Wharfside, or me, or anyone. Oh why didn't she stay with Seb? He'd have taken her in, or at least found her somewhere to go and contacted one of us."

"There's no point in thinking like that. What's done is done. We can go back tomorrow. We'll manage in the apartment until we find something else."

"I wish it was that easy," Jo gnawed her lip. "I think that whatever it is has to be dealt with, or it will follow us for the rest of our lives."

"Ghosts don't travel, Jo. If they exist at all, they are locked into a place."

"I know. But Strif's called him Nicholas and who's to say that at some time in the future she won't be back here. Look at me. When I left Weston Ridge I didn't think I'd ever be back." Richard took her hand and squeezed it.

"You didn't have to come. Nothing made you. You were the one that insisted on The Granary. If you hadn't bought this house, then I would never have got the rest of the estate."

"I don't know about that. I don't think it was that simple. Don't you remember how desperate I was to get this place?" Richard nodded and she went on. "On one level it didn't make any sense. It would have been much more sensible to buy some closer to Wharfside, but for me there was no question, the studio had to be here at Kingsfield. It was as if I was being driven. My past was catching up with me. If I didn't face it then, it would never let me go."

"You weren't well. It was only a few months before that that you'd had that miscarriage. The one where you'd nearly died. It was still preying on your mind. You weren't acting rationally."

"I know. And we weren't speaking. You wanted to give up on having a family."

"I wanted to make sure that never happened again. Oh God Jo, you don't you know how close we came to losing you." Jo nodded. Richard lifted her hand to his lips and kissed it. "I couldn't bear to go through all that again. Knowing that it was my fault. If I hadn't made you pregnant then you wouldn't be bleeding to death."

"It was my choice too."

"True, but you weren't about to lose the person you loved most in the whole world," Richard said bleakly. Jo got up. She went over to Richard and pulled him close. He rested his head on her breast and she held him for a moment or two.

"There was so much anger and grief in our lives and that's what she works on," Jo said after a while.

"Knowing Strif she'll have her fair share of that."

"If life doesn't deal it out to her, she'll find it somewhere," Jo agreed a little shakily. "Or maybe not if we can help her. Whatever happens we can't guarantee that she will never be enticed back. Her or Nicholas. We simply can't leave them with that possibility."

"OK. What do you suggest?"

"There's someone I can ring," she said. "I'll call him in the morning. He's a priest I know, he'll help us."

*

"Father Damien can't take calls. He's still very unwell," the nun's voice was reproachful.

"I didn't know…"

"Maybe not, but if it's important you can speak to him when he gets back. He's off to convalesce in the morning."

"Right, but if you could…" Before Jo could finish, the nun's tone changed.

"Oh very well Father if you insist."

"It's all right Sister. I won't talk for long." Damien's voice grated as if his throat were raw.

"What's happened? Are you OK?"

"I'm getting better. There was an accident. It happened the day before I was due to see Father King. I was called out in the night to this old man. They said he was dying and needed a priest to give him the Last Rites. He wasn't even a parishioner but there was no one else." Damien's breathing was jagged. "I was on my way to Sea Mills, when it happened." Jo's stomach lurched. The sound of the accident rang in her head. She knew what he was going to say next. "I saw her Jo. Sophia was waiting for me on the bridge. She means to hurt you. There's only one person, who can help you. You have got to go and see Father King."

CHAPTER THIRTY-ONE

A single shaft of light filtered through the stained glass. It fell like the finger of God on the figure behind the desk. As he rose to greet her, Jo saw that the priest was thin as paper, his eyes dark sockets in a face stretched over bone. He appeared wracked with fever, but his grip was dry and firm, denying any suggestion of sickness.

"Please make yourself comfortable," his voice was strong and cool. A skeletal hand gestured towards the chair opposite him. Jo sat down. Knees together, bag at her feet she kept her hands neatly folded. Memories of school, of being in Sister Edwina's office, surfaced and were hastily discarded. She must not let herself be intimidated. Peter King leaned back, his drooping eyelids giving him the look of a basking reptile. Jo's stomach fluttered as she waited for him to speak.

The room was sombre, heavy with Victorian furniture, the windows hung with velvet curtains, the walls covered in embossed paper and religious paintings in ornate gilt frames. Jo glanced at the crucifix directly above the priest's head and wondered if he had chosen the shining image of a triumphant Christ, so different from the maudlin suffering of the rest of the art that surrounded him. If it was his choice then what did it say about this man whom she was going to have to trust with a child's life?

"Would you begin by telling me exactly why you are here Mrs. Avery."

Jo resisted the temptation to moisten her dry lips.

"I came because Father O'Connor said you could help me."

"Ah yes. Father O'Connor."

Was there some hidden meaning in the priest's tone? Was he trying to imply something about Damien? Whatever it was, Jo resolved to stay calm.

"I talked to him when it first began. He thought he could

help me, but after the accident, he realised the situation was beyond our control. That was when he suggested I came to see you."

The hooded eyes half opened.

"In what respect did Father O' Connor think I could I help you?" Peter King steepled his fingers.

"I'm sorry. I don't think I understand."

"Let me make it clear. I take it we are talking about the realm of the supernatural and not the emotional?" The priest's eyes were directly on her, their darkness unfathomable. Jo's fingers tightened. She could feel her anger rising.

"What do you mean by emotional?" she parried.

The four feet of Father King's chair touched the ground. His lips distended into a smile.

"You are troubled by something beyond the physical," he said.

"Yes," Jo admitted. "But they're not emotional things. What I've seen and what I've heard is not something I've imagined. I don't have hallucinations. I'm perfectly sane."

"Of your sanity, I have no doubt. If Father O'Connor had had any concerns in that area he would not have referred you to me. He would have suggested some other form of assistance."

"You've spoken to him?"

"I have. He had made an appointment to see me. The accident, however, intervened."

"So you do believe me."

"I believe that you have seen and heard things that are beyond your power to explain. My role is to establish what they are and, if they are in my area of expertise, how I can help you."

"You can make them go away?"

"The Church has laid the duty of exorcism on my shoulders. If you are prepared to trust in that and to put yourself in my care, then I am sure the matter can be resolved." Once again the dark glance. "If that is indeed what you want."

"Of course it is," Jo bridled. "That's why I am here."

"Forgive me. You must understand that not everyone wants to free themselves of the dark elements. For some people they add an excitement and meaning to their lives that they are loathe to lose. In spite of anything they may say."

"I want it to be over. I've had enough and so have my family."

The priest nodded. He positioned an old fashioned tape recorder in the middle of the desk.

"I trust you have no objection if I record our conversation. It will assist me in keeping track of the data, that is, time, place and number of appearances. These facts can be crucial to building up a picture of the manifestation. I will need as much information as possible, so I can make a decision as to the best course of action. Are you ready to begin, or do you need to compose yourself?"

"No, I'm OK. I came prepared." Jo smiled thinly.

"Then let us begin. Tell me everything, including how you felt before and after each occurrence. Don't concern yourself with making sense of the phenomena. That will be my task."

"I understand."

"The analysis will come later."

Jo took a deep breath.

"It started when I was ten years old..."

Father King listened intently as her tale unfolded. Occasionally, with a sharp downward flick of the hand he gestured for her to stop. Then he switched off the tape and wrote swiftly in his notebook, before nodding to her to begin again.

"I thought, when I found the remains of Sophia's baby, it would be over. That if mother and child were re-united then she would be at peace and perhaps even forgive me for what I had done."

Father King let out a meaningful breath.

"Interesting that you should put it that way. From what you have said I have gained the impression that you see yourself as guilty. However, it appears to me that you were a tool,

- 234 -

rather than a perpetrator. You were not the one who used evil spirits to gain what she wanted."

"Ann wasn't evil, she was afraid." Jo looked the priest in the eye. "And I think she was right. If she had not done something to rid herself of Sophia then I believe her life was in danger. Sophia would have done anything to have Nicholas to herself."

"Hmm," the priest half closed his eyes.

"When we sent her through the Stones, Sophia died soon after. Whether Ann meant that to happen or not I don't know. Sophia's spirit is here, but her body is buried in a churchyard in Bristol and I helped to kill her."

"It was not your intention."

"No," Jo cried. "I told you, I didn't understand what was happening and I don't think Ann did either. She wasn't versed in magic like Sophia. She was fighting for her life. She'd seen me come and go and all she wanted was to send Sophia to where I had come from."

"Then she appears to have succeeded. She has unleashed a troubled spirit into our time. A soul that requires sending to its rest. Tell me, have the episodes of possession become more frequent, or more intense?"

"Neither. Sophia seems to have left me alone."

"Then what exactly is the problem?"

"I think the baby's at risk."

"Spiritually, or physically?"

Jo was taken aback; she had not considered the risk to the child's soul.

"Certainly physically. Three things have happened where he could have been seriously hurt, or even killed."

"None of these incidents have anything to do with you." It was a statement not a question. The priest went on to explain, "In most cases the manifestations are caused by the victim's own psyche, but in your case I do not believe that is so. In the first place, you have been refreshingly honest about your feelings towards your stepdaughter and her child. Secondly, these occurrences were happening before you were even aware of the pregnancy. They stem back to your childhood, where again there are emotional factors, such as your need for love and the forging of a close bond with a child in similar circumstances to your own. However, never once did you use what was happening to you to gain attention from others. This is a typical scenario particularly in cases of poltergeist infestations, when very often the problem stems from the victim themselves. Thirdly, we have to consider the question of Kingsfield House itself."

Once again the chair tilted at an impossible angle, the fingers linked on the chest, the lids drooped. "Kingsfield has a long history of such incidents. From Medieval times the Stones have been associated with fertility rituals, which is no doubt a folk memory of their initial purpose. There have been rumours of child sacrifice, although I do not believe them to be of any significance. What is of importance is that even before the house was built, Kingsfield was a place both revered and feared.

There have also been more recent deaths. Just after the war, a child was murdered in the grounds, another went missing only two years ago and there have been sightings. During the period when the house was used as a home for unmarried mothers one of the sisters reported seeing a dark haired woman in a red dress in their nursery."

"Sophia!" Jo let out a pent up breath.

"Possibly," Father King said dryly. Jo clenched her fists.

"Did she hurt any of the babies?"

"There is no record of anything untoward."

"So nothing was done?"

"No doubt the good sister made the sign of the cross and wished the spirit on its way."

"Nothing more?" Jo was incredulous.

"It was before my time. The home was closed not long afterwards."

"And that was it?"

"I've heard nothing more, until you came to me."

That doesn't mean anything Jo thought. *If it hadn't been for Damien, then I wouldn't be here. New people, new families would move into the estate and whatever it is up there, would have gone on and on.*

"What happens now?" she asked.

"After you leave, I will listen to the tape and study my notes. I will pray and then I will make a decision to determine the best course of action."

"You'll do an exorcism?"

"I have yet to decide. In my opinion, the spirit that haunts you does not know it has died. She is trapped in this world and needs to be released into the next. It may be that all that is necessary is to bless the house. However, that in itself gives rise to certain dilemmas as the spirit has been seen and experienced in a number of different locations. Logically, therefore, since you appear to be the link then you must be the focus of our attention." The priest shut his eyes. "I will consider and I will pray."

Jo leaned her arms on the desk.

"There isn't time."

Eyelids rose like shutters over blank windows.

"I admit that the danger to the child gives cause for alarm. Tell me, has he been baptised?" Jo shook her head. "In that case, I would advise Baptism without delay. The sacrament in itself may be enough to protect him."

"I'm not sure his mother would agree."

"His father then."

Jo said nothing.

"It would not be possible to ask him?"

"It could be difficult," she conceded.

The priest rose to his feet.

"I am sure you will do your best," he said putting an end to the interview. He led Jo through a corridor hung with paintings of saints. At the door she turned to him.

"When will you come?"

The dark eyes flickered and for the first time, she saw a recognition of her fears.

"I will ring you tomorrow," he said and raising his hand,

he traced the sign of the cross above her head. "God go with you, Mrs. Avery."

"Thank you," she murmured in response.

"And may He and His holy angels protect you and keep you safe from all evil," the priest added as she ran down the steps to the car.

CHAPTER THIRTY-TWO

Strif stood by the sofa, her baby in her arms. "Dad! Do something!" she screamed.

"My God, Strif. Don't worry sweetheart. We'll get him to the hospital."

"He can't breathe. He's choking and I don't know what to do."

Standing on the threshold of The Granary, her key still in the lock, Jo stared in horror at the scene in the living room. Hissing and spitting the kitten tore past her. Nicholas gave a strangled cry and fell limp against his mother's shoulder.

Please don't let him die, Jo prayed. *Holy Mother of God not now. Not after all she's gone through, don't let Strif lose her baby.* She reached for her phone to dial the emergency number, but before she pressed the key, the baby's body heaved, his eyes flew open and he vomited, then began to cry.

"I'll call the doctor," Jo said.

*

"There were marks on his throat," Strif muttered defiantly.

The doctor snapped her stethoscope back in its case. "It's good that you called me, but in my opinion the child is fine. There's nothing to worry about." She wrote on her pad; tore out the page and handed it to Richard. "I've prescribed a mild tranquiliser. A first baby, a young mother. It's always stressful."

"She's breast feeding," Jo said.

"In that case a tranquiliser won't be suitable. Just keep your daughter calm. Take some of the responsibility off her shoulders. Perhaps you could take care of the baby at night. To give her a break, that sort of thing."

"We will do whatever we can," Richard said, as he showed the doctor out.

As soon as she had left, Strif subsided onto the sofa and began to weep. "I don't want to be here," she sobbed. "It's not safe. You saw it too Dad, didn't you? You heard him choking, like someone was pressing on his chest."

Richard glanced at Jo. "I saw it," he said. "But it's OK now. He's fine. You heard what the doctor said. There's nothing wrong with Nicholas."

In his basket by their feet, the baby gurgled and waved his fists in the air.

"I want to go home. I don't want to stay here." Strif's face was blurry with tears. "I want to go now."

"You can't. Not yet, not straight away. I'm going to ring Father King and ask him to come over. There's something we have to do first," Jo said gently.

"I don't want to." Strif rubbed her eyes. "Dad, don't make me stay."

Richard's face was very serious. "I think you'd better listen to Jo," he said.

*

"It happened when you were on your way back from seeing me," Father King's voice on the other end of the phone was tense. "In that case we have no choice. Have you prepared your family? "

"They know what has to be done."

"Good. Then I will be with you tomorrow, at noon."

"Tomorrow? But what about tonight? Anything could happen," Jo's voice rose.

"It is the earliest I can come," the priest said. In the meantime, take the child and his mother away from the house."

*

They spent the night in a hotel. It seemed simpler than going back to Wharfside. Richard booked a suite and Strif insisted on sleeping on the sofa in their sitting room.

"I won't sleep. Not on my own. Stay with me, don't go." She clung to her father.

"It's all right. I'm not going anywhere. There now." Richard sat and held his daughter's hand until she fell asleep, then crept in beside Jo, leaving the door between the rooms open.

In the morning, a blue sky arced over the river and a lemon coloured sun floated amid trails of white cloud. Jo stretched out in the tangle of sheets. "A new beginning," she murmured.

"I hope so." Richard turned on his side and kissed her. "Let's hope this guy is as good as you say he is."

Or else, the words hovered unspoken in the air, *we will never be free of this.*

*

The sun brightened into a deeper gold. In The Granary Jo swept soft drifts of dust from the four corners of the living area. She rubbed polish into wood, breathing in the smell of lavender and wax. She sprayed windows with blue liquid from a plastic bottle, then polished until the glass sparkled and the room dazzled with light. In the kitchen, taps and tiles gleamed. Fresh linen lay crisp on every bed. Rubbish was emptied and the cat banished to the garden. On the unit that divided the kitchen from the living area she placed the glass bowl, she had bought that morning.

When she had finished, she showered and put on clean clothes, so did Richard and Strif. Their dirty garments were placed in a plastic bag and locked in the boot of Richard's car. The baby was changed and dressed in white.

Father King arrived promptly with Sister Rosemary. His manner was brisk and business-like. "First let me explain to you what I propose to do this morning. As our priority must be the safety of the child, I would suggest, most strongly, that he should be christened." He looked at Strif and she nodded. "Good. Mr. and Mrs. Avery will stand as godparents and after the sacrament the mother, the newly christened child and you, Mr. Avery will be required to leave the house."

"Is that necessary?" Richard asked.

"Most certainly. The rite of exorcism that I will perform on Mrs. Avery demands that only those who believe can be present. The young are especially vulnerable to demonic possession and it is a requirement that any children present should be blessed and sent to a place of safety. Sister

Rosemary will take you, Mr. Avery, your daughter and her child to Our Lady of Sorrows."

"I'm not a Catholic, Father, but I was christened and confirmed and if Jo is at risk I want to be with her."

The priest considered. "You accept there is a danger here. That may in itself be enough."

"I know there is a danger here. What kind and where exactly it comes from, that's what I don't know." He took Jo's hand. "On the other hand, if you think my being with her will make things worse, then I will leave."

"There's no need. You can stay. Your love will give her added strength."

Jo's fingers tightened around Richard's. He returned the pressure and gave her a quick smile. Father King opened his case. He took out a white cloth and a pair of silver candlesticks, which he placed on the counter and beside them he set a vial of holy water and a small silver box. Murmuring a prayer, he slipped a white silk stole over his shoulders then motioned to Strif to step forward.

They stood in the sunlit room, Strif holding her baby, his head positioned over the bowl as the priest poured the holy water and said,

"I baptise you Nicholas, Richard, Joseph. In the name of the Father and of the Son and of the Holy Ghost. Amen." As the water ran over the back of his head, Nicholas gave a yell and mother and godparents exchanged glances and smiled.

There should be champagne and cake to celebrate, Jo thought irreverently, then stopped herself. W*hat's wrong with me? Why can't I concentrate? This is serious for God's sake. Father King has come here to face Sophia and all I can do is think of parties and cake.*

"Go in peace and may the Spirit of Our Lord Jesus Christ protect you and keep you safe from all danger." Father King made the sign of the cross over Strif and her child then Sister Rosemary picked up the baby's bag and led them out to her car.

The house felt warm and light. Dust motes danced in shafts

of sun. Jo stifled the urge to yawn.

"Are you ready?" Father King asked. She nodded. "In that case we will proceed with the exorcism." The priest turned his gaze on Jo. "Mrs. Avery, I do not believe that you are possessed of a demon as such, but I do believe that the unquiet spirit, who has made her home in this place, uses you for her own ends. For that reason, it would be beneficial, if you underwent the ritual of exorcism."

"I understand."

"Good. Mr. Avery will you place a chair in front of our temporary altar and position yourself behind it, so that you are ready to restrain your wife, if it becomes necessary. If the spirit is within her and does not wish to leave, there can be a physical as well as a psychic struggle. To prevent harm to the person being exorcised it is helpful if they are held. You understand?"

Richard nodded. Father King's face was taut, his voice dry.

"We begin with the blessing of the salt and the water. These two elements will work with us to drive out the spirit." He poured holy water into the bowl and taking a pinch of salt from the small silver box sprinkled it three times over the surface in the shape of a cross praying that, "Wherever this creature of salt and water be sprinkled with the invocation of Your Holy Name, spirits will be repelled and the fear of evil banished."

Jo felt Richard's hands on her shoulders. His touch was warm and firm. Inviting. Hurriedly, she closed her eyes against a sudden vision of Sophia leaning against the wall of the barn; her voice husky, her breasts rising and falling above her tightly laced bodice as she opened her lips to her lover.

The priest made the sign of the cross. He took Jo's hand and led her to the chair.

"If she moves, throws herself about, or shouts, hold onto her shoulders and keep her as still as you can," he told Richard.

Jo leaned her head back and looked up at her husband. His face was grim and set, as if he was the one about to do battle with demons.

He's taking it seriously, she thought. *So why can't I? What is wrong with me? I know how important this is, but somehow I don't seem to be able to concentrate as I should.*

Father King began with the Lord's Prayer. The familiar words came firmly and resonantly from those thin lips, but instead of finding comfort and strength Jo's mind skittered like a leaf caught in the wind.

"Deliver us from evil." Richard's voice, clear and firm brought her back to herself.

"For Thine is the Kingdom, the Power and the Glory, now and for ever Amen," she responded.

The priest raised his hand for the blessing, then taking his bible began to read from the gospel of St. John. "In the beginning was the Word and the Word was with God and the Word was God."

Words, thought Jo, *have such power. Pictures show what is, or has been, or even might be, but for most of us it's words that make things happen. They make us what we are. Melinda said I was beautiful and I stopped seeing myself as a plain little girl. Kit said I had talent and look what we achieved together. Richard tells me I am loved. My promise to Ann bound me to her. Ann's words sent Sophia out into time.* She shuddered. Richard tightened his hold on her shoulders and the warmth and comfort of his touch calmed her fear.

Sunlight caught on mirrored surfaces and refracted arcs of colour over white walls. Father King swung the censor and incense rose drowsily into the air. Jo shut her eyes. Flecks of gold shimmered behind her eyelids, deepened to amber, then ochre, sliding into scarlet, silken skirts that rustled, echoing the mocking laughter that grew fainter as the priest's voice strengthened.

"I command you to depart from this creature of God and return to the place appointed to you, there to remain for ever." Drops of water fell on Jo's face, she raised her hand to make the sign of the cross and Richard grasped her wrists. "Leave her." The priest was smiling. "She is no longer in any danger."

"Is it over?" Richard said.

"Except for the blessing of the house."

"Jo, are you OK?"

"I'm all right." She turned from him to the priest. "I didn't feel anything." Father King held her gaze.

"People react in different ways," he said neutrally.

Frankincense and cinnamon smouldered on a bed of charcoal, blue grey smoke drifted up to the ceiling, as each corner of The Granary was blessed and its spirits exorcised in the Name of the Father, the Son and the Holy Ghost. Then Father King took holy water and sprinkled it along the thresholds, sealing the doors against all evil, before going outside.

The late afternoon sun dipped behind the trees, throwing into relief his dark figure as he asked to be admitted with the words,

"Peace be to this house and all that dwell herein." Then the priest stepped back inside; Jo crossed herself and so did Richard.

"It is finished," Father King said softly.

"There will be no more ghosts?" Richard said.

"This house is at peace," the priest said.

CHAPTER THIRTY-THREE

Jo stood at the door of the barn and watched the Porsche disappear down the drive. Richard had business in London, but he would be back in a few days. In the kitchen the washing machine purred and Strif sat on the edge of the table, gnawing at a piece of toast.

"I've fed him and he's clean," she snarled.

Jo took out her sketchpad and drew Strif as an angry goblin, her arms and legs elongated, her face twisted with spite. The girl scratched absently under her arms and Jo pencilled in sharp tufts of hair and a row of metal rings spiked through one ear.

"What you doing?" her stepdaughter demanded.

"Working."

"Yeah well," Strif shrugged and sloped off to play with her baby.

Jo gritted her teeth. What were they going to do with Strif? Until Caro came back she would have to stay with them, but when she returned would Strif want to go and live with her mother? Would Caro want her daughter and her baby? It was unlikely that she would prove a responsible, let alone doting grandmother. On the other hand, she would give Strif the freedom to do exactly what she wanted, which for a rebellious fifteen year old was bound to be a great attraction. And what in that case would happen to the baby? Who would look after Nicholas?

She can go, but the child belongs here. The thought, or was it a voice in her head, startled her. The first, faint feeling of unease slid up her spine. Nicholas had been born at Kingsfield so he would always have a connection with the place. But was it more than that? Was there still something here that would hold him and never let him go?

"That can't be right. It's all over. He's been christened. There are no more ghosts," she said out loud. "You agree with me, don't you?" The kitten, sunning himself on the windowsill, opened one eye then shut it again. "You do," Jo persisted and her voice had an edge of desperation to it.

I need someone to talk to, she thought. *Or I'll go crazy.* She glanced at her watch. Richard would still be on the motorway. Who else could she call? Damien was convalescing and it would not be right to trouble him, even if she could find out where he had gone. Father King had gone to Rome for a conference, but he thought his job was done and if it wasn't then he was not the one to help her. Jo frowned. There was no one. Then the phone rang.

"Jo," Helene's voice was urgent. "Cecile and I need to see you. When can we come?"

"Come to supper tonight," Jo breathed. "You have no idea how glad I am you called."

*

Jo looked at the vegetables spread out on the work surface. The aubergines with their bitter flesh and crowns of thorns, the fleshy folds of the red peppers, the thrusting shape of the courgettes, the dark red onions each layer stained as if marinated in blood. Her hand shook as she cut and sliced, sweat stood on her forehead and she had to stop and wipe it away from her eyes.

"I've got him off to sleep." Strif wandered into the kitchen, hair lank, T-shirt stained, jeans ripped at the knees. "He won't stay like that for long," she added ominously.

Oh go away. Leave me in peace. Jo swept the thought from her mind. The air in the kitchen clotted with tension. Her stepdaughter's boredom and dissatisfaction radiated through the room. In spite of her decision that Strif could live with her and Richard, moments like this were never going to be easy. Jo's skin crawled with irritation. She knew Strif couldn't help it, that she was both a confused and mixed up teenager and a very young mother, whose hormones were still in overdrive, but the stupid girl had everything Jo had ever wanted and she couldn't see how lucky she was. Jo's anger coiled ready to strike, an explosion only averted by the arrival of a car in the courtyard. Strif threw her stepmother a baleful glance and stamped off into the living area, where she hunkered down on the sofa.

"Behave," Jo hissed through gated teeth. "Please," she added as she hurried to the door.

Helene stood with her hand on the doorpost, her fingers searching the surface of the wood. "The sign of protection, it's gone. That's not good," she murmured as Cecile stepped forward, arms open and swept Jo into her embrace.

"Jo, I'm so sorry. We should never have left you like we did," she cried.

"We have to talk." Helene strode past them into the living room. Her face was stern and drawn and Jo felt her stomach churn and sweat prickle the back of her neck.

"Perhaps not in front of ..." Cecile nodded towards Strif.

"It's OK. Whatever it is, I can take it. It can't be worse than what I've already gone through. We had to be exorcised," the girl said with a hint of pride in her voice.

"Then she's gone?" Cecile spoke, as if there was no need for explanations.

"I don't know." The feeling of dread that had been lurking at the back of Jo's consciousness could no longer be denied. "Father King said the house was at peace, but..."she shrugged. "I'm not so sure."

"This will help." Cecile held up a small fluted bottle. The glass was opaque, the colour a deep, rich blue. "It's a concoction of blackthorn, oak and Hyperion. For protection."

"What? We're going to do aromatherapy?" Strif snorted.

Jo spun round. "Stop it," she snapped.

"Sorry!" Strif snarled.

The visitors ignored her. "So much has happened since we were last here." Helene's eyes moved around the room, her expression serious and intense.

"I've had a baby." Strif was determined to be centre stage. The two women exchanged a horrified glance then Cecile said carefully,

"How lovely. Is it a boy or a girl?"

"A boy. I've called him," the merest pause, the slightest intake of air, before she said the name, "Nicholas."

Cecile's eyes widened, but Helene forced a smile. "A good, strong name," she said.

"He was christened," Strif said.

"Then let us hope that is enough."

"You don't think it is?" Jo's throat was dry, as fear struck a belly blow. She clutched the back of the sofa and only Helene's hand under her elbow stopped her from falling.

"We'll tell you all we know, but first there are certain things we must do," the older woman said.

At Helene's direction they sat around the table. Helene lit candles, then Cecile pulled the cork from the bottle and circled them, sprinkling its contents and murmuring words of protection as she did so. When she had finished, she took the chair next to Jo and began,

"Helene and I have been away at a conference."

"Of witches," Strif interrupted wide-eyed.

"It was a meeting with like-minded women, some of whom have highly developed psychic powers," Helene said dryly.

"Witches," Strif repeated and no one contradicted her.

"Because we were concerned about you, we talked to other women about the threat we'd sensed here and we performed certain rituals," Cecile drew in her breath. Her eyes focused on the flickering candle flame and when she looked at Jo, her pupils were black pools rimmed with a faintest line of blue. She was very pale and her body swayed slightly as she spoke.

"When the trance caught me, I found myself walking down the avenue of oaks. The moon was up and the trees cast a ladder of light in front of me. I moved between the shadows and all I could think of was the power of the Stones. I knew I could use them to destroy her," Cecile's voice rose, grew stronger, thicker. "Oh how I hated Ann; how I longed for her destruction. Blood would bring blood, vengeance and death." Cecile's body shuddered. Her face contorted. Helene put her hand on her arm.

"Enough of Sophia," she said sharply. "Cecile come back

to us." Her daughter's eyes closed. Her head fell forward. The air crackled, then slid away, draining their lungs. Jo clutched the edge of the table. Strif whimpered and moved closer to her stepmother.

"I was her. I was Sophia." Cecile's eyes were calm. She seized Jo's hand. "If we'd known, we'd never have left you unprepared."

"Was she so dangerous?" Jo said.

"For you and Strif, yes," Helene said.

"Why?" Strif clenched her fists, her eyes fierce.

"She wants your baby," Cecile said.

CHAPTER THIRTY-FOUR

"Stop it," Strif shrieked furiously. "You're making it up. You're…" her voice faltered as she looked at the faces of the women, pale and solemn in the candlelight.

Jo leaned forward and touched her arm. To her surprise Strif did not flinch. "Shall we listen to what Cecile has to say," she suggested.

"You said she was gone. You said it was over," Strif snarled, but her hand clasped Jo's.

"That's what Father King told me," Jo said.

"Did you believe him?" Helene asked.

"I wanted to. But somewhere inside me I knew it was not over."

"That was your inner eye, your sixth sense if you like." Helene looked directly at Jo. "If you let it, it will always show you the truth."

Cecile nodded.

"Over the centuries that she has spent outside her time Sophia's hatred linked to the power of the Stones has made her increasingly powerful and dangerous," she said.

"Too strong for Father King?"

"His rites will not banish a spirit bent on evil," Helene said.

"What has that got to do with Strif and the baby? I can understand why she hates me, but why Strif and Nicholas?"

"Yeah why me? What have I done?"

The two women looked at each other.

"We don't know," Cecile admitted. "All I can guess is that she will use the baby to harm you and Jo in some way."

"But he's not mine," Jo murmured.

"No, he's not," Strif said. Helene put her hand over Jo's pressing it in a brief moment of sympathy.

"He is in some way linked to you and to the past."

"I can understand that. He was born in the house where

Ann had her child. Is Ann then the link? Is it because Ann was my friend?"

"Ann could be the reason. It is possible that your link with her was something Sophia intended to use. We've puzzled over it, but we cannot make the connection. All we know is Sophia hated her and would have done anything to destroy her," Helene said.

"It was only Nicholas that stopped her," Cecile added.

"He cared for her," Jo said.

"He needed her." Helene's judgment was harsher. "From the start Ann was the victim, a pawn in the game between Nicholas D'Aubeney and his foster sister."

"Sophia was his sister!" Jo's stomach lurched.

"Possibly not by blood, but we don't know for sure," Cecile said. "Sophia's mother Aphra did nurse both children. She was Sir William D'Aubeney's mistress and he brought her back to England from Jamaica when he inherited the title. She was his slave, but he was completely in her power. It was rumoured that it was Aphra's skill in the black arts that caused the deaths of his father and brothers so that he inherited the title he had always wanted. Whatever the truth of the matter, he bought her a house in Bristol, settled money on her and tried to put her out of his mind. But you cannot cross a woman such as Aphra. Time had no meaning for her. She knew that all she had to do was wait.

Word spread about her powers and although witchcraft was against the law, people came from far and wide to consult her. For her own protection, she took lovers, who were always rich and powerful men and all the time she waited," Cecile paused. The air outside the circle seemed to tremble with menace.

"Do you want me to go on?" Cecile asked. Mutely Jo nodded.

"Then something totally unexpected happened. Instead of acknowledging his mistress and legalizing their relationship Sir William fell in love with a young woman and married her. Kingsfield House was to be a symbol of their great love, where they would raise a new dynasty. At first it seemed all would be well. Even before the building was completed, Lady D'Aubeney fell pregnant. However, she was not very strong and when it looked as if she would lose her child Sir William summoned Aphra. Throughout the pregnancy she treated her master's wife, promising them both, on her life, that the child she would bear would be healthy and strong. As indeed he was.

His mother, however, died when he was born. Sir William was plunged into despair. He abandoned Kingsfield leaving his son to be nursed by Aphra, who had not long had a child of her own.

The two children, Nicholas and Sophia were brought up together. Sir William travelled abroad, returning to Kingsfield from time to time, but never staying for long. Eventually he died in France."

"Which is why there was no grave for him in St. Michael's," Jo said.

"He wouldn't have wanted it," Cecile said. "He hated the place and spent no time here. As soon as Nicholas was old enough he was sent away to school. Aphra returned to Bristol, but she left Sophia behind. Whether it came from the child or the mother I don't know, but there seems to have been an understanding that Sophia was to stay close to the Stones. The village girls used them to practice white magic. They asked for strong lovers and healthy babies but as Sophia grew older she studied the dark side, the way of power.

When Nicholas was nineteen, his father died. Sir William had squandered his fortune, the estate was almost bankrupt, there were no servants left, the house was empty except for Sophia. She was waiting for him. I saw her," Cecile's voice grew warm and dreamy. "She was there in the hall to greet him, her hair falling down her back, her skin glowing like dusky silk. He could not resist her. He did not try. They had loved each other since they were children, so…"

"They saw nothing wrong with the arrangement," Helene finished dryly, her astringent tone cutting through the overheated atmosphere.

Jo moistened her lips. "They went on being lovers, didn't they? They were in The Granary, or rather the barn that it used to be. I saw and heard them. No. It was more than that. It was as if I were her. It was the first time, she…" Jo put her head in her hands unable to continue.

"It's not your fault. She is a very powerful being and you had no way of knowing what was going on so you could not protect yourself. Even when I knew, I had to be so careful," Cecile added, giving Jo an understanding look.

"What did she make you do?" Strif asked.

"I think that does not concern you," Helene said firmly.

"OK. I was only asking. Why if they were so mad about each other didn't they just get married?"

"Because in those days they couldn't," Cecile replied. "For a start Sophia was coloured. She was the daughter of a slave and Nicholas needed a wife from the right social circle. She also had to be rich. A wealthy bride was the only way he was going to save himself and the estate from total ruin.

A couple of times he almost made it to the altar. Once to a young heiress, who died suddenly a month before the wedding, then to an older woman, a widow with a vast fortune, who rejected him, when she was visited by a gypsy who told her that if she married a man younger than herself she would not live out the year."

"Sophia," Jo breathed and no one contradicted her.

"What about Ann?" Strif asked.

"She was a distant cousin," Cecile continued. "She was orphaned when she was six, and her family was very, very rich. Sir William was her godfather and once he had died Nicholas, as her only remaining relative, was appointed her guardian. It was too good an opportunity to be missed. Ann was brought to Kingsfield and put in Sophia's care and it was understood, from the very beginning, that when she was old enough she and Nicholas would marry."

"But he was old," Strif screwed up her face in disgust.

"She loved him," Jo murmured, remembering Ann's face

- 254 -

when she spoke about her cousin Nicholas.

"So did Sophia and you can see how things began to take shape. Nicholas's kindness to his ward fuelled Sophia's hatred. What made it worse was that she was growing older as Ann was growing up. Ann was never beautiful, but she was young and desperately in love and after they married Nicholas appeared to fall for his new wife."

Strif rubbed her eyes fiercely. "He was with her at the end," she whispered. Jo stared into the surrounding shadows, reliving the night that Strif had given birth in Kingsfield House. "He held my hand and said he was sorry," her stepdaughter said.

"Poor child," Helene murmured.

There was a wisp of sound, like the faint echo of laughter. The women looked at each other. They waited, ears straining to catch the slightest noise. Silence settled into the corners. The candle flames burned steadily. Strif gave a loud sniff,

"Then what happened?"

"Nicholas left. Sophia and her child were dead, Ann too. Like his father, there was nothing to keep him at Kingsfield. He fled to Europe, where he drank and whored and did everything he could to blot the past from his mind."

"What about his kid?" Strif said.

"He didn't die with his mother, at least he's not buried with her," Jo said remembering Ann's plain stone.

"And no one knows for sure? That's horrible. I don't want to hear anymore." Strif stood up. Her face was a whitish grey her eyes huge.

"I know," Helene soothed. "Why don't you go and see your baby, while we figure out what has to be done."

"Fucking shit." Strif rounded on Jo. "You promised when Father King did his stuff. You said it was OK. You said she'd gone." She gave an angry sob and fled from the room.

"I'll go and see if she's OK," Jo said.

"Will she let you?" Helene asked.

"I think she might. She's not as hard as she appears. She's afraid and confused."

Cecile caught hold of Jo's arm. "Let her go. It's better if she's not here. She's too young and volatile for this."

Even as she spoke the cry came from the garden. A screech of terror followed by hissing and spitting, then a strangled gurgle, a whimper and silence.

"Diablo," Jo cried. Flinging open the door, she rushed out into the night. The light from the house spilled out onto the lawn, but it did not reach the bushes at the edge of the woodland, where an injured cat would crawl to hide. Jo called and called, but there was no answering miaow. Helene brought a torch and the three women searched the shrubs and the long grass.

Cecile found him. He lay in the shadow of the door, quite still. She knelt down and stroked the cooling fur, then she called Jo. Jo wept as Cecile covered the kitten's body with her scarf. "He was trying to keep you safe." Cecile's face was grim.

"It's Sophia," Helene cried. "I think she is in the house."

CHAPTER THIRTY-FIVE

Jo raced up the stairs. When she reached the bedroom door, she made herself stop and knock, hoping against hope that she would find Strif sprawled out on the bed, the baby beside her, or asleep in his crib.

The room was empty. She called her stepdaughter's name. There was no reply. Her heart thumping against her ribs, Jo searched the other rooms. In the bathroom, the baby's bath stood upended against the wall, his towel hung over the radiator, his dirty clothes were in the hamper. He had been bathed and put to bed, so where was he?

"She's not here is she?" Helene was standing at her shoulder, Cecile beside her. Jo stood by the crib and looked at the soft indentation of the baby's body on the mattress, smelled the sour scent of regurgitated milk. She put her hand on the sheet. It was cold.

"She can't have gone. We would have seen her."

"We were in the garden searching for Diablo."

"Where would she go?"

"I think you know the answer to that," Helene said grimly.

"Sophia has them. She has them both," Cecile said.

"I knew she hadn't gone, but Father King said we were safe and I wanted to believe him. Oh God, we should never have brought Strif and the baby back."

"Don't blame yourself Jo," Helene said.

"I trusted him."

"You had no reason not to. The priest believed that the exorcism had worked. He thought he had sent Sophia on her way."

"Then why didn't she go?"

"Because she is very clever and very powerful. Father King has had only one lifetime to learn his craft; she has had two centuries," Cecile said.

"Her powers are female," Helene said slowly. "That perhaps is the answer. Maybe she will only listen to her own kind."

"She knows how to manipulate men," Cecile added. "And she had no belief in a Christian God"

"I should have known. When he did the exorcism, I felt nothing. I couldn't concentrate properly. I knew it was serious, but all I could think of were things like who should we invite to the christening party. And I heard her laugh."

"She was playing with you. She wanted you to think that Strif and the baby were safe."

"Where has she taken them?" Even as she asked Jo knew the answer. "They've gone to the Stones haven't they?"

Cecile nodded solemnly. She turned to her mother.

"We may still be able to stop her."

The two women faced each other. Looking deep into each other's eyes, they joined hands and stood silently for a moment, gathering their strength. Then Helene turned to Jo.

"You stay here."

"No. I'm coming with you."

"There's nothing you can do," Cecile said.

"I don't care. I can't stay here."

Cecile looked at her mother.

"Tell her, she can't come. It will be hard enough for us without worrying about someone else."

Jo clenched her fists.

"I am coming with you. I must. Strif's my responsibility. If it wasn't for me, if I'd never got involved with Ann and Sophia none of this would have happened."

"It will be dangerous," Helene warned.

"I know, but I have to be there. Please. I can't explain, I don't understand it myself, I just know."

Helene put her hands on Jo's shoulders. At first her palms were cool and firm, then they grew warmer and warmer and as the heat flowed from her, Jo's mind opened up. A tumble of images seethed through her consciousness. A heavily pregnant Ann leaning on her as she helped her towards the house; Ann and Nicholas on their wedding day, shadowy figures in St. Michael's church; Jo and Ann at the Stones, Ann chanting her spell the sky dark with menace and foreboding; then a younger Ann racing down the great flight of stairs to throw herself into her guardian's arms and Ann taking a pair of scissors and stabbing them into her hand. Two hands joined together, a trickle of blood seeping between the palms.

Helene leaned forward and drew Jo into her arms. She held her for a moment, then stepped back.

"You're right Jo. We can do nothing without you. You are the focus for what is going on. We can't help Strif, or her baby, without you. Come." Jo took her hand, Helene joined with Cecile, who took Jo's other hand and they circled, three times clockwise, three times widdershins, as Helene chanted,

"Spirits of earth, air, fire and water we beg you protect us and keep us safe." She loosed their hands and traced the sign of protection first on Cecile's forehead then on Jo's. Then Cecile did the same for her mother. Helene took salt and sprinkled it into their pockets. She blessed them again and then grasped Jo strongly by the hand.

"May Mother Earth grant you the strength and protection that you need this night," she said.

In the courtyard their cars hunkered beast like on the cobbles. The dark bulk of Kingsfield loomed in front of them; walls leprous with mould, windows staring like empty sockets. The moon hung low above the roof, its light sickly in the hectic glow rising from Weston Ridge. Cars roared through the estate, a siren shrieked, brakes squealed.

In the shelter of the ancient oaks the sound of traffic was muffled, the light of the sky dimmed. Dark against a darkness that thickened as they approached stood the Satan Stones. At their foot was a small figure clutching a white bundle to her chest.

"We're not too late," Helene breathed. "Go carefully, don't startle her."

"Strif."

Helene frowned a warning, but neither Jo nor Cecile had

spoken. Out of the darkness a woman's shape materialised.

"Give me the child," her voice was gentle. Her long, dark hair flowed down her back, her dress was pale in the shimmer of light that pierced the centre of the Queen Stone. Strif bent her head. She kissed her baby. Sophia held out her arms.

"No," Jo stumbled forward. "Strif don't."

The girl did not move, but in Sophia's arms a baby wriggled and kicked.

"Hush my little one. Hush Nicholas." Sophia raised her head; she looked directly at Jo. "Now I have his son, he will love me again. I have waited for you for so long and now you are here, you can make up for what you have done and all will be well." Sophia began to move towards the Stones, her outline merging into the light.

"Don't let her go." Cecile's fingers dug into Jo's arm.

"If she does, the child is lost," Helene said.

Jo hesitated. Strif would recover. She was young. She had the rest of her life in front of her. In a short while, it would be as if she had never had a baby. She could go back to school, life could go on as it was and Jo could forget how easy it was for Strif to bear a child. Let Sophia take the baby, it was for the best.

"Jo, call her, keep her here," Helene's voice was insistent. The light grew stronger, dazzled.

"She's going," Cecile cried. She released her grip on Jo, but Jo did not move. Deep within her, she wanted Sophia to take the child; wanted Strif to suffer as she had. Why should the ungrateful brat have what she had been denied, over and over again? Her shoes sunk into the damp grass. The light began to grow dimmer and what had been unbearably bright became opalescent, as Sophia, holding the child, stepped through the Stone.

"She's gone. We were too late," Helene said heavily.

Strif sank to the ground. Holding the limp body of her baby in her arms, she rocked on her heels and began to weep.

CHAPTER THIRTY-SIX

Strif's weeping echoed around the Stones. The sense of loss, of universal grief was almost unbearable. She was both an awkward teenage mother and all mothers since the dawn of time mourning the death of their children. Watching her, pain sliced through Jo's body, leeching the air from her lungs, the strength from her legs. Sinking to the ground, she pressed her arms against her chest, as her heart contracted in an agony of loss.

Then Strif called out his name and gazing across at her Jo was shaken by the realisation that this was partly her doing. If she had acted sooner, moved faster, Sophia would not have reached the Queen Stone in time, but she had given into to her worst feelings and if the child was lost it was her fault.

"No. Not this time. Not again. I won't let it happen again." Staggering to her feet she stumbled towards the top of the rise, but it was as if some invisible power was holding her back. Fighting her way upwards, every breath burned, every gasp seared her throat, sending her head spinning, until she was conscious of nothing but a deep overwhelming need to sleep. Fragments of darkness danced before her eyes. She fell to her knees and as she did so, her hands clutched at the King Stone. She pressed her face against the cold surface and the pain began to ebb, leaving in its wake an unshakable determination that she would not let this child die.

Her body felt weightless, cleansed. Knowing what she must do, Jo stood and turned towards the Queen Stone. The entrance was narrow, like all sacred paths, but she had only to bow her head…

"Jo don't," Helene's voice called out in the darkness. "Don't go through the Stone."

"I must. It's my only chance." Dimly she sensed Cecile scrambling up the rise towards her, Helene following calling her back. Jo focused on the pearlescent light shining through the Stone.

"Jo," Helene's voice rang out. "Do not follow her."

"I have no choice."

"That's not true. Turn around. Look at us. Listen. You must listen. If you go with her, she will take what you hold most precious. You can't save him without paying her price."

"I must bring him back."

"It's too late," Cecile wept. "The child is dead."

All my children are dead, Jo thought. *Each and every one of them. They leave the warmth and safety of my womb in a tide of blood.*

"Don't," Helene cried.

For me and for my children there is no hope. Unlike Strif and Helene and no doubt one day Cecile, I will never know what it is to be a mother and to have my own child, but I will not, I cannot let this baby go. Whatever it costs I will pay the price.

Jo stepped through the circle.

*

For one moment she appeared in its centre, her figure dark against the light. Cecile threw herself forward, her arms outstretched to pull her back, but before she could reach her, Jo had gone.

"It's too late. Why didn't we stop her? Why didn't you tell her? It's always a life for a life," Cecile cried.

"I did not think it would come to this. I thought we could fight on our own ground. I did not think Sophia was so strong," Helene said.

"She's stronger than all of us and now she has Jo. The light is going. She is leaving. We can't let her go."

Helene put her arm around her daughter's shoulders.

"I am not sure there is anything we can do."

*

Jo was falling, falling through and into a white mist, which held her suspended, weightless, as if she had already parted from her body and was nothing more nor less than spirit.

"Will she die?" Cecile asked.

"Her body will. In this time. As Sophia's did in hers, when she made that final journey through the Stones."

"We can't leave her."

"We can't stay." Helene glanced towards Strif. The weeping had ceased and the girl sat motionless, hugging the body of her baby. "There are others who need what help we can give."

"Strif's not ready to go. She's not ready to give him up. Give her a little more time, Jo too. The way back is still open. The Stones are not yet dark. We don't know what might happen. We should wait," Cecile argued. Helene glanced up at the top of the rise then looked at her daughter and nodded,

"We will stay, for as long as we have the strength." Standing before the Stones, Helene raised her arms to the skies. "Mother of Earth and Heaven listen to the prayers of your daughters. Keep open for us this portal between the ages, so that she whose time is now can return whole and in safety to those of us who wait."

"Bring her back to us, let her come to us," Cecile chanted softly. "Jo," she whispered. She shut her eyes and filled her mind with an explosion of light. In the centre of the Stone the light brightened. The circle within the circle widened. Cecile concentrated. For a long time she held the brilliance, then as it began to fade, she felt Helene join her. The light held steady.

*

Jo was standing at the Stones looking down the avenue towards the lighted windows of Kingsfield House. In front of her, Sophia with the child in her arms hurried towards the building, behind her a dark tunnel was closing in on itself.

"Give him to me," Jo cried. "He's not yours." Her voice sounded weak and feeble and as she began to run towards the fast retreating figure her legs were heavy and her breathing ragged.

"He is Nicholas, his son and mine." Did she hear a note of triumph in Sophia's voice? Was the battle already lost?

"No," Jo cried and forced herself onwards. She had to stop

Sophia, because the closer she got to the house and the further away from the Stones the smaller was Jo's chance of saving the baby and herself.

*

Strif screamed. The sound seared through the brilliance; it wavered, whiteness was streaked with strands of scarlet that spread like cracks across a mirror. Around the edges of the circle a deep blue line appeared, it grew thicker, darker, closing in on the light.

*

Sophia was at the steps of Kingsfield; the doors of the house were opening. Jo cried out in despair, then in a final desperate effort she sprinted towards her.

A figure stood at the top of the steps. Backlit by candlelight her pale blue dress was almost transparent, her white skin bloodless.

"Cousin Sophia, you and your bastard child are not welcome here." Ann's voice was cold.

"Indeed. How little you know. I have his son and he will acknowledge us both." Like a snake about to strike, Sophia drew herself up, but Ann held her glance.

"My husband will not countenance any such thing. There will be a legitimate heir to Kingsfield." Ann's lips curved into a smile and her hand rested fleetingly on her belly. Enraged, Sophia started forward and in that moment Jo reached her. In one despairing lunge she tore the baby from her arms and holding him close to her heart she ran.

*

The circle of light in the Stone became smaller. Strif began to sob, a low, dull, heart-breaking sound, which beat through the mind, bringing despair in its wake. Helene broke away and crouching down beside the girl she put her arm around her shoulders. Cecile, still holding firm, thought of sunlight, gold quilting the waves on a deep blue sea, dazzling through young leaves, falling in molten puddles on a bare floor.

*

The ground was rough and pitted. Tree roots snaked out to trip her, stones littered the avenue.

If I fall I am lost. I will never be able to go back. I will be trapped in this time forever. I won't be me. Jo Docherty, artist and wife. Richard's wife. I'll never see him again, feel his arms around me, or lean my head on his shoulder.

The child in her arms stirred. She felt his warmth, the sleepy heaviness of his limbs. If he was here in this time did it mean that Strif's child was dead?

No, Jo thought. *That can't, that won't happen. I won't let it.*

Only a little further and she would be at the Stones. But where were they? All she could see was a faint glimmer in the blackness of the night.

"It's gone. The portal is closing." Sophia stood before her. "You opened it and sent me out into an endless torment of unending time and now I have brought you here. You will feel what I felt. You will live a half-life, trapped forever on the edge of existence, longing for a time when you were human and knowing that you will never, ever be so again."

Sophia's hand closed around her wrist. Her nails dug into Jo's flesh. The twist on her arm almost brought her to her knees, but Jo clung onto the child holding him with all her strength. Sophia towered above her.

"All these years I have waited. I watched you, when you were a child, sharing your secrets with her, sharing your blood. You became one. She died, but you lived in your time and now you are mine."

"I have to go back. I do not belong here."

"No more than I did in all those centuries. Now I am home and the way is closing. I have sealed it forever. See." In her triumph Sophia loosened her hold and Jo staggered forward. Her legs buckled, but her will drove her on. "Run if you must, but you are too weak. It is too late. I have the child. I have condemned you to everlasting torment and I will never let you go."

*

I'm losing it, Cecile thought. She was dizzy with the effort of holding the light. A kaleidoscope of colours swirled in her head. Then like a child's palate they began to merge into a murky brown.

"Mother!" she cried.

"I am here. I am with you," came the reply. Blindly, Cecile stretched out and met the firm grasp of her mother's hand. The light stabilised, but the circle had shrunk.

*

A mere pinpoint at the bottom of a dark pit; the light through the Stones was dying. Could Jo reach it in time? Hardly able to move her legs, she lost her balance and half fell. For a moment, her grip on the child slackened, then her arms closed around him again. His little body grew heavier and heavier dragging her down, holding her back. Without him she would be free to sprint up that final distance to the rise, back to her own life, her own self. His heart beat against hers, she breathed in his breath and she knew she would never let him go.

*

Just a little longer, Helene's thoughts wavered.

"We can't give up. We can't," Cecile urged, but she saw the darkness encroaching and knew she was nearing the end of her strength.

*

From somewhere behind Jo, Sophia's mocking laugher snaked through the trees. It was too late. In the centre of the Stone a splinter of light flickered wanly.

*

Cecile sank to the ground and covered her head with her hands. Helene still stood by the Stones, shoulders drooping, so weary she could scarcely stay upright.

*

One hand on the ground, the other holding onto Nicholas Jo clawed her way up the rise. There was nothing now, but darkness. Behind her she could hear the swish of Sophia's skirts. Hands grabbed at her legs, tore at her waist.

"Give me the child."

- 266 -

"You will not have him," Jo cried. And dived into darkness.

Pain moulded her body. It stretched and tore, pressing on her chest, until her lungs folded. Gasping and choking, heart pounding, blood thudding through her veins she slid onto cold earth. Too weak to rise, she rolled her head to one side. At the edge of her vision, stood Helene and Cecile, their arms uplifted, their voices ringing out, powerful and strong.

"Spirits of the earth bind her."

"Spirits of time hold her."

"Mother Earth take this unquiet spirit and let her find peace in your arms."

"Spirits of earth, air, fire and water, bind her and keep her."

"Forever."

The darkness at the heart of the Stone thickened. Helene and Cecile sprinkled salt at its base, then stood silent, heads bowed. With their stillness, came peace and with it the energy began to return to Jo's body. As she struggled to sit up, Cecile came to her and took her in her arms, letting her rest against her warmth.

"We've bound her. She won't come back." Cecile put her hand on Jo forehead. "You did it," she whispered.

"I lost him." Jo closed her eyes. "I had him with me, but when I came through the Stone, he had gone." A tear slid down her cheek. She lifted her hand to brush it away. "I'm so sorry Strif," she whispered. "So very, very sorry."

A baby's yell, strong and healthy tore through the air. The child on Strif's lap kicked out his legs and screwing up his face bellowed out his hungry rage.

"He's here Jo." Helene knelt beside Strif. "It's all right," she murmured gently taking the young mother's hand. "He's OK."

Strif's eyes were blank. Helene took Nicholas and held him against his mother. The baby's mouth began to work, he snuffled and burrowed into Strif's breast.

"I think you should take him in. It's too cold for him out

here," Helene said.

Strif's head jerked, her arms flew up to hold her child.

"I thought," her voice trembled. "I thought he was dead."

"Shh," Helene put her finger on Strif's lips and helped her to her feet.

"Was a dream? Or was it her?" Strif glared towards the Stones. "Did she take him?"

"Sophia's gone now," Cecile said.

"Oh yeah!"

"I promise," Helene said.

Strif looked at them uncertainly.

"It's true," Cecile assured her.

"It better had be." Strif choked back a sob.

"It is. Nicholas is safe. Jo brought him back for you." Helene's arm was around Strif's waist turning her gently towards the spot where Cecile sat holding Jo.

"She did?" Strif said.

Helene nodded. Clutching her baby Strif came over towards the two women.

"Thanks," she said sharply. Then turned and strode down the avenue.

Jo's feet shrank from the hard ground. Like a new born child her legs could not carry her weight. Her skin bristled against the soft collar of wool around her neck. Her flesh ached from the pressure of the belt at her waist and her head hung forward, too heavy to lift. Helene and Cecile put their arms around her and helped her down the slope. With each step, Jo grew stronger and as a faint line of grey appeared above the trees they released their hold and she walked beside them towards the light and warmth of The Granary.

14885472R00159

Printed in Great Britain
by Amazon.co.uk, Ltd.,
Marston Gate.